SOFT WILD ACHE

A Crown Creek Novel

THERESA LEIGH

Created with Vellum

To Kacey Musgraves, for Slow Burn and Lin-Manuel Miranda, for Wait for It, both of which I listened to on repeat while writing this book. I think it's no coincidence it's the longest one I've written yet!

I'm alright with a slow burn
Taking my time, let the world turn
I'm gonna do it my way, it'll be alright
If we burn it down and it takes all night
It's a slow burn, yeah...
- Kacey Musgraves - Slow Burn

Chapter One

RACHEL

I smiled at the bartender and waved my empty glass. "Another Long Island Iced Tea?" he asked over the noise of the party.

I grinned and nodded my thanks. Sticking with iced tea was a wise choice, and I was proud of myself for making it. The last thing I wanted was to ruin my housemate Everly's party. She was my only friend, and she watched out for me. But I didn’t want her thinking I couldn't handle myself when she was gone.

“Thank you!” I shouted once he handed me my drink. Everly’s goodbye party had gotten really noisy in the past few minutes. It seemed like the entire town of Crown Creek had come out to wish her and her rockstar, celebrity boyfriend, Gabe King good luck as they headed overseas to shoot his TV series. This was the kind of party that would have gotten me in trouble a month ago. But I’d wised up since then.

Yes. Drinking only iced tea was a good choice. I grinned to myself. Pride made me feel loose-limbed and slippery.

Seized with the urge to move, I shimmied back onto the dance floor, taking another big sip of my iced tea. It was hot in here, I suddenly realized, then spun in a circle to get closer to the open door. Everly was watching me with an odd look on her face. I grinned at her and waved. “I love you!” I shouted. It was true. She was like a sister, no, more than a sister since my sisters and I had never really gotten along. I waved to her and Gabe. "Hey guys!" I shouted over the music. “Come dance with me!”

“Nah, I’m pretty comfortable right here!” Gabe called back, draping his arm over Everly. Then he shot me a wicked grin. “I bet he’ll dance with you though!”

I felt heat on my skin and turned to see that Gabe’s brother Beau was watching me. When Everly and Gabe had started dating, she’d dragged me along and introduced me to Gabe’s younger brother, who had also been dragged along. I knew that all four King brothers had been in a band at one point, which should have scared me. But there was something about Beau.

Something completely confusing.

He was calm. He was quiet. Being with him was almost...restful.

That is, until he looked at me like I was the only thing worth noticing, with warm hazel eyes that seemed to heat my skin to scorching.

He was over in the corner now, sitting with his twin brother, but his eyes were on me. If I went over to him, I knew that would be the end of the night. When Beau and I got to talking, I lost all track of time. And I wasn’t here for Beau tonight. I was here for Everly.

I needed to focus on her. She was my friend and she was leaving. My *best* friend. "I can't believe you’re leaving, Everly!" There was a strange echo in my head and I wondered if I had already said that.

Then I felt her arms squeeze me tight and wondered how I was already hugging her when I didn't remember crossing the room. "It'll only be a few months," she said and I heard that same echo in my head.

This time I was certain we'd already done this, so why couldn't I stop my mouth from whining, "Who's going to teach me about secular life?"

My drink suddenly lifted itself from my hands. I blinked and realized she was setting it on the bar. "Right, well I'm clearly a bad influence, how much have you had?"

"Nothing!" I protested. I leaned in, stumbled and braced my hand against the bar. "It's just iced tea!"

But even as I said that I knew it was wrong. I was drunk. I had no idea how it had happened, how iced tea had made the room start spinning like this, but it had happened and now I was far drunker than I ever had been before.

"Goodness," I mumbled, turning away from Everly. She was asking me a question, but I was too preoccupied with remembering how to put one foot in front of another. Guilt was pouring into my veins like I was standing in front of my community during a Shaming.

I needed to get out of here. I stumbled, then cursed myself silently as I pushed open the front door and staggered out into the cool night air. A chill shivered up my overheated skin and I vaguely remembered leaving my jacket in Everly's car, but there was no way I could turn around and ask her for it. She'd be horrified at me.

No, I needed to get out of here and get home before I ruined Everly's night. Guilt was throbbing in my head right along with the drunken haze. Drunk... how was I drunk? How had I gotten this drunk when I didn't even mean to...

That thought cut short when I felt myself suddenly go airborne. I was falling, no I was flying, no I was floating parallel to the ground, borne up in a pair of arms.

I knew who they belonged to, without having to turn and look at him. I knew by the way my skin heated under his gaze.

Chapter Two

BEAU

"Put me down!" she shrieked in a voice that was half squeak, half slur.

It was really cute.

I obliged her, setting her gently back down on her feet. "You were going to fall," I explained. Then stepped back.

Even when she was as drunk as a sorority girl during Rush Week, Rachel Walker was beautiful. She had the kind of beauty that crept up on you. I'd first met her when my brother explained that he needed me to come be his wingman. I was tasked with dealing with his girlfriend's housemate so they could engage in some serious PDA without Everly feeling guilty about it. My first impression of Rachel was that she was a shy girl who was weirdly oblivious to my pop culture references and deflected most questions I asked her about what she liked to do. It wasn't until the second time we hung out that I noticed how shiny her long braided hair was. The third get-together I noticed the amber flakes in her brown eyes. By the fourth meeting, I couldn't keep my eyes off the way her hands fluttered like birds when she got excited and was willing to make a complete fool of myself just to see the pretty way her cheeks pinkened when she thought she was being bad. I started keeping an eye out for her around town and calling to check in with her at night. Slowly, without me really noticing, Rachel Walker had become someone I cared about.

And I took care of the people I cared about.

That's why, when I saw her stumbling to the front door like that, I'd immediately jumped up to follow. Which was why I had been there to catch her when she fell.

Now she was looking at me through half-slitted eyes. Probably trying to understand why I'd picked her up in the first place. Sure I'd caught her before she pitched forward and wrecked that pretty face of hers on the blacktop. But I definitely didn't need to keep holding her cradled against me for several paces.

I exhaled. That had been for me. I took advantage of the situation to have her in my arms for a second. But she was drunk, and that definitely made me an asshole.

Fuck.

"Can you walk?" I asked, putting a steadying - friendly - hand on her shoulder. "I'm right here if you need to lean on me."

"I'm fine," she mumbled, and very deliberately put one foot in front of the other, making sure it was fully planted before lifting her back foot. She looked like she was walking on some planet with stronger gravity and the way she was concentrating was so adorable I had to bite back a laugh. I had a feeling she wasn't in a laughing mood.

"Good," I said, instead of laughing. "I'll just walk you home then."

"You don't have to," she said quickly.

I shrugged and tried to look like I wasn't watching her every move. "It's a nice night," I said.

And it was. There was still a bite of chill in the air, but it had softened enough that it felt good to be out without a jacket. The rush of the creek from last month's flood had died into a burble after a month with no rain, and the gentle shushing sound was a soothing backdrop to the quiet evening. Above us, the little spring peepers trilled out their high, piping calls, talking to each other in the trees. That was probably my favorite sound in the world.

Second favorite, I thought to myself when Rachel spoke up. "You were watching me," she said.

She turned her head to look at me as she said this, which made her stumble a little. I reached out a steadying hand. "Was I?" I said, even though I very clearly was. I hadn't been able to keep my eyes off her the whole party. Even when my twin brother Finn was talking to me, I was still captivated by the sight of her dancing. Even when I was talking to Gabe and Everly, I'd been worriedly counting the number of drinks she'd been buying.

I had no right. I knew that. For one thing, it was her business how much she cut loose. Hell, if anyone had a right to party hard, it was Rachel Walker. I only had the vaguest inkling what she went through, growing up in that environment, but I definitely understood why she'd want to break free of it. She had every reason to go crazy.

The problem was that she had no idea what she was doing. I was pretty sure that growing up in a restrictive, fundamentalist cult didn't exactly prepare you for knowing your own boundaries. Which was another reason I had no right to have my eye on her the way I did. Rachel was a grown woman - beautifully grown too - but she had the life experience of a young child. She was naive and sheltered and she trusted me to be her friend.

"I guess I was," I confessed. Then I lied. "Just a friend looking out for a friend, right?" It was such a bold-faced lie, but Rachel was pure enough to believe it.

"Just a friend?" she repeated. "Really?"

Damn how soft her voice sounded. Damn that note of pleading. I was this close to kissing her already and her wide-opened eyes weren't helping. "Yeah," I grunted and looked away from her. At the rising moon, the fading light in the sky, the first stars winking into existence. Anywhere but at that face, those lips. She was drunk, and I was not an asshole.

She opened her mouth, about to say something, but mistimed her odd, heavy steps. She stumbled, pitching forward.

It was all instinct. I had her back in my arms before my next breath, sweeping her up to cradle her against my chest. "I've got you," I said, and that was instinct too.

The light was draining from the sky, but there was enough shining down from the streetlights so that I could see the way she was looking through her lashes at me. And if I didn't see that, I could feel the slow slide of her fingertips before she laced them around my neck. Her lips parted a little and I spotted the pretty pink of her tongue. The blood was pounding in my ears and every part of me was laser focused on that mouth. I could feel it already, the softness, the slow slide of that pretty tongue against mine. I was already bending my head to kiss her when she closed her eyes all the way. "Yoou'ff got meee," she slurred.

That slur went through me like a jolt of electricity. Instantly I straightened back up again. My blood still felt super-heated, but it was cooling rapidly.

She's drunk, Beau. You fucking asshole. She's completely shitfaced drunk.

I clenched my teeth together and started to jog. She made a little whooping sound as her head jostled, and then rested it against my chest. With every jogging step I cursed myself for how wrong I was for enjoying how it felt there, but at least I wasn't trying to kiss her anymore.

The little three room cabin she shared with Everly was situated on a spit of land that bordered the creek. Even though it was only a half a mile from the bar, and she was pretty light, my arms were still burning by the time I reached their sunken porch. "Rachel," I whispered.

"Mmm," she protested, half asleep.

"I need your keys."

"Pocket," she mumbled, snuggling into my neck and sighing.

"Jesus," I hissed through my clenched teeth. I braced her up with my knee against the porch rail and then slid my hand into her pocket. I wasn't feeling the heat of her thighs, I wasn't thinking about how close my hand was to... to... "Rachel, can you stand up for me?" I growled, setting her down a little too roughly.

She was too drunk to notice how I tugged at the crotch of my jeans. She just leaned against the side of the house and mumbled something before smiling. I was clenching my teeth so hard I was getting a headache. "Thank fuck," I muttered when I finally got the door unlocked. "Can you make it in?"

She mumbled again, her head lolling. Fuck, she was really far gone. I stepped in, catching her just as she pitched forward. "Okay," I winced as my hand accidentally brushed her breasts. "Fuck, ah, okay, right in here, right? Let's get you in bed. Right, good girl, just like that, no, lie on your side, here, I'll get the wastepaper basket." I set it on the floor right next to her head. "There."

"...iced tea," she slurred.

"What was that?"

But she passed out.

I stood there for a moment, unsure what to do. Her waist length hair was tumbled all over her in a curtain, which would get pretty gross if she ended up puking. With my lips pressed together, I gathered the silky strands up in my fist, pulling them back from her face and then tucking them all back into her shirt. She let out a muttering sigh and shifted in her sleep, then moaned.

"Okay," I said aloud. "You're okay now, right?" Of course there was no answer. I shifted in place, watching her breathing even out. “You're going to be fine now," I said, more for my benefit. But I still wasn't moving away from her. I still wasn't leaving her alone.

I couldn't leave her alone.

"Fuck it," I grumbled. I took one more look at the beautiful face, those plump, parted lips.

Then I undressed and made a pillow of my clothes. I checked her one more time, then fell asleep on her floor.

Chapter Three

RACHEL

Everything hurt. My head hurt. My stomach hurt. My hair and my eyelashes somehow even hurt.

I tried to open my eyes and moaned when I finally succeeded. The sun was like a knife driven right into between my eyebrows. I tried to clap my hand over my face, but the motion made the room start spinning. "Merciful God," I groaned and shut my eyes again.

There was a soft sound of footsteps outside my bedroom door. I must have woken Everly. "Hey," I croaked, licking my parched lips. "Would you mind getting me a glass of water?"

"If you have water right now, you're just going to puke," came a deep, sleep-clogged voice.

I shot straight up in bed and stared at Beau. Merciful heavens, what was he doing there, standing in my doorway all shirtless and rumpled and looking like every kind of sin I'd been warned against? I stared at him just long enough for his mouth to kick upward into a smile...

And then everything hurt again. I wondered if I had the flu. My little sister Miriam had said it felt like this when she got it. Everything hurting,

I fell back onto the bed, feeling like I'd been kicked in the stomach by a cow. "Dear Lord above," I panted.

"Do you have any juice in the house? I'll mix you up something to help your electrolytes."

I had no idea what he was on about, but I nodded weakly. "In the fridge." Talking felt like dying.

I heard his step on the floorboards as he walked back down the narrow hall that separated my room from Everly's.

Everly who had left for Gabe's house early this morning.

Everly was not here.

But Beau somehow was?

I squeezed my eyes shut - even that hurt somehow - and tried to piece together how it was that Beauregard King was in my house right now. We'd become friends once Everly and Gabe started dating, but there was no way anything more had happened. He was famous in the secular world. He'd want a girl who didn't seem so sheltered and naive. He wasn't... oh heavens no, he hadn't been in my bed last night... right?

A flutter of terror in my stomach made the contents rise. For all his sweetness, Beau was from a family steeped in worldliness. And while I didn't follow the laws of the Chosen anymore, I couldn't shake the warning voice inside of me. *He was in a rock and roll band,* it hissed. *Satan's music.*

And he had stayed the night. Where? In here?

I clapped my hand over my mouth and rolled to the side, noting with muted surprise that there was a garbage can already sitting there at the ready. "Oh no," I breathed, touching my lips, my body, checking, checking...

Everything felt fine. Normal even. Flu aside of course.

I swallowed hard and willed my stomach to settle. Beau - terrifying, fascinating Beau - was in my house, but it seemed like he had... slept on the couch?

Why?

"Here you are." Beau reappeared at my doorway, and I was relieved that he had put on a shirt. He handed me a glass and laughed when I squinted at it suspiciously. "It's apple juice with honey and some salt." He grinned wider when I wrinkled my nose. "It'll replace what you lost drinking last night. It should help that headache, as should this." He opened his fist and offered me two white pills.

I glanced down at what he was offering and back up again. It was sweet that he was trying to take care of me, but there was one small problem. "I didn't have anything to drink last night."

He raised an eyebrow.

I shook my head and then regretted it. But he was wrong. "I didn't drink last night," I protested, louder now. "I didn't want to miss any of Everly's goodbye, so I specifically stuck with iced tea... why are you laughing?" I demanded.

He was. I scowled as he laughed so hard he had to set down the drink. My mouth was a desert. I wanted so badly to reach for it, but not when he was laughing at me like this.

He caught a glimpse of my face and tried to pull himself together. "I'm sorry, you said iced tea, right?"

"Yes," I grumbled. My thirst won out and I reached for the drink he'd brought me. The salty, sweet mixture felt odd on my tongue, but I was too parched to care.

"Hey, hey," he said, reaching out and pulling the glass from my lips. His hazel eyes were concerned. "Slow down," he said. "You're going to make yourself sick."

"I'm already sick," I said. "I think I have the flu. It's too hot in here, can you open the window?"

He was smiling for some reason when he leaned over my bed to push my sticky window up, letting in the cacophony of birds. "Oh hush," I spat at them, flinging my arm up over my eyes. "There's nothing to be singing about."

"You don't have the flu, Rachel," he said, pushing back from my wall. He looked down at me and I sulkily took another sip of the odd tasting drink. My head was starting to actually feel a little better. He was sweet for making it for me. Sweet and handsome and way too big for my tiny little bedroom. "You're hungover."

At the sound of that, all nice thoughts I'd been having about him vanished. "I told you," I said, mustering up as much dignity as I could while lying sweating and squinting in bed. "I didn't have anything to drink."

"Long Island Iced Teas are alcoholic, Rachel," he said gently. "They're actually one of the strongest drinks you could have. It's no wonder you were falling down drunk last night."

Long Island Iced Tea. I remembered the name on the menu and immediately flushed hot. My heart started racing and my fingers curled in panic. I should have known. I hadn't known.

Panic was closing my throat. It was the way he looked down at me. It had nothing to do with his expression, which was concerned and faintly amused. It was the way he was looming over my bed in the morning. It was the way he was informing me of a mistake I swore I hadn't made. It was the hot, bright shame that slithered through my veins. I could almost see the eyes of the congregation, watching impassively, doing nothing, waiting for the first blow to be struck...

I sat up. Ignoring the way the world slid sideways, and squeezing my eyes shut against the pain in my head, I forced my words out between teeth gritted in panic. "You need to go."

My eyes were still shut, so I couldn't see his face, but I could feel the shift in the air. He was surprised. "Rachel, it's okay, you didn't know..."

There was that note in his voice. Whether he heard it or not made no difference, because I sure did. The note of confusion. Like I was some kind of puzzle. Like the way I'd grown up meant I belonged in a zoo, or in a lab to be studied under a microscope. "You're right, I didn't," I said crisply. "And it's not right for you to make me feel silly for not knowing. I'm not silly, Beau."

"No, of course you're not, it's just—"

"Don't laugh at me," I said. "Please. Don't laugh at me ever again."

He inhaled sharply and then held it. Then let it out in a long exhale I could feel rushing across my cheek. I kept my eyes shut until he finally said, "I won't."

"Good."

"Is there anything else I can do for you, Rachel?" His tone was more formal now, and part of me wanted to tell him it was okay. To ask him to go back to teasing me and taking care of me.

I licked my lips and steeled myself to do the right thing. The way I had countless millions of times before. "You can go," I said.

He held his breath again. I kept my eyes shut, not even daring to peek at him. If he wanted to stay, there was no way I could stop him. I was alone here in this house with this man, this rock and roll musician, completely vulnerable. I felt so helpless, I was almost able to pray again.

But after a moment, I heard his tread on the floor. I held my breath until I heard the front door slam, then opened my eyes to see that he had done what I asked.

I wasn't sure why that surprised me so much.

Chapter Four

BEAU

The birds hopped and twittered in the trees above me as I walked back to the Crown Tavern, flitting and calling like they had questions that needed answers.

Me too, birds. Me fucking too.

I had no idea what had set Rachel off. One minute she was half laughing and asking me to open the window, the next minute she was kicking me out of her house fast enough to give me whiplash. There was a steady tick-tick of guilt in the back of my brain, like the sound of a dripping faucet late at night. Keeping you from relaxing all the way.

I was confused and I didn't like being confused. I liked to have everything laid out and making sense. I liked to know the reasons why people did what they did. Things that were irrational I couldn't help but view as a challenge. I was going to figure this out.

But first I had to pick up my car from the Crown Tavern and get back to my parents' house. I slid my phone from my pocket and winced at the time. Our first showing was at eleven. Guess I wouldn't have time to grab a shower before we headed to the first house.

My oldest brother Jonah was now living with his fiancée, Ruby. Gabe had left early this morning to go film his TV show. That left Finn, Claire and me left in the family house. And all three of us were way too old to still be living under our parents' roof. Claire, being the baby and the only girl, was immune from the deep sighs and long-suffering silences from our father and was oblivious to the sidelong glances from our mother. But I saw them all. And I felt them too.

Getting my twin brother to realize we needed to move the fuck out and live on our own for once had been a process. To say that Finn was stubborn was like saying water was wet. His first instinct was always to say no, to anything, and if you pushed him on it, his temper would flare.

My car was still where I had left it, all alone in the empty lot. Perks of living in a small town where everyone knew your name. I opened it - I never bothered locking up around here - and slid into the cool interior and let my head fall back on the seat.

Sleeping on Rachel's floor had left an ache settled right between my shoulder blades. I still wasn't sure why I had stayed. Her reaction hurt more than the stiffness in my back.

I pushed that thought from my brain. Right now, I was headed from one prickly reaction to another.

It was time to go find a house with Finn.

Yeah, he wasn't the easiest person to deal with, but dealing with him was something I had a lifetime's worth of experience in. "We get a place together," I'd informed him a few weeks back. "It makes sense, right? No one else knows how to deal with your shit." I laid out the printouts from the real estate website. "And look, you want a place in the woods, right? These are all up in the hills."

Finn had only glanced at the results of my careful research. I was ready with Excel spreadsheets and monthly budgets, but it turned out I didn't need any more persuasion than a house in the woods. "As long as it's far away from people," he'd mumbled and then rolled back over and fallen asleep.

Living in the middle of nowhere - even more so than we did right now - wasn't exactly appealing to me. But I was willing to make the effort for Finn.

Whether he was going to make the effort was another story, I thought to myself as I pulled into our driveway next to Claire's white

Jeep. He wasn't standing by the kitchen window, watching for me. It would have surprised the hell out of me if he was.

"Mornin'," my sister said, eyeing me over the top of her coffee mug.

"Where's Finn?" I asked, ignoring the significant looks she was shooting me. The fact that she had no idea where I'd been was killing her, I could tell. Claire was physically incapable of minding her own business.

She set down her mug and pressed her lips together.

"Oh for fuck's sake," I sighed without the least bit of shock. She shrugged as I went past her and up the stairs.

"Yo!" I called as I knocked on the door of the bedroom we'd shared as kids. He'd claimed it when we all moved back home again, leaving me to sleep with the spiders in the basement. I didn't mind and as soon as Jonah moved out, I'd claimed his room for mine again. "Hey, you decent?"

When there was no answer, I slowly pushed the door open and then sighed heavily. "Finn, hey, Wake the fuck up, man, we're looking at houses today."

My brother mumbled a curse and slapped a pillow over his face. "Go without me," he grumbled.

"And pick the wrong one?" I yanked on his blankets, making him curse again and tug them away. "No way. I'm not giving you any reasons to back out on this because the house is the wrong color or some shit. You're going with me. We're doing this together."

Finn was quiet.

"Fuck, did you just fall asleep on me?" I laughed, shaking my head. "Look, I'm tired too. I spent the night on a floor."

Just like I knew it would, that made him open his eyes. "Rachel?" he grunted.

I sighed. "Fucked that right up," I confessed. "Though I don't exactly know how."

"Welcome to my life," he groaned as he sat up, scratching his bare torso. He glanced up at me with eyes the exact same shade of hazel as mine. Now that we were older, it wasn't so much like looking in the mirror, but growing up it had always felt that way. I held his gaze for a moment and we conducted the kind of silent conversation that always pissed Jonah and Gabe off when we were on the road together. "We're really doing this?" his wide eyes asked me. "Come on," my eyebrows answered. "You can do this."

He sighed and spoke aloud. "Fine. I'm up. Give me five minutes."

He took ten, but I held my tongue, just happy to see him up and moving. Gabe leaving was a change, and Finn got weird about change.

"So today's the day?" Our mom appeared out of nowhere, carrying a laundry basket on her hip. She stopped on her way to the basement and looked at the three of us - Finn, Claire and me - with an unreadable expression on her still-pretty face. "And Gabe snuck out this morning while it was still dark too." She let out a sigh. "All my little birdies are fleeing the nest."

Finn and I looked at each other, both of us thinking about how we'd fled the nest at age eight when the King Brothers went on their first tour. Mom didn't seem to count that though.

Claire was laughing as she poured another cup of coffee. "I'm not fleeing anything, Mom," she said, softening the brattiness of her declaration with a quick kiss on Mom's cheek. "At least for the time being."

"Hooray," Mom said, and she was either happy about that or annoyed by it. With our mother, it was sometimes hard to tell the difference.

"But these big boys!" Claire went on, punching Finn in the bicep. "So grown up!" She ignored Finn's grumbling and looked at me. "I'm coming, by the way."

"Um, excuse me?" I went over and poured some coffee for myself. This morning had been confusing enough without Claire's added drama.

She set down her mug and reached way up to sling her arm over Finn's shoulder. "You guys need my help," she said. "I'm an expert. I work for a developer."

I narrowed my eyes as Finn chuckled. "Yeah, as PR." He grabbed her mug and slurped some of her coffee, ignoring her shrieks of protest.

He held it way above her head and she planted her hands on her hips and glared at him. "I know the area, and I know the desirable markets," she said with a haughty lift of her chin. "A house is an investment and you two idiots need all the help in that area you can get."

I held my tongue, choosing not to remind her that I had invested all of my King Brothers money as soon as I earned it, and was now drawing down a healthy income without even touching the principle. Because Finn hadn't done that. Not even close. And that was one of the reasons why we were moving in together. He didn't know it yet, but I planned on keeping a close eye on his money for him.

"Whatever," Finn sighed as he drained the last of her coffee. She glared at him and he grinned. Finn and Claire should have been the twins. They were so much alike. "If you want to tag along I'm not going to stop you."

"Ha! I'm not tagging along. I'm driving."

"Um, excuse me?" I said again.

Claire snatched her mug away from Finn and lifted her chin again. "You four were all famous, but none of you have decent cars." She reached into her purse and jingled the keys to her Jeep. "Who wants shotgun?"

I let Finn have shotgun without a fight - because we're not *twelve* - and settled myself into my sister's cramped back seat. I gave her the address of the first place and she headed out.

It was a bright, sunny Sunday morning, which made all the houses look pretty okay to me. "This one is nice," Claire murmured approvingly as we pulled into a place about an hour from our parents' house. Red and white balloons danced above the open house sign.

Finn glared at it without saying a word. "What!" Claire exploded. "You really hate it already?"

I could see that without him even having to say a word. Rather than argue - even though that was Claire's favorite pastime - I just sighed. "It's pretty pricey," I volunteered after swiping through the info on my phone.

"Lord grant me the strength," Claire muttered, but she pulled out of the driveway without pressing the issue. "You're the most impossible person I've ever met."

"You love me," Finn announced.

"Lucky for you."

"I bring joy and meaning to your life."

"You bring irritation and confusion to my life," Claire said, but she was smiling as she said it. "So what was wrong with that place?"

"Too close to the neighbors."

"You want to be a fucking hermit or something?"

"Sounds good to me."

"You too, Beau?" she glanced back at me, causing the Jeep to swerve alarmingly on the country road.

"Why not?" I shrugged.

"Now this is more like it," Finn said as we pulled into the long gravel drive of a secluded, lodge style house. It was surrounded by dense pine trees, giving a feeling of the woods being claustrophobically close.

I opened the window and inhaled the sharp smell of pine.

"This is what you want?" Claire squeaked. "This looks like a nice place to get axe murdered."

I agreed with her but kept my mouth shut. "It's even more expensive than the last place," I said instead. "We're gonna have to start up the band again to be able to afford it."

"Yeah but this time I'm in it, right?" Claire laughed.

I pressed my lips together. Her tone was light enough to make it seem like a joke, but I knew that being excluded from the family band for being a girl was still a sore spot for my sister. Our old manager had wanted a boy band and wasn't even willing to consider her, in spite of her talent. Claire was the best singer out of all of us, by far, but she'd never had a chance to share that gift with the world. "Definitely," I said, reaching over the seat to squeeze her shoulder. "I mean, if you can spare a moment from your hectic PR schedule."

She gave me the finger and then shoved Finn with her shoulder. "So should we get out?"

He nodded and all three of us got out and stood in the drive. I looked at Finn and then surreptitiously glanced at my phone. We were still early for the showing, but, "You gonna go in or..."

"Don't rush me," Finn glowered.

I held up my hands. "No it's cool," I said. I heard the unnatural brightness in my voice and hated it. Claire must have heard it too because she shot me a warning glance. "Take your time," she said to Finn, putting her hand on his shoulder.

"Cut it out," he said, shrugging her back off again. "I don't need you guys being all careful with me."

Claire and I exchanged glances. That was a bad sign. The more Finn protested he was okay, the more it meant he was freaking out. "All we have to do is go inside," I said. "Just go in and see if it feels right."

"Will you stop it?" Finn shouted, his face suddenly beet red. "Stop *pushing* me! Christ!"

"I'm not pushing you..." I started to say, holding out my hands. Worry was coursing through my system, which sucked.

"You're pushing! You're fucking rushing me, and I hate to be rushed!"

"Finn—" I said calmly just as Claire shouted, "Will you cut the shit?!"

We both turned and stared at her. "Get in the fucking Jeep," she cried, her voice strained. "Obviously this is the wrong house. You!" she said, stabbing a finger at me. "Stop pushing him." I didn't even get a chance to protest before she stabbed her finger at Finn. "And you! Stop shitting on everything before you even get it a chance, got it?" She got in and started the engine then threw up her hands in a "well?" gesture.

Finn didn't look at me as we walked back into the Jeep. And he didn't say anything, didn't try to apologize. I didn't expect it. I knew better. And maybe I was pushing him a little. It was just that, without a little pushing, he stayed stuck right where he was.

Round and round these thoughts went, an endless loop of worry. I couldn't help it. I worried about those I loved.

The next house was way out by the college. "Well, if you moved out here, you'd be closer to Ray-chel!" Claire sing-songed, breaking the silence.

"Shut it," I mumbled, but I found myself looking a little too keenly out the window as we slid by. I was almost convinced I could see her there by the dumpsters, her long hair braided in a rope down the center of her back. If that was her, then she was up and working on a

Sunday with a killer hangover. Hard work, too. Being a janitor wasn't easy.

She was right. I shouldn't have laughed at her. She was tough, tough in ways I was still finding out about. Leaving her insular world and living out here with us took guts. It wasn't her fault she didn't know that Long Island Iced tea wasn't non-alcoholic. She was smart enough to learn, she just needed someone to teach her.

I could teach her.

I sat up straighter in the back seat. My brother's moody depression was still an enigma I was no closer to figuring out. He didn't want my help, but Rachel? I could help her.

Chapter Five

RACHEL

I have had worse days.

That's what I had to keep repeating the whole wretched time. I have had worse days. Days of hard work and misery far worse than being a janitor at a college on a quiet Sunday afternoon. And thanks to Beau's magic potion, my headache was close to gone by the time I had boarded the sporadically-running rural bus that took me to my job.

I closed my eyes against the fading dizziness and reminded myself that cleaning up after college kids was no worse than cleaning out stables. And I was helping out Juanita, whose kid was on the third day of some truly nasty stomach bug. I tried to help out the mothers as much as I could. It made me feel a little better about myself.

So I powered through my work and by the end of the day I was bone-sore and exhausted, but at least the hangover had faded.

The bumpy, swaying bus ride home would probably reawaken it though. Remembering this, I grabbed my bag and paused as my hand slid into the pocket for my beat up old brick of a cell phone. Everly wasn't around to pick me up in her old death-trap of a car. I'd forgotten and almost called her.

Sighing, I slung my bag over my shoulder and then hoofed it to the far end of campus where the bus stop was. The driver took pity on me and waited as I sprinted the last fifty yards. I sank into the seat, pouring sweat through my clothes, and lifted the heavy weight of my braid off my neck to let the relatively cooler air hit my skin. It was the warmest night yet, hot and sticky, the air heavy with night-blooming flowers. I caught whiffs of their scent through the open window of the bus, in between wafts of diesel fumes and the smell of my own perspiration.

I fell asleep, exhausted and sticky, against the window pane, and woke two minutes before my stop on reflex.

Home.

Thank you, God.

After the most blessed shower in existence, I was two seconds away from falling face first into bed when I heard a knock at the door.

I froze. Then scowled. My bed was calling. "Who is it?" I shouted.

"Beau," came the muffled reply.

I froze in place. A loud voice in my head that sounded just like my grandfather's booming condemnation of sinners told me to stay put. I was in my pajamas, and I was alone. To open the door would be like inviting Satan right into my home.

But Satan had already *been* in my home, and while he'd been here, he'd tried to take care of me.

I padded over to the front door and stood on my tiptoes to look out the narrow window.

When I caught sight of him on my porch, my heart did a little racing hop before galloping like a frightened horse. He was standing there, looking clean and put together in a plaid button-down shirt and a pair of dark washed jeans. But it was what he had in his hand that had my heart speeding like a freight train.

Flowers.

I opened the door and hesitantly peeked around it. This morning when I'd sent him away, I was certain that his pride would mean I'd never see him again. "What are you doing here?" I asked, clutching the door so tightly my knuckles were white. All traces of exhaustion had fled my system and my heart thumped with excitement. Seeing him had me feeling like I could run for miles now.

"Saying I'm sorry," he said as he extended the bouquet to me.

"Yellow roses?" I asked, reaching out as if I expected the thorns to leap out and attack me.

"They mean friendship," he said, looking sheepish. "At least, that's what my sister told me. I hope she was telling the truth, but you never know with her." He straightened his shoulders a little. "You're right. I shouldn't have laughed at you. I'm sorry."

I exhaled and then suddenly felt like I could take a much deeper breath. My fingers closed around the long, paper-wrapped stems, and I searched my brain, trying to figure out what the Elders would have said about this. But my memories came up empty. There was simply nothing in the laws of the Chosen that dealt with what to do when a man handed you flowers and apologized. There would be no need for a law because it would never happen.

"Thank you," I said. They felt heavier in my arms than I was expecting. "You didn't have to do this."

"Yes, I did," he said with conviction. "You're not silly, you just didn't know." His smile softened his face in a way that made me think of the sun peeking out from behind a cloud. "I'd be honored to teach you."

Warmth spread through my body, making me all tingly inside. It wasn't just that he'd apologized, it was also the effort he'd put into it. I hadn't... I never even thought to expect that kind of effort, from any man. "Okay," I said softly, then cleared my throat and spoke louder. "You can, ah..." I couldn't believe what I was about to say, but I could no more stop myself from saying it than I could stop my heart from beating. "You can get started with teaching me right now."

He grinned and then dragged his teeth over his bottom lip like he was trying to catch it before it got too wide. I know I was smiling so wide my face hurt. It was dangerous and wrong to want to be with him alone like that, but once I'd started sinning, I couldn't seem to stop.

"Right now?" he asked.

"Yes, ah..." I drew back as my bare toes hit the cold cement of my front step. I'd been out with Beau before. But never right after he'd brought me flowers. That was why I felt all giddy and strange, I told myself. That was the reason I was forgetting how to speak. "Wait, yeah, uh..." I held up my finger. "I'm going to go change out of my pajamas first, okay? Don't go anywhere."

"I'll be right here," I heard him chuckle as I raced inside to change.

Chapter Six

BEAU

"So what's this?"

Rachel was leaning over the table I'd snagged for us way in the back of the Crown Tavern. It was the best I could do with the only real bar in town. It was a little too warm in here and a lot too loud. For the first time, I found myself wishing that we had some kind of upscale place. An intimate, first date kind of place with plinking piano music as the backdrop. A place where I wouldn't run the risk of hearing my own band's songs played over the PA system.

She was eyeing the next drink I'd ordered for her. We were running down the list of drinks on the back of the battered looking card that had stuck to the table when I'd tried to lift it. I figured one sip from each was a good enough baseline for her to know her way around a menu. Though it was sorely lacking in decent wines.

She certainly looked pretty enough for a high-end wine bar, though she'd probably disagree with me. In the few minutes it took her to change, she'd transformed herself. I loved the way that red sheer top fit around her shoulders, and the black tank underneath was cut just low enough to give me a nice view of the tops of her breasts...

"This?" I echoed, suddenly remembering that she had asked me a question. "Well, this is a Dark & Stormy. Ginger beer and rum. I think we established you like rum?"

"I like rum." Her eyes looked really dark as she blinked up at me with a wicked little smile.

"Me too." I cleared my throat and looked away. Those yellow roses of friendship I'd given her were also a big yellow caution sign for me. *Slow down* they reminded me. "So, with this one, it's not a cocktail, which are just spirits right?"

"Like a Long Island Iced Tea," she winced.

"Right. A Dark & Stormy isn't as strong. It's a mixed drink."

"Ginger beer isn't the same as beer?"

I held in the laugh. "No."

"This is very confusing," she whined, making me laugh.

"Well, try it and see if you like it," I told her. The more she knew about drinks, the less I had to worry about her.

But why was I even worrying about her in the first place? I shoved that thought aside to think about another time. "It's a good idea when you're unsure," I went on, hoping she didn't notice my pause. "To have one basic mixed drink you know you enjoy. That way you know how many you can drink safely."

She bit her lip and glanced at it like it was going to bite her. Then squared her shoulders dramatically. "Okay," she said.

I tried not to watch as she closed her lips around the rim of the glass. *Slow down.* "You like it?" I asked.

She narrowed her eyes and swished it around her mouth. "Spicy. Ooh, I like how it feels all warm in my stomach."

"Good, right? Now take a sip of water."

She rolled her eyes. "Again?"

"Staying hydrated is really important. That's how you avoid the kind of hangover you were dealing with this morning. And always make sure you have something in your stomach too."

"Like nachos?" She looked really eager all of a sudden.

I laughed. "Sure. Nachos." I signaled to Taylor behind the bar. "And can you bring out a gin and tonic for her to taste?"

"Isn't it a lot of money for you to be getting all these drinks and then not letting me finish them?" she asked.

I licked my lips. "You let me worry about that. This is important shit."

She colored a little and looked away. I wondered if it was because I swore. It was a bad habit, and one made worse by spending the day with Finn and Claire. As far as I knew, Rachel didn't swear, but that didn't seem to stop her from getting those wicked looks in her eye. To be honest, I loved seeing the moments when her strict upbringing clashed up against her mischievous, pleasure-seeking nature. So much so that I decided I needed to swear around her more often.

I was just about to ask her, her favorite cuss word when Taylor came back with the G&T. "Thanks, man," I said as I lifted the glass over the bar.

"Is this the next step in my education? Have I moved up a grade level?" she asked with a glint in her eye.

"Yep. This isn't nearly as sweet as the stuff you've been trying."

"Hmm." She gave me that same glance over the top of her glass. One I was certain was innocent. She couldn't possibly know what she was doing to me, peering out from under that thick fringe of lashes. Even her long hair, usually a pretty good reminder of how off-limits she was to me, was tumbling down her back in a thick rope just made for winding around my fist. She couldn't possibly know how sensual she looked right now, lifting that glass to perfectly pouty lips and...

"Pew!" she spat, she gagged and sprayed tonic water all down her front. I leaped to my feet at the same time she did, but I was faster with the napkins, mopping and dabbing the spill from her front, not even realizing where my hands were landing until she looked at me again and I became aware of the rapid beating of her heart under my fingers.

My hand was right over her left breast. I snatched it away. "Okay then!" I said. "So, you don't like gin."

The corner of her mouth quirked up. I pressed my lips together, but I couldn't hold it anymore. I burst out laughing and this time Rachel joined in, a long, joyful sound that made me want to hear it again and again. "That was terrible," she groaned, gulping down the rest of her water.

"Well, now you know."

"This one time, when I was a little girl?" she said, and I stilled because I wanted to hear all about how it was for her growing up on the God's Chosen compound. "I climbed up a pine tree." She looked at me and rolled her eyes. "Yeah, I know, and in a skirt too. You just have to reach through your legs like this and then tuck it up in your waistband and you can climb just fine."

"You found a workaround," I nodded approvingly.

"Of course. So, I was climbing this big pine tree, and I couldn't have been more than five but I knew about maple sugaring, you know for syrup? I knew that the syrup was made from the sap. So..." She smiled softly as the memory stole her backward in time. "When I was climbing the pine tree and got a glob of sap on my hand I thought, 'ooh, candy!' and licked it right up."

"Oh no."

"Yup, it was terrible. I couldn't get the taste out of my mouth for days." She wrinkled her nose. "And that gin and tonic just now tasted *just like it.*"

"That's awesome," I laughed as she grinned at me. "How were you supposed to know, right?" Curiosity tugged at my thoughts. "So you made your own syrup in the... the..."

"Community," she supplied. "Yeah, there's a stand of trees on the northwest corner of our land." I was close enough to her to notice the way her lip twitched when she said the word 'our.' She shook her head. "It was always such a treat to have syrup because it is a *lot* of work, but it wasn't *hard* work because everyone was working together, you know?"

I licked my lips, choosing my words carefully. "Sounds like you have some nice memories."

Her smile was wistful. "Yeah, I guess I do." She picked up the Dark & Stormy glass and drained it down while her eyes stayed far away. And sad.

We have nothing in common, my brain insisted. Her life inside the cult was so different from my childhood spent touring all the continents and playing in huge arenas. And yet there was... something. Something about her...

"Do you miss it?" I asked.

"Sometimes," she said.

I hesitated. "Why did you leave?"

She dropped the glass back onto the bar with a loud *clack*. "Let's go dance," she said, her voice suddenly bright again. She reached down and grabbed my hand.

"Oh no, are you feeling it? Drink some water."

"I'm *fine,"* she huffed, exasperated. But her voice sure was louder than it had been a minute ago.

I was too wrapped up in how her fingers felt sliding across my wrist to really dwell on the fact that she hadn't answered my question about why she had left the 'community' as she called it. Around here, the word most often used for God's Chosen was 'cult.' But I wasn't about to argue semantics with her. I was too busy trying not to put my hands on her as she started to move with total abandon.

Shit. Here we were again, with her way too close to drunk for this to be okay. I felt like a middle schooler, reaching for her and then dropping my hands to my sides.

"Do you know this song?" I asked her, totally nonsensically. But I needed her to stop wiggling like... like that.

"Oh yeah!" she laughed. And then, just to prove it, she started to sing.

She may as well have punched me in the gut. Rachel... Rachel could *sing*. She raised her voice above the noise of the bar and started belting out the lyrics to an Ed Sheeran song in a clear, strong voice. I stood, frozen in place as I listened, feeling like she'd just revealed some deep secret that she'd trusted me to understand. I was blown away.

I was so blown away that I stepped back on my heels. Stepped back right into the path of another bar patron loaded down with beer.

A bump, a whoop and then I was suddenly showered with Bud Light as four pint glasses drenched me right down to my skin.

Rachel clapped her hands over her mouth as I turned to the stunned looking guy who'd just lost all of his drinks. "Hey, you okay? Sorry about that, let me buy you another round."

His face went from 'I will fight you' to sheepish in one breath. "Nah, it's coo. You okay? Here's a napkin."

I shook out the front of my shirt. "A napkin isn't going to cut it," I laughed. "I need a hose."

"You're not mad?" Rachel hissed as I waved to Taylor, signaling for four more beers to go on my tab.

"Why? It was my fault. I wasn't looking where I was going." *I was listening to you sing.*

Chapter Seven

RACHEL

I fully expected to feel terrible. But I didn't.

I stood at my tiny kitchen sink and tried to keep the smile off my face. Then gave up and grinned ear to ear as I sipped my coffee and stared out at the creek. It was my first day off in eight days, and it was a bright, sunny morning filled with the rasping cries of the red-winged blackbirds over in the marshy parts. After a night of drinking, I would normally be cursing the sun and the birds and the noise of the creek. But thanks to Beau - sweet, careful Beau - I felt just fine. Good even.

Like I'd gotten away with something.

I frowned down into my coffee mug. Coffee was still a new drug for me. As was alcohol of any kind. Having fun without consequences, without guilt hanging over my head, that was new for me too. I was seized with the need for - not penitence, no, something else.

When I was little, the men would gather in each other's homes and break the bread. Women and children were barred from this sacrament, but they pretended not to notice me and my sister as we hung quietly in the doorway and watched the ceremony. Always the men began by breaking off a little piece of the loaf - the loaf I'd helped my mother bake - and leaving it on the plate as an offering to our Savior.

An offering, then. I needed a way to say thank you. For a night filled with happiness and a morning free of pain.

All at once I knew what to offer. When it was our turn to provide the bread to the community Elders, I always whined and pushed my mother to bake something other than the usual hard brown loaves. I loved the fluffy white crumb of the potato bread that was her specialty. She'd taught me the recipe. My mother was a gifted baker whose loaves were always lighter than air. Chosen were not allowed selfishness or vanity, that was the explanation she gave me for never sharing her loaves with those outside of our family. But I liked to think it was some tiny spark of rebellion against being barred from the bread-breaking that made her keep it to herself.

She never shared it. But I wasn't Chosen anymore.

I could.

I picked up my coffee, took another fortifying sip and then started walking around the kitchen and gathering the ingredients, humming a little as I put on a pot of water to boil the potato. The song from last night with Beau was stuck in my head, the one I only knew because Juanita at work had it playing on repeat on her phone all the time. Beau had seemed surprised I knew the words. He'd been staring at me like I'd sprouted a second head right up until that guy dumped his beer all over him.

I smiled down at the potato I was peeling, remembering how funny he'd looked, standing there soaked in cheap beer. He had just... laughed. No temper, no yelling at the other man to watch where he was going. He'd even been kind enough to buy the man another round to replace the spilled one.

I dropped the potato into the water and wrinkled my nose. Chosen held themselves apart from the world, saying that secular, worldly people were selfish and lacking grace. But last night, all I'd seen was grace. Grace from a hedonistic pop star.

It didn't make sense.

Turning the flour out onto the counter, I started kneading it, pushing as hard as I could against the cool dough. This was the part where my mother always took over. With the quiet murmur of the creek in the background and the smell of the yeast filling my nostrils, I could almost be in her kitchen, helping her as my siblings ran riot through the house. She'd wipe her floured hands across her perfectly clean apron and smile at me as she rolled and beat the dough into submission. "Don't be afraid of it," she'd encouraged me.

Swallowing back an unexpected lump in my throat, I slammed the dough into the bowl, rolling it into a tight ball to start rising, then wiped the tear away from my eye before it could fall. Baking had brought my mother's presence so strongly, I could almost hear her voice.

Guilt washed over me. I *could* hear her voice. The community had a telephone, one line to call out if there was an emergency. If I called it, my mother might pick up.

Or one of the other seventy-five people counted among the Crown Creek Chosen. They were the ones I had left. They were the ones who had driven me out for not being whole. The rest of the community. But not my parents, and most certainly not my mother.

I clenched my fists, digging my nails into my palm. My silent house, my solitary life, they were nothing like what I once had.

Hastily, I wiped my eyes again and headed over to shower while the dough rose, hurrying past Everly's shut door without looking. Once I was dressed and the bread was in the oven, I turned on Everly's TV and put the volume up as high as it went, pretending that the cacophony of voices belonged to people here in the room with me.

Since leaving the Chosen, I'd been floating like a leaf caught in a current. It took Everly to pull me out of my solitary drift and feel connected again. We were connected as friends.

My connection with Beau.

That felt... different.

The awful screeching noise of the oven timer broke through the noise of the TV and my thoughts. I rushed over and opened the oven, letting out the warm smells of home that made my heart swell too big for my chest. I wrapped it loosely in a towel, and then stood there, suddenly nervous.

Last night he'd asked me why I left the Chosen. I hadn't answered him because that reason was still too painful to speak aloud. A lot of people had asked me that question, most with their own ulterior motives, most gawking at me like I was some kind of zoo animal when they asked it.

Beau had done something no one else ever had. "Sounds like you have some nice memories," he'd said.

That was why I had baked this. To share it. To share my good memories. But what if he laughed again? Or worse, what if he looked at the bread and saw it only as something to eat and not... not...

A connection?

I'd been brave before, I reminded myself as I tucked it into a tote bag and grabbed my keys. I'd done much braver things in my life than wait for the lumbering bus with bread in my hand and my heart on my sleeve. I'd struck out on my own, leaving behind everything I ever knew and facing down a world I'd been taught to fear, so it should have been no big deal at all to pull the cord to stop the bus and get off. I'd listened to a somber-faced doctor as he told me that surgery was the only way to keep me from bleeding to death, so it should have been the easiest thing in the world to walk past Everly's parents' house and then turn at the big yellow farmhouse on the hill.

A shadow flickered past the window as I stood there in the drive, nervously twisting the straps of the bag in my hands. I jumped a little when the front door opened and the screen door swung wide. "Rachel?" Beau called.

I let out a long breath to see him smile. "You're up," I said.

"I've been up." He looked happy to see me. My heart was soaring up like a bird. "You look well rested too."

I smiled and stepped onto the porch, then stopped and sniffed, then laughed. "Are you sure you're not hungover?" I teased. "You still smell like beer."

"Aw man, really?" He rubbed his shaggy head and then sniffed his hand. "I swear. I've already showered twice." His eyes grazed over me, leaving those trails of heat wherever they lingered. "But what have you got there?"

"Bread," I said, holding out my tote. "Potato bread."

He looked down at the bag and then up at me, clearly confused. "That's really nice but..."

"You said carbs help with hangovers, so I thought—" I stopped explaining mid-sentence, caught up in the way his grin was broadening, getting prouder. "Bread," I finished lamely and almost threw it into his hands.

He caught it easily. "Come help me eat it," he insisted, stepping out onto the porch and pushing the screen door wider.

I hesitated. From inside I could hear the sounds of people, of a family going about their morning business. Sounds of clinking dishes and shouted plans. I blinked away the stubborn tears that had been threatening to fall since I'd started baking. "Sure," I said.

And stepped into the Kings' house.

It was the first time I'd been in a secular home. I don't know what I expected. Certainly not a perfectly normal, rambling farmhouse stuffed with the clutter of family life. A wide staircase to my left, a high-ceilinged living room straight ahead. I could see through the doorway into a light-filled sunroom full of plants and over in that same corner a huge grand piano hulked, taking up half the room. "Whose piano is that?" I wondered.

"Mine." Beau wandered over to the bench and sat down, then swiveled to look at me. "Hey, I'm glad you're here by the way. I wanted to ask you something."

I licked my lips, suddenly wary. He'd given me no reason to fear him, but it was hard to go against a lifetime of warnings. "What is that?" I asked, clutching my purse to my body.

He leaned in, tilting his head as if to study me. My breath was coming in short, shallow gasps as I felt the heat of his gaze everywhere my skin was exposed. I tugged on the sleeve of my T-shirt, nonsensically trying to shield my arm.

He leaned back then, like he sensed my discomfort, and dragged his gaze back up to my eyes. "I just wanted to know. Where did you learn to sing like that?"

I gasped out a shocked laugh. "Like what?"

"Rachel," he said, leaning in again. "Don't you know? You sing like a goddamn angel."

Chapter Eight

BEAU

She colored, ducked, looked away.

The smell of her bread was filling my nostrils and the sight of her here, in my house, was filling my heart up. Talking about her singing seemed to make her uncomfortable, so I stood up. "I'm starving and this smells too good," I declared, picking up her threadbare tote. "I hope you don't expect me to share this with the rest of my family or anything, because that's not happening."

"Are they around?" she asked, looking suddenly eager.

I shrugged. "Somewhere, yeah. Mom's probably in her room with a stack of biographies until she heads out to her part-time job at the library. Dad's most likely found something around the house that needs fixing, whether it was broken in the first place or not. Finn?" I shrugged. "My brother sleeps like it's his job these days, so I don't expect him to stumble down the stairs until mid-afternoon, and my sister is the only one of us with a regular job, so she's up in Reckless Falls doing whatever it is she does for that Granger Development guy." I smiled at her. "So, at the moment, your bread is completely safe." I clutched it to my chest. "Except from me."

She laughed, that big, throaty sound I'd heard last night. "Don't build it up too big in your head," she admonished me. "It probably didn't turn out that great. I'm not as good a baker as my mother."

I cocked my head at her. "You have a hard time accepting compliments, don't you?" I prodded gently.

She colored again and looked down, mumbling something I could barely hear. Something about the sin of pride. "Well I don't think it's a sin to share the gifts you were given," I said, reaching out to squeeze her arm. When she didn't stop me from touching her, I got bolder, brushing my fingers up to lift the weight of her hair off her shoulders, marveling at the length of it, as well as the silky strands. "Your hair is beautiful."

"Is that one of my gifts I should share?" she asked softly.

I looked down at her. "If you don't mind."

"I don't mind," she breathed. "And, ah. Thank you."

Feeling no small amount of triumph, I gestured for her to head into the kitchen ahead of me. She settled onto one of the stools along the kitchen island while I got out a cutting board and a knife. "What's good on this?" I asked her. "Butter?"

"It's pretty delicious just plain," she said. When I looked up in surprise, she smiled again. "Another gift," she said, somehow looking both shy and sly at the same time.

I was speechless then, and I was speechless again once the still warm bread hit my tongue. "Jesus Christ," I swore, then glanced at her and mumbled an apology. "This is fucking delicious. Sorry. But seriously, how the fuck did you bake this? Sorry again."

"It's my mother's recipe," she said, a note of wistful pride in her voice.

I heard it and that same curiosity overtook me again. "It's a gift," I said. "As is that voice of yours."

She licked a crumb from the corner of her mouth and watched me. She wasn't saying anything. But she also wasn't ducking away.

That was progress.

I extended my hand. "Come over here with me."

"Where are we going?"

"Just to the piano. I just want to hear you again, is that okay? Without all the noise of the bar and everything?"

She hesitated and looked like she'd rather bolt out the front door than follow me. But then she let her hand slip into mine. I felt a jolt of electricity when her skin slid against mine and I was surprised by the strength in her fingers and the roughness of her palms. These hands knew hard work.

God, I really fucking liked her.

I led her back into the living room and let go of her hand as I slid onto the piano bench. I couldn't help but sigh with pleasure as I brushed my fingers over the keys. Wherever Finn and I ended up moving, we needed to find room for this, my favorite instrument. Light was streaming in through the windows, and little dust mites danced crazily in the beams. If you squinted, it was almost like we had a spotlight shining on us.

I remembered how last night she had sung to an Ed Sheeran song, so I started playing the intro to "Perfect." But when I got to the part where the vocals kicked in, she only looked at me blankly.

"Don't know that one?" I asked.

She pressed her lips together and shook her head.

I shifted on the bench a little. "That's okay, you'll know this one, I'm sure." I picked out the melody of "Shape of You," and raised my eyebrows.

Her face was still blank, although a trace of anxiety had crept into her expression.

"No problem, I'm sure you know the words to this." I started playing "I Will Always Love You," figuring everyone on earth knew that song, whether it was the Whitney version or the Dolly Parton one.

She shifted from side to side but didn't open her mouth. I trailed off, letting my fingers slide from the keys.

"Maybe I should go," she said, picking up her bag.

"No!" I said, far more loudly than I intended. She looked startled and I quickly held up my hands. "One more time. Sorry."

Turning back to the keys, I wracked my brain. Popular songs were out. She'd grown up in a different world from the one I'd occupied. I knew this on some intellectual level, but this really drove home the fact that we were speaking different languages. I had no idea what musical language she spoke, what songs would speak to her and let that voice of hers shine out again, except?

Except I did.

I lifted my fingers and started plinking out the barely remembered melody and then looked up. Rachel's face, which had been contorted in anxious confusion, smoothed out. She tilted her head, listening as I felt out the melody and added the chords.

And then she sang.

First halting as she watched me watch her. But then her eyes fell closed and the song tumbled from her lips. "Amazing Grace, how sweet the sound..."

The sound was sweeter than any I'd heard before. My fingers played on their own, all my attention was wrapped up in the way her head was tilted up to the sunbeam, awash in the light. She looked like an angel, a piece of my personal heaven.

When the last chord rang out, we both stilled. The quiet lasted for one breath.

And then I was on my feet. Kissing her.

Chapter Nine

RACHEL

First kiss.

It was screaming through my head. Two words.

First kiss.

First kiss.

First kiss.

The words clanged so loud that they drowned out all other thoughts. Leaving me shocked, soft and pliable when Beau's teasing tongue swept a tentative taste across my bottom lip.

A bolt shot through me, raising the hairs on my scalp and making my toes curl in my shoes. Sudden and slick and all-consuming, and it felt so good that terror froze my blood. It seemed fitting that at that moment the sun slipped behind a cloud, sending the room into hazy darkness.

I pushed him back and stepped away. My hand fluttered up to my cheek and I expected my skin to be ice cold in fear.

The heat - my heat - almost burned me.

Beau's hazel eyes were still closed, but they fluttered open now and the second they fixed on me I had to fight the urge to run. Just run as far and as fast as my legs could carry me. The softness drained from his face as he watched me, eyes darting all over me, heating my skin. If you flicked water on me, I was certain it would sizzle upon contact. "Are you okay?" Beau asked.

Mutely, I stared at him but inside I was screaming. *What was that?!?* my brain shouted. *What was that feeling? What did you DO to me?*

Shame dumped hot leaden guilt into my veins, making my limbs heavy and sluggish. But even as it coursed through me, a little spark burned hot and eager inside of my breast.

Whatever you did to me, it whispered, *could you do it again?*

Hurriedly, I shook my head. "No," I breathed, and then made to turn into the kitchen, nonsensically fixed on grabbing my loaf pan before I bolted from the house.

And nearly ran straight into Finn King.

"Oops," he drawled, reaching out to steady me, but the feel of his hand on my arm was too much, I swerved to the side like a cornered bull and stopped dead when I saw Claire King.

The Kings' house was huge. The living room itself was larger than some houses in the Chosen compound. Houses shared by a family of thirteen or more. This house was a palace in comparison, so big that Beau and I should have gone completely unnoticed, but here were his brother and sister right in the doorway. Finn smirking, Claire smiling.

They had seen, what had they seen?

Merciful heavens, *what had they seen?*

In a flash, I was twelve years old again, squirming in my seat during fellowship, looking down at my thick-soled shoes, because if I looked up, I ran the risk of making eye contact with the girl - my *friend* - who was now crying in the center of the room. Her skirts were raised, fisted in her shaking hands as she tried to hold back her yelps of pain. I couldn't see the angry red lashes that crisscrossed the backs of Ruthie's thighs, but I could hear every harsh whack of the switch, and I could hear the curt monotone of the Elder who was dispassionately counting out each stroke. Twelve lashes. That was the punishment for contact outside of marriage. Ruth Wall had been caught kissing Zeke Clemstead - and Zeke was standing in the middle of the circle with his head bowed in red-faced agony as he awaited his turn - and the price for being welcomed back into the fold after the sin of fornication was twelve public lashes and a month of hard labor.

"Was that you singing?" Claire gasped, clutching her hands to her heart and bringing me sharply back to the present.

"It sure wasn't Beau," Finn reminded her, as I tried to still my shaking and remember that I lived in the secular world now. That getting caught in a kiss wasn't something that brought condemnation and shame. I wasn't Chosen anymore.

"That was her," Beau said from behind me.

I winced as Claire shook her head. "No way, Rachel. You are *fucking* amazing."

"Claire," Beau rumbled under his breath and I knew he was correcting his sister for cursing near me, but I was too preoccupied with what this meant.

"You... you heard me?" There was some small part of me that wanted to turn a cartwheel at the news of this, but it was drowned out by the voice of the Elders in my head. *Vanity,* they intoned. *Pride is a terrible sin.* The sin of vanity was not lash worthy. No. Vanity meant having your head shaved and your face scarred. Vanity meant having your possessions stripped and "returned" to the community. Vanity was the accusation you shouted in fellowship if you were jealous of your neighbor's tidy house and happy children. Vanity was something you had to be ever vigilant against, lest your children find themselves waking up in a strange house and being asked to call someone else mother. All Chosen steered cleared of anything resembling pride or vanity, of calling attention to themselves and giving themselves glory.

Vanity was the worst sin there was.

The Kings were chattering on easily around me, unaware of the storm that was raging inside of me.

"You have the voice of an angel," Beau was saying as Claire nodded, but his voice was little more than static in my head. I hugged my arms around my body, but my skin was still buzzing from that bolt from Beau's lips. The mere brush of my fingers over my own skin was enough to make me feel feverish.

"Is that what you all are doing down there in that cult of yours?" Finn piped up. "Singing hymns like a freaking gospel choir and shit?"

"*Finn!*" both Beau and Claire hissed.

I lifted my chin. This was more familiar territory, one I was used to navigating. "The Chosen are not a cult," I corrected him. "The word cult implies that we aren't free to leave when we want to. I think I'm proof that's not the case."

It was a practiced speech, and Finn seemed to hear the rehearsed nature of it because he just rolled his eyes and hefted himself up off the doorframe. "Sure," he said.

I looked from Finn back to his brother. They looked so alike, but the difference between them seemed to be down at the soul level. I'd been drawn to Beau from the first time I saw him, but Finn almost repelled me.

"Whatever, it doesn't matter," Claire jumped in. Beau's sister reached out and grabbed my hand, giving it a squeeze. "You've never taken lessons though, right? Like, please don't take this the wrong way because you've got natural talent falling out of your ass, oops!" She clapped her hand over her mouth and I grinned, deciding that I liked Beau's sister way more than I did his brother. "Sorry! I use cuss words like commas."

"It's fine," I said. It really was. Cursing no longer sounded foreign to my ears. After all, I wasn't Chosen anymore. I had left.

I'd left willingly, and I'd also willingly come to Beau's home for...

For what?

My fingers went to my lips again. That kiss was lingering there, haunting me like a ghost. "It's fine," I repeated.

"You sure?" Claire exhaled, eyes wide. "It's fine if it's not, like I don't want to offend you and everything, I know it's like against your religion to cuss and whatever." She leaned in, a keenly interested light now shining in her eyes. "You're like, out-out, right? Like fully and completely not in it anymore?"

"Yes."

She stepped back a little at my curt, one-word response, but then brushed it off. "Okay, well yeah, duh, obviously, because you're here. I just wanted to make sure because like..." She trailed off and gestured to my head. "You've still got the, the..."

I reached back and touched the heavy braid that hung like a rope down the center of my back. "Yes," I repeated and for some reason, I glanced at Beau. He was watching his sister carefully, not saying anything to halt her litany of questions. Not that I would have expected him to, except.

Except I couldn't help but notice the way he had shifted his body weight. He'd unobtrusively, but very deliberately, placed himself half in front of me. Shielding me if not from her questions, then at least from her gaze.

I shifted my balance to my other foot. Beau's broad, muscled back now formed a wall between me and his siblings and for some reason this made it easier to speak. "It's symbolic," I said. "I mean, to me anyway."

"What does it symbolize?" Claire's voice floated up from the other side of Beau.

I lifted the rope of my braid and let it fall back down, feeling the reassuring weight on my scalp. When I was a kid, I thought of the long braids of the Chosen women as tethers. A way to keep us anchored to the community.

It still did that now. "When I left," I said, softly, haltingly. "It was not because... it was not because I really wanted to. It was because... because I had to."

Beau shifted a little and turned to look at me. A quick flick of his eyes had me nodding that yes, I was okay, even though I had no idea how I knew that was what he was asking.

Claire caught the pain in my voice. "Why's that?"

The words seized in my chest and only came out on the heels of a strangled cry. "There was no place for me," I whispered.

And in that moment, I missed my family so intensely I could barely breathe. I could only stand there, rooted to the spot, watching as if on the other side of a glass wall while Beau herded his siblings away from me. Claire's apologies were a jumbled mess in my head, but Beau's words were loud and clear. "Get out of here," he rumbled. "Give her some fucking space, Jesus, she's not a goddamn zoo animal!"

"I'm sorry," he said when he turned back to me. His strong hands gripped my upper arms, squeezing me. I found I liked the contact, liked the pressure. Without it, I might shatter into a million pieces. "Claire means well. The second she meets someone she likes, she wants to know everything about them. I'm sure she's practically ready to adopt you at this point." He squeezed a little tighter. "But you don't need that right? You're doing just fine. Come on, let me take you back home."

The tightness in my chest released enough that I was able to gulp a swift breath. "Yes. Thank you."

He quickly turned on his heel and disappeared into the kitchen, returning with my loaf pan. I looked down in surprise. "This is what you were heading for, right?" he teased me gently. "When you were trying to run away from me?"

My chest loosened by another degree and I was able to look up at him again. "Yes, it was," I said, taking it from him and clutching it possessively to my chest. He hummed out an amused sound and then gestured for me to follow him.

I fell into step behind him so automatically that it took a second for my brain to catch up and realize what I was doing and when it finally did, I stumbled forward in a clumsy stutter step. Beau had a hand out in a moment, and once again the natural reaction of my body to rely on him, to lean on him, to follow him made me widen my eyes in disbelief.

This wasn't okay. Me being here. Me letting him kiss me. Me catching his arm and brushing my fingers against his warm skin. None of this was okay.

But it felt that way. It felt intensely...

Right.

It felt right to sit in companionable silence as he drove me the few miles back to my house that I could have easily walked. It felt right to brush against him as I shifted in my seat, and the crisp hairs of his forearm lightly tickling mine felt more right than anything ever had before. I had to work to conjure the disapproving voices of the Elders and when I finally did, their voices were far fainter than the one whispering "stay."

Stay.

Stay with me.

He pulled into the rutted gravel drive in front of my shabby cottage and put the car in park. When he shifted in his seat to look at me, there was a momentary flash of something in his eyes that had me ready to run away and hide, but it was followed quickly by the warm glow of something that made me desperately want to stay here with him in this car forever.

"Sorry again about my sister," he said. "I hope she didn't scare you so much you'll never come over again."

"She didn't scare me," I said, although the quaver in my voice made me sound like a liar.

He leaned in a little, close enough so that the warmth of his breath hit thc shell of my ear. "Did I?" he murmured.

I swallowed. What was the right thing to do here? Was it to lie and say no? Or tell the truth and say yes, he terrified me, but I wanted him to do it again?

"I'm not scared of *you,*" I finally said.

He pulled back from my ear and gazed at me a moment. I was close enough to see the ring of dark emerald around the iris of his eye. "What are you scared of?" he asked and before I could answer he went on, "Is it how I make you feel?"

I opened my mouth to tell him the truth, but my words were swallowed by the brush of his lips. It was the barest hint of a kiss, nothing like the soul-devouring one in his living room. But I could feel his restraint, the effort he was making to hold back and that...

"Yes," I breathed against his mouth. And I didn't pull away.

Chapter Ten

BEAU

I'd kissed her for only a moment, though I could have easily gone on kissing her forever, in awe of how soft her lips were, how sweet her mouth tasted.

It was the small noise she made in the back of her throat when my tongue found hers that made me remember myself. Remember where I was and what had just happened.

And who she was. And whatever she had been through that made her voice catch in a quiet sob as she remembered it.

I pulled back from her, alarmed at how I'd forgotten all of this so easily. Apologies sprang to my lips but died there when she quietly turned and opened the door.

I watched her cross the driveway and head into her little house and only then did my shoulders slump. "Fuck!" I shouted, slamming the heel of my palm into the steering wheel. "You fucking asshole!"

For the rest of the day, my glum self-hatred rivaled Finn's in its intensity. After she got home from work, Claire started hanging around, getting in my eyeline and being super chipper. Her way of apologizing for being a nosy little gossip, I supposed, but I wasn't feeling charitable to anyone. Least of all myself.

For fuck's sake, Rachel was off-limits. Wanting her this much was wrong. Only some douche-bag asshole would be thinking about a sheltered girl like her this way. And now that I knew she had the pure voice of an angel to go along with those innocent brown eyes and full, pretty lips?

No way. Look but don't touch, that had to be the rule from now on.

But even as I spent the day admonishing myself, her words kept running through my head. She wasn't scared of me.

She was scared of how she felt about me.

That makes two of us, angel.

The next morning, Claire was still hovering, purposefully getting in my path as I stumbled and cursed my way to the coffee maker, still not awake even after a freezing shower. "Good morning!" she trumpeted.

"Too loud," Finn snarled from his position slumped over the kitchen table.

"Don't we have some houses to look at today?" she asked me, ignoring our brother.

I let out a long exhale. "Fuck," I hissed. I was not in the mood to do anything other than beat myself up for how I'd crossed that line with Rachel, but Claire was right. "Yeah, Finn, you ready?"

"I'm not coming," he snarled.

Claire and I looked at each other. Some of my worry about Rachel slid away as heavy meaning settled like a wet blanket over the both of us. "Aren't you interested in what kind of house you and Beau end up in?" Claire asked. I bristled. That was far too on the nose. One of the first signs of Finn's depression setting in was him losing interest in everything that used to be important to him. I knew why Claire was asking, but Finn wasn't dumb. He was going to hear the subtext.

I was right. My brother leaned back in his chair and glared at Claire. "Nope!" he said. He sounded cheerful enough, but I knew him too well. He was pissed. "Not interested at all. Beau can just go ahead and make the decision for me," he said, meeting my eye. "Like he always does."

I shifted and stood up straighter. "What the fuck did I do?" I asked.

He turned away with a grunt. I rolled my eyes and shot my sister a knowing smirk.

She didn't return it, only bounced once on her toes. "I'm coming with you again," she informed me.

I could hear something under her words, something she was trying to tell me, but I didn't know what it could be. Shrugging, I went over and grabbed my keys. "I'm driving this time," I told her. "There is nothing wrong with my car."

She whined about it all the way out into the driveway and right up until we were seated in the busted up old Crown Vic my dad had restored for Finn and me for our sixteenth birthday. I tuned out her complaints as she bitched about the lack of Bluetooth, thinking about the last person who'd been in that seat.

The more I told myself to stop thinking about Rachel, the more I thought about Rachel. The more I wanted to see her again, hear that clear, pure voice of hers and watch the corners of her mouth tip up in a sweet smile as she sang. The more I reminded myself that she was and should stay off limits, the more I wanted to hear that noise again, the one she'd made as her tongue sought mine. Because it almost sounded like she liked kissing me as much as I had liked kissing her.

What would she do if I kissed her again? Would she tell me no? She had never told me no, it had all been the guilt-ridden voice inside my head.

Would she see me again? If I came over? But why would I come over?

"You're quiet this morning," Claire said, interrupting the spiraling vortex of my thoughts. "Worried about Finn?"

I sat up a little straighter and tried to push Rachel from my head, but she refused to budge. "Yeah," I grunted. It wasn't exactly a lie, because I *was* worried about my brother. I just... hadn't been thinking about him right then.

"What are you thinking we should do?"

She caught me. "Actually, I was thinking about Rachel."

I could practically hear the record screech in Claire's head. "Ray-chul?" she sing-songed in the most annoying way possible. "Rachel the Chosen girl *that you kissed?"*

"Yes, thank you, I'm glad for you that your eyes work." I took my eyes off the road for a second to narrow my eyes at her, but that only made her cackle louder. "I'm thinking maybe I shouldn't have done that."

Claire threw up her hands. "Jesus Christ Beau, I swear you *like* feeling guilty. Did she slap you?" When I didn't answer, she shoved me in the arm, making me swerve a little. "Hey!" I said as she shook me.

"Did she slap you?"

"No."

"Then you're fine. You and Finn, I swear, it's like mirror images. He doesn't feel bad about *anything*, you feel bad about *everything*. Oh, it's right up on the right." She pointed at the last second and the Crown Vic sent up a shower of dust when I yanked the wheel to the right, narrowly missing the nearly hidden drive. "Oh shit," Claire breathed reverently as we rolled to a stop.

I sat back heavily in my seat. "Yeah, you can say that again."

It was perfect. Set back against a stand of pines, the timber-framed house resembled a log cabin on steroids. A huge deck wrapped around the front, overlooking a sloping lawn that led down to a picturesque little pond. I stepped out to inhale the smell of pine tree warmed in the sun. Dragonflies hovered over the water and a single noisy frog was piping up quite a melodic little racket, but otherwise, the only sound was the slight rustle of the wind through the cattails that ringed the banks. There was no sound of passing traffic and no sign of any neighbors except the slight hint of wood smoke that spiced the air.

It was exactly what Finn wanted.

"This is it, yes, yes," Claire danced over to me and excitedly shoved her phone under my nose to show me the listing. "And it has enough bedrooms that like, you could have *us* over for dinner and to crash for once."

"Us?" I teased, even as I took the phone from her and scrolled through the listing.

And then sighed.

I'd put this house down on our list for, well I wasn't exactly sure why I thought we needed to see it, other than catch a glimpse of what we could never have. "It's too expensive."

"Seriously?" She snatched her phone away and squinted at the screen. Then whistled. "Yeah okay, that's a lot, but you have it, right?"

"I have half of it."

"Okay, but isn't that all you need?"

"Do you really think Finn has his half?" It was impossible to keep the edge out of my voice when I asked that question. Claire knew all about how I'd covered him when the four King brothers gave a portion of our earnings to our parents so they could retire. After all, we owed the band's success to them running us to a million far-flung festivals and appearances when we were first starting out. "Maybe back when we were touring," I went on. "But you know it's gone now."

Claire fell silent - for once - and lifted her face to the sun and closed her eyes. "You know he's spiraling, right?"

"'Course I do."

"His demons are getting to him again."

"I can see that." The sarcasm, the bitterness. I knew what that meant. "And there isn't much we can do except—"

"Head him off at the pass with a giant change," Claire interrupted me. "He's going to start picking fights again if he doesn't find something to distract him."

I looked back up at the house. "This would be a distraction."

"It would."

"But he needs money. Or hell, the both of us do."

"Yeah, too bad you are both completely unqualified for anything resembling a job." Claire loved getting in those little jabs.

"We're qualified to play music." An idea was starting to snowball in my head. "Hey, come on. Let's go let him know we found the perfect fucking house and we're gonna drag him to a showing if it kills him." My sister was already nodding and getting back into the car when another idea piggybacked onto the first. "But can we make one stop beforehand?"

Chapter Eleven

RACHEL

I spend all day cleaning up other people's messes so usually I left mine alone.

Not today.

"Come on," I mumbled as I turned the sponge over and attacked the stain with the scouring side. "I'll get out the bleach if I have to." The pink ring had lived happily in the bathroom sink since Everly and I had moved into the place, but not anymore.

The mysterious fluorescent mold around the drain was not the first casualty this morning. I'd been at it since I woke, flustered and breathless after some very confusing dreams, at five AM. On my day off. Lying in bed and trying to go back to sleep had only brought frustration, and the third time Beau's hazel eyes popped unbidden into my head was when I finally propelled myself out of bed and right to the cleaning supplies.

Hard labor was part of the penance for fornication. There was no one here to flog me - except myself, with my own mind - but maybe if I cleaned my house, I could clean my soul in the process. First I'd opened all the windows and doors, letting in the fresh smell of early summer. But the fresh air wasn't enough to blow away the thoughts of Beau from my mind.

What would my parents say if they knew that I had kissed him? A debauched rockstar, the very definition of a worldly sinner? "Come on," I snarled at the stain, ignoring the way the cleaner burned my hand. I scrubbed so hard that my finger knocked against the faucet, opening a scrape on my knuckle. I ran the water and let the tinge of pink swirl down the now sparkling drain. The sink was whiter than it had ever been, and all the battered nickel fixtures gleamed like they were new. I lifted my knuckle to my lips and absently sucked on my knuckle then spat into the sink. "Guess I need gloves now."

I padded out into the kitchen and was pulling on the bright yellow dishwashing gloves that lived under the sink when a sharp rat-a-tat-tat jolted me out of my mumbling-to-stains reverie. "Oh!"

Beau was there on my sunken porch, just on the other side of the screen door. I blushed in immediate guilt, certain that I had somehow managed to conjure him from thin air just by thinking about him non-stop.

"Sorry, are you busy?" He was looking right at the bright yellow gloves.

"Uh." For some reason, my fingers went right to my lips. Where his kiss still lingered.

The dreams I'd had last night came flooding back, overloading my senses and heating my cheeks. As my heart rate sped up, I ducked away from his hazel eyes, wanting to feel anything but delight at seeing him here. Even though I was wearing one of my old Chosen undergarments, loose and shapeless, tucked into a pair of ripped and paint-spattered jeans, I still felt beautiful the second his gaze heated my skin.

And that's when I knew that my cleaning had done nothing. My soul was still tainted with the memory of his kiss. And what's more, I liked it.

"I just wanted to ask you something." He was still on the other side of the door, unaware of the turmoil he'd unleashed inside of me.

"We wanted to ask you something." Claire popped out from behind her brother, startling me out of my introspection, and opened the door to let herself in. "It was my idea in the first place, wasn't it?"

Beau followed her in with his lips screwed up like he was trying not to smile. "Sorry." He glared pointedly at Claire. "We probably could have called but—"

"Man, this place looks fantastic!" Claire looked around appreciatively and took a deep breath. "Smells amazing too. Like... bleach and pine trees."

"I was cleaning." I held up my gloves as if they needed a deeper explanation as if they couldn't see that every cupboard was open, every dish was out on the counter and the floor was still wet in some places. "So, um..."

Beau picked up on my confusion immediately. "Claire and I were out looking for houses when I had an idea."

"It was my idea!" Claire stepped in front of him. "So I want to say it. Rachel?" All that brash, little-sister confidence drained from her face and she looked suddenly shy. "You have such a pretty voice. Can I give you voice lessons?"

I dropped my sponge. "What?" Crouching down to grab it again hid my blush of pleasure. At least I hoped it did. I was suddenly reminded of the time our barn dog had puppies, and the way they'd tumble around, tails wagging, basking in the pleasure of being loved and petted. If I had a tail right now, it would be wagging just like that. "You want to teach me?" I repeated.

"I'm not a professional like my brothers." She punctuated that statement with a hefty eyeroll. "But I helped my friend Ruby with the school play last spring and I really enjoyed teaching those kids how to sing."

"My sister was in that." At their shocked expressions, I straightened a little and took off my gloves. "My parents started sending her to secular school this past fall." And I had been more jealous than I wanted to admit, that she'd been given the opportunity to do something I'd so desperately wanted for myself. Those same bad feelings had sent me into a cleaning spree at the hotel I'd been living at when I heard the news. "She loved being in the play."

At least I thought she had. Lydia hadn't been allowed to contact me since I left the compound. My mother's last letter had mentioned it in passing, buried in news about the children being born or fostered in the community and a whole paragraph about one of the cows getting stuck in the mud by the creek. I'd had to read between the lines.

Claire's eyes had widened into saucers. Then she snapped her fingers. "Little Lydia!" I smiled when I heard my little sister's name and Claire nodded. "Oh my God! It makes so much sense now! You guys have the same color hair, like, exactly. She's a mini-you, why the hell didn't I see that? Anyway," she grabbed my ungloved hand and squeezed. "That means it's fate. You *have* to let me teach you. You have such a talent."

I half-nodded before I even thought to distractedly worry about the vanity laced in that statement. My sister had been allowed to sing in a play and bow to the audience's applause.

Why not me?

I wanted it. I wanted to learn, to get better. I wanted to do something I was *good* at, something I *loved,* and I didn't want to feel bad about it.

"Yes."

She and Beau froze in place and looked at each other. I took a deep breath. "Okay yeah, that sounds great." As soon as I said it, I felt a spark inside of me. Like a match struck and held to a wick, it flickered and then burned bright to life. I squeezed my sponge and then set it deliberately on the counter, then blinked confusedly at the fury of bleach and scrubbing that surrounded me, as if it had been done by someone else. The only connection I felt to the penance I'd designed for myself was the way my knuckle throbbed dully. Distracted, I exhaled. "I think I'm done cleaning."

The Kings sprang into action. "Here." Beau grabbed a stack of plates. "Where do these go? I'll help you put them away."

"Singing while you work helps pass the time, you know." Claire was shoving my colander into the wrong drawer, but I didn't stop her. I just cleared my throat and started humming the melody of an old hymn that was as familiar to me as the lines on my palm. "Breathe from your diaphragm," Claire said idly. Then reached out and pressed the flat of her hand just below my ribcage. "Make my hand go up when you breathe, in. See? See how that brings the tone down from your head? Yes!" Her smile was wide and proud. "Listen to you!"

"Listen to you," Beau echoed. His fingertips were pressed to his lips. I'd only glanced over at him for a second, but his hazel gaze seemed to trap mine in a snare and suddenly I was singing right to him as I watched his face transform into wonder. "You have to do this," he said. "You have such a beautiful voice."

I closed my eyes. I could feel it, the compliment, how it traveled through my body right to my tingling fingers and curling toes. This flush of pride was something I had never allowed myself before because it was a full-on, open defiance of the way I'd been raised.

Rebellion.

It was seductive and sudden, and I knew I should fear it, but I was too busy smiling proudly. I opened my eyes again. "When can I start?"

Chapter Twelve

BEAU

It felt like there was a balloon in my chest. It inflated every time I was within fifty feet of Rachel and I was practically floating now.

But when we walked back into my parents' empty house, it popped. "Where is he?" Claire spoke my thoughts aloud.

"Bed," I grumbled, not even needing what Jonah and Gabe called my "scary twin sixth sense" to know that that was where my brother was now. Wrapped in a blanket - in spite of the warm June afternoon - and staring at the wall.

Claire turned to look at me, cheeks white, "You want me to go?"

"I've got it." I was already climbing the stairs.

His door was shut all the way, latch though hopefully not locked. I knocked hesitantly, then called myself a pussy and knocked louder. "Yo, Finnegan. I've got news."

There was no reply, but I heard the sound of his bed creak, so I knew he was awake. "Hey, I'm coming in." I tested the handle. Not locked. I opened it slowly, giving him time to get used to the idea of me intruding. "How are you doing in here? Jesus." I paused and fanned the door. "It's hot as balls in here, how are you not sweating to death under those blankets like that?" I strode to the window and made to open it, but it was stuck. "Jeez, this is bad, why didn't you tell me? I could have fixed this for you, I think the wood must have swelled or something. All that rain last month." I couldn't seem to stop making stupid observations. He was my own twin brother, but his silence made me feel awkward as hell. "Hey, you know, when we have our own place, we can turn on the A/C without Dad having a coronary, wouldn't that be awesome?"

Finn gave me no sign that he was listening. His dull eyes were fixed intently - but disinterestedly - on the ceiling.

His room it smelled... sad. The air was heavy and stale, and the faintly acrid odor let me know that he'd stopped showering, probably days ago. It hit me all at once that him coming downstairs and having breakfast with us was just him going through the motions. His laughter was false, his participation was just for show. Nothing was reaching him anymore, except...

I could. "Speaking of which. We found a house," I said, plopping myself at the foot of his bed. He obligingly shifted his feet to give me space, but he didn't say anything, not even when I started telling him all about the secluded place Claire and I had found. "It's so quiet there, Finnasaurus Rex. Exactly what you're looking for. It's even got this little fishing pond and I think we scared some ducks. There's definitely a frog, a loud little fucker too, so you most likely could hear him from the big wrap-around deck that overlooks his habitat."

"Cool."

One word. He didn't even lift his head. Gritting my teeth, I pressed on. "We can schedule a showing, but we should do it soon. I doubt a place like that is going to stay on the market for long. You're probably not the only pseudo-hermit in the Crown Creek area." I waited, giving him time to collect his thoughts, and as I did, I couldn't help but do a sweep of the room. Was he taking his meds and this was just a normal downturn? Did he need a higher dose? Should I be badgering him to go see his shrink? Oh Christ, there was another fight I'd have to gear up for. "Finn?" My brother was still silent, but I knew he was listening, I could feel his tension and knew that the only thing that was keeping him from bolting from this room was the heavy weight of his depression that kept him lying down. "So the only problem is that it's a bit out of our price range, but that's to be expected since it's a pretty kick-ass house." I swallowed and then nodded to myself. Yes. This was the right move. "But I know where we can get the money, man. Easy-peasy. I just have to make some phone calls. Sounds good, right?"

I waited in the deafening silence for him to give me something. Anything. Hell, even a sarcastic comment shooting me down would be preferable to this apathetic silence. "Finn, where are your meds?"

"Fuck off." My brother rolled back to the wall.

I stood up. "You're taking them, right?"

"Fuck off, I said."

My chest tightened in a snarl of anger. I tried to push it back down again. *This isn't him.* "I'm going to schedule the showing though. So is there a time that's bad for you? Like maybe you have a doctor's appointment coming up?"

"Beau, I swear to God if you don't leave me the fuck alone I'm going to..."

He drifted off in mid-sentence, already bored with threatening me. I would have taken it. I was used to Finn's temper but this apathy...

I couldn't take it. I turned on my heel and stalked out of the room, burning with the need to move, to run. The tight bud of anger was blooming, and the rushing heat of my blood thudded in my ears. "So?" Claire was right in my path as I stomped into the kitchen, but I veered around her and made a beeline straight for the door off the kitchen that led into the garage.

I wasn't even fully aware of what I was doing or why I was grabbing the hand-axe until I was running full tilt through the yard and straight down to the creek.

Last month's flood had left our yard a mess that my father was only just starting to tackle. The tangled mass of branches and debris was dry now thanks to the string of warm, sunny June days.

And that made it easy to start hacking.

The first thud of the axe into one of the branches unleashed something. I blinked away the sudden blurriness in my eyes and then grunted as I split the log in two. "Fuck!" Yanking and heaving, I wrestled the unruly mass back up the hill to the fire pit. I wiped the sweat out of my eye and then went back in again.

Thunk. Yank. Thunk. Yank. The rhythmic sound of the axe and the hard labor went a long way toward soothing my soul and letting me think clearly again. Clearly enough for the both of us since my brother was in no shape to be making decisions at the moment. It would be up to me to find a way to get the money together. I could do it.

I just had to make a few phone calls.

As I hacked away at the fallen underbrush, the plan solidified in my brain. One appearance. That was all we needed. Call it a King Brothers Family Reunion, yeah, that had a nice ring to it. Maybe a festival or a one-night only event down in New York City. That was all we needed. It would kickstart our sales, start the royalties flowing again.

Re-fill Finn's checking account and get him on his feet again.

The pile in the fire-pit was getting bigger now. I paused, and wiped my forehead again, wishing I had thought to bring out a glass of water. The brush was nearly clear, and the banks of the creek were visible again. I only needed to cut up a few more branches.

As I split the last big, sprawling oak branch, I tried to keep my misgivings away. This was a good plan, a solid one. And it didn't matter if I actually hated playing pop music.

Yeah. There it was. My dirty secret.

I hated playing pop music. I loved classical, the swooping grandeur, the meaningful silences. But I had never said a word because being in a pop band was how I spent time with my brothers, how I kept a watchful eye on Finn. I had sucked it up, believing that it was better that three people were happy and one person was unhappy, rather than make all three of them unhappy just for my sake. When we'd broken up, I'd been sad about losing that closeness, but I hadn't mourned the loss of the music at all. Those simplistic little songs did nothing for me.

But they paid the bills. And that's what I needed them to do again.

With one final heave, I sent the last of the branches up to the top of the pile. I paused and massaged the stitch in my side. I definitely needed water now, I'd damned near sweated myself into mummification, but it was hard to pull myself away from the mindless, comforting toil and head back into the house. I knew what I would find there. A worried sister and an uncommunicative brother. And me back in the middle again, trying to make everything right.

As I trudged back up to the house, my steps got lighter before my brain registered the reason why.

Music. The sound of my piano drifting out of the house, a simple little chord progression and then—

My heart quickened. "Rachel?"

I ran full-tilt - not even sparing a thought for my aching muscles - up the sloped lawn. The door off the back deck was closer to the living room where the piano sat, so that was the one I burst through just in time to hear Rachel belt out a perfect high C. She turned at the noise of the door slamming shut, and the corner of her mouth quirked ever so slightly as a happy blush spread over her face.

I pressed my fingers to my lips. I wasn't going to interrupt. Not this. Claire was working on scales, taking Rachel through a series of warm-up exercises. It was nothing I hadn't heard a million times before, but somehow the silly little "ah ah ahs" and "ee ee ees" sounded like something rare and beautiful when they came from her mouth. She closed her eyes and tilted her chin up as if she were singing right up to the angels she sounded like. The tips of her fingers grazed the top of my piano and I resolved never to polish it again.

I swore I was only standing there for a minute, maybe two, when Claire closed her book. "We'll leave off there. I don't want your vocal cords to get fatigued."

"Okay," Rachel said, kneeling down to gather her things.

"Stay!" I blurted, like the biggest, lamest asshole in the world.

The two of them looked at me, Claire scoffing, Rachel confused. "What for?" my sister asked, and I wanted to smack her.

"We're having a bonfire."

"We are?"

"Yep. To celebrate the beginning of summer."

"We are?"

I glared at my sister, sending her silent 'not helping!' vibes with my eyes. She widened hers dramatically - and completely obviously. "Oh! Yes! We are! Definitely, yes, we are definitely having a bonfire to celebrate the beginning of summer. As we do. It's a thing that we do."

"You're invited," I said, raising my voice over Claire's fumbling. "We'd love to have you."

The pink was still there in her cheeks, the dreamy expression. I would be kissing her right now if my sister weren't standing there, I knew it. My fingers itched to hold her. I wasn't above begging. "Please say yes."

She licked her lips. "Yes."

Chapter Thirteen

RACHEL

The eastern sky was a band of turquoise, growing deeper blue by the second. But if I stood in the middle of the Kings' expansive lawn and tilted my head upward, the sky slid back to faded pink and then orange. Deep magenta clouds hugged the western edge of the sky where the sun had just finally slipped down to sleep.

"When was the last time you watched the sun set?"

Beau's voice was low in my ear as he leaned forward, offering me a plate. I darted a quick smile at him and then resumed my hunched silence as I stared into the fire. "It's been a while." There was a sigh I didn't mean to exhale on those words, but I was relaxing. In spite of all the reasons I should be on edge; the fact that I had eaten at the same table as the worldliest family in the world, the fact that I was calling attention to myself by taking lessons with Claire, and most importantly, the fact that Beau's body was warm enough next to me that I could feel him there even though he'd been careful not to touch me at all, I was relaxing.

I couldn't help it.

There was some awareness deep inside of me that was turning cartwheels and sounding alarm bells. The hypervigilant Chosen-bred vigilance that insisted that I was deep in the lion's den. It expected Satanic sacrifice and wouldn't be surprised if Beau jumped up and suddenly devoured a baby. Any minute now, it insisted. Any minute now he's going to eat a baby.

But that vigilance was faint. Smothered under a blanket of something that felt almost like bliss. The fire crackled, the occasional knot in the pine exploding in a pop and a shower of sparks. The night was soft and warm, with enough chill curling around the edges to make me grateful I had Beau's warmth nearby. The crickets had quieted their racket, for the most part, only the occasional creak and whistle from a loud guy down by the woodpile, but the frogs had picked up the slack, bellowing in deep echoing brawwwpas that made us all laugh every time they went off.

Us. The four of us. I'd always been part of a group, and now, suddenly, here I was in the middle of one again. I had forgotten how I missed being part of something.

Claire was across the way, perched on a stump that Finn had wrestled into place with her. She was talking now, pontificating on how to properly toast a marshmallow, and then shrieking whenever Finn deliberately set hers on fire. The fact that Finn was down here with us seemed to make Beau relax too, although I could feel the way he was watching his brother and the careful way he was talking to him about neutral topics. Something had happened between the two of them, and that knowledge should have made me on edge as well, but then the fire popped again and the shower of sparks was mesmerizing enough to drag a yawn out of me.

"Are we boring you?" Beau teased.

I sighed and leaned back in the rickety chair that Beau had dragged out of one of the seemingly innumerable sheds that hugged the perimeter of their property. "I'm sleepy." I stretched my arms overhead and yawned again.

"You need sugar," Claire announced, springing from her log and snatching the bag of marshmallows up.

I grinned and sat up a little. "I've been meaning to ask you. What *are* those?"

Claire gasped and placed a shocked hand over her heart. "Please tell me you've had a marshmallow before."

Heat tinged my cheeks, but when I looked over at Beau, I saw nothing but interest in his eyes. No pity. So I shook my head. "I can't say I've had the pleasure." I took one from Claire and gingerly squished it between my fingers. "It feels like a mushroom."

The fire was bright enough for em to see Claire's horrified disgust. "A mushroom?"

"Well, then? What does it taste like?"

"I'd tell you to eat it right now and see, but toasted marshmallow is far and away the superior marshmallow." She handed me a thin, sharpened stick. I stared at it, feeling the hairs on the back of my neck raise in fear at how closely it resembled a switch, but then she speared one of the marshmallows on the end of it, neutering the horror.

I swallowed back the memory. "Am I supposed to set it on fire?"

"No!" Claire shot Finn a look, making him lazily wave his hand. "Finn is just an asshole and a weirdo who likes to eat the charred parts."

"I'm just trying to teach you to appreciate the finer things in life—" Finn drawled.

"Whatever." She cut him off with an airy wave of her hand. "No, you want to toast it. Hold it far enough above the heat so it gets all toasty brown and perfect."

I allowed her to minutely adjust the height of my stick. She furrowed her brow in concentration.

"That's it." Beau leaned forward, brushing against my arm and knocking it so that the stick dipped too close to the fire.

"Oh no!" I cried as my marshmallow burst into flames. I leaped up, horrified, apologies springing to my lips as tears suddenly stung my eyes.

Beau jumped up too and in one deep breath, he extinguished the flames.

I stood there, panting. Unsure as to why my heart was racing, as I waited for Claire to chastise me.

"Finn!" She reached over and slid the charred part of the marshmallow off. "It's your lucky day."

Her brother jumped up and came over, gravely accepting the blackened bits. I watched in wonder as he crammed it into his mouth, licking like it was some kind of delicacy, then sighed. "Well, I guess that's it then."

"No, you can try again, look." Claire pointed at my marshmallow.

It was smaller, but it looked untouched. Pristine. Like nothing had happened. Like I hadn't made any error at all.

Something in my chest that had been pulled taut like a rubber band suddenly snapped. I gasped in a deep, full breath and looked at each of them in turn. "That's it then? Just... try again?"

Claire shrugged. "Yup," she said, completely distracted with the surgical precision to which she was rotating her marshmallow.

Needing... something... reassurance? I turned and looked at Beau.

His eyebrows were up, but he just silently made a go-ahead gesture with his hand. I turned and tried again, and this time I managed to cover my marshmallow in a perfectly brown and toasty exterior. "Now what?" I asked.

"You eat it." His gentle grin was all the encouragement I needed. I tugged it from the stick, yelping squeamishly at how sticky it was and making Beau laugh, then pressed it to my lips gingerly.

"Oh my God!" The slightly burnt sugar clung to my lips and I licked them with my eyes wide. "This is... this has to be a sin." I gobbled up the rest of it and licked the sticky traces that clung to my fingers. "Have you had one?"

"Many times." He leaned in and pulled one from the package, producing a spear out of nowhere. "But I like mine more charred, like my brother." He dipped his stick into the fire, and calmly pulled back the flaming tip and blew it out. "It's terrible for you, but hey, you only live once, right?"

It was the very antithesis of what the Chosen would say. Life was supposed to be about readying for the next one, keeping clear of the worldly indulgences and hedonistic pursuits of the secular world. But I only knew this life. Here, with Beau, this was the only thing I could imagine, and a part of me wondered if he was right. Life could be... enjoyed.

He jammed the blackened bits into his mouth with such gusto that I had to laugh. "See?" Finn spoke up. "Beau eats his the same way and you don't give him shit? What the heck?" He punctuated his indignation by yanking Claire's stick from her hand. She shrieked as he went running, his laughter echoing across the dark lawn.

Beau sighed. "Haven't heard that in a while." He sat down and motioned me closer.

I jammed another marshmallow in my mouth. "Heard wha?" I tried to say around a mouthful of sugar.

Somehow he understood me. "Finn laughing. He hasn't seemed to be able to have much fun lately."

I leaned back in thought, and as I did, my head brushed against Beau's arm. When he didn't move it away, I licked my sugary lips, my heart racing a little. "What's going on?" I asked.

His fingers brushed my shoulder as he shrugged. It was an accident, I told myself, but then they did it again. "Something. I mean, I know that's not exactly an answer, but yeah, something is definitely going on."

"You worried about your brother?"

"I always worry about him." He sighed, and his hand fell down alongside my arm and all at once I was snuggled into the crook of his arm. His warm body warded off the chill of the night air and for a moment we just listened to the night sounds. Above us came the slam of a door. "Finn must have chased her back to the house."

"What are you worried about?"

Beau sighed again, a heavy sadness in there that made me feel bad for prying. But then again, with his arm around me and his breath brushing past my ear, I felt like now was the best time to get to know him. More than the rumors and gossip and condemnation. "I know my brother can come across as a bit of a—"

"Dick?" I supplied, which made him laugh.

"So you can say dick?"

"It's a proper name, right?" I smoothed my hands demurely down my lap which made him laugh harder.

"Exactly." He sobered a little. "He's got this kind of 'I'm going to hate you first before you can hate me' defense mechanism because he was pretty badly bullied back when we were kids."

I sucked in a breath. "The big rockstars?"

He turned and looked at me. "We're just people," he said. "People who played music." I swallowed, keeping my eyes turned away from him as I reflected on how wrong every one of my assumptions had been. He continued, "Finn can get pretty down sometimes. Still."

"And it's your job to take care of him?"

"Why not? I'm his older brother."

I grinned at him. "By how much."

"Five minutes. Five extra minutes of wisdom."

"It's a good thing he has you."

"It's a good thing I have you," he said, pulling me a little closer. "To keep me warm, I mean." He brushed his lips across my forehead, startling me, but before I could react, he stood up. "I'm putting more logs on. Want another marshmallow?"

"Please." I leaned forward, and he laughed at my eagerness. The fire popped as he poked the coals, then threw on another load of wood. The dry log caught with a whooping sound and I let out an inadvertent "ah" as the heat hit my chilled legs.

"Better?" His arm was settled back around me again. "Because I'm still cold."

"I'm not really, oh..."

I drifted into silence as his other arm settled around me and he pulled me close. I stiffened and then eased into his body. He brushed his hand up across my cheek and then gently cupped my head back until it was resting on his shoulder. I could feel his chest fall as he let out a long sigh. "Watch it," he said casually.

Confused, I looked and then squeaked to see that in my distraction my marshmallow had caught fire. "Merciful heavens!" I cried, waving it dangerously through the air.

Beau stilled my hand and put out the blaze with one strong puff. "Just the way I like it," he said, lifting the char to his lips. I grinned my thanks and then devoured the sticky, melted center. "You got some on your lip."

"I do?" My hand went to the side of my mouth. "Where?"

"There." I inhaled sharply as his thumb dragged across my bottom lip. "Ooh, it's a little stuck, I'm going to have to—"

His lips brushed mine, opening a sudden ache in the pit of my stomach. Soft and warm, and waiting. For several heartbeats, he kept his lips pressed to mine, and the longer he went without moving, the more the ache throbbed, bubbling up into a frustrated sound that burst from my lips.

He heard it and answered with a sound of his own, reaching up to wrap his fingers around my braid and pull me into him. The tip of his tongue probed gently at my lips, teasing my mouth open. When his tongue met mine, the ache sharpened, making me catch my breath.

In the course of one night, Beau had challenged every assumption I'd ever made about him. Now that he was kissing me, the last little bit of Chosen that lived in my heart insisted that this was it, that now he was making his move, angling to take advantage of me.

But he wasn't taking advantage. He was only kissing me, going exactly as far as I wanted him and no further and as I relaxed into it, I realized I wanted him to go further still.

How could this feel so good? It was just lips and teeth and tongues and breath but the more he kissed me, the more insensible I became. The combination of his hands at my face, holding me to deepen the kiss more, and the insistent softness of his lips on mine was driving me to distraction. When he wrapped his arms around my waist and pulled me into his lap, I almost leaped into his arms, and when he cradled me in his lap, peppering my forehead, cheeks, and shoulders with kisses, I felt for the first time that I had found a place where I belonged. I snuggled up to Beau King and for the first time in my life, I surrendered to what felt good.

Chapter Fourteen

BEAU

Since the day I met her, I'd been wondering how she would feel in my arms.

It was somehow even better than I'd imagined.

"Do you like this?" I breathed against her neck. I could feel her shiver, whether from pleasure or fear, I couldn't tell.

And that was the problem.

As far as I wanted to take this - and heaven knew I wanted to take it right to the very end and then some - I knew that I didn't yet know her well enough to know the difference between her gasps. Was she loving how it felt to have my lips against her rapidly beating pulse or was she aghast that I was kissing so close to her breast? Rachel was naive, this much I knew for sure, and she kissed me back with more passion than skill, but her clumsy, enthusiastic touch had me harder than I'd ever been in my life.

It was full dark now. Above us, the stars were popping out, one by one. "Ever wish on a star?"

"Hmm?" Her eyes fluttered open and then fixed on the sparkle of lights above us. "Wow."

"You probably didn't grow up with this," I murmured against her ear, pulling her back up so her cheek was against mine as we both gazed upward. "But we always said if you made a wish on a star it had to come true."

She blinked. "I'd have to think."

"I already know." I pulled her even closer, burying my face in the place where her neck met her shoulder. "And it is coming true as we speak."

She hummed a soft sound of contentment and we both fell silent. The crickets that had been making their evening racket were falling silent now and the sigh of the wind through the trees had died down, leaving the rushing of the creek in its place.

Then from the woods came an ear-shattering scream that made us both jump. She leaped to her feet and looked at me, utterly panicked. I was half out of my chair ready to call 911 when we both realized. "Fox."

Her eyes sparkled. I felt a laugh bubble up in my chest. "Jesus, those things sound like they're getting murdered." From deep in the woods, the vixen screamed again, making us both jump and then cling to each other. "Who is saving who?" She laughed against my chest and held me tighter. "Good, I'm so glad you're here." I tilted her chin up. "I wouldn't want to be alone right now." She had such amazing eyes, so full of trust and gentle humor. "I'm going to kiss you again, is that okay?"

She tugged me down to her. I felt her smile curl against my mouth as I kissed her. White heat coiled at the base of my spine as she pressed against me and I allowed us both to tumble back on to the chair. She was fully cradled in my arms now, and she flung her arms up around my neck with such sweet abandon that a sound I'd never heard boiled up from inside of me. "God you smell good," I growled. She moaned and arched herself into me as I trailed my lips dangerously close to the top of her breasts. "Can I kiss you here, Rachel?"

"Yes." She squirmed a little in my lap, intensifying my hard-on.

"Shit." Her skin was soft on my lips and it took everything I had not to tug her shirt down and expose her further. "If you don't like where my hand is, you move it, baby, but I just want to feel you. Does that feel good?" Her soft moan into my mouth was all the answer I needed as I slipped my hand under the hem of her T-shirt and smoothed my fingers over the softness of her belly. "Ah Rachel, what are you doing to me?" I had my mouth at the top of her other breast now, and forcibly wrenched my lips back upward to her mouth rather than explore lower. When her mouth met mine, her lips parted immediately. Groaning, I fisted her hair, twining it around to grip more tightly. The enthusiasm with which she entangled her tongue with mine drove all thoughts of caution from my brain. On their own, my hand drifted down, seeking that heat between her thighs and...

"Oh!" She stiffened and drew back.

Shit. "I'm sorry." I snatched my hand away, but it was too late. She was staring up, wild-eyed and gasping and even by the low light of the fire I could see how pink her cheeks were.

She inhaled sharply and sat up, not looking at me. "I should..." Her voice was high and not at all like her normal one. "I need to go home."

"I'll drive you." I leaped up and then tugged at the seam of my pants. My body hadn't quite gotten the message that it was all over yet, but it quickly caught up with my brain.

Shit.

Chapter Fifteen

RACHEL

Don't run away. Don't run away.

But when Beau pulled up in front of my house, that was exactly what I did to get away from... from him and the terrifying thing he had just done to my body.

Chosen girls got married young. Before I left, I had known several girls my age who were on their second or third child. I knew what had happened to get them in that condition. What I hadn't understood was how they could possibly... like it.

"Oh, you'll see," Suzanna Heath had crowed, primly flicking her braid back and then bouncing her firstborn on her hip. Then she'd leaned in and whispered something to my younger sister Rebecca that made her blush and giggle and then look at me with such sorrow and pity in her eyes that I had left before I could find out any more about what I was missing as an unmarriageable girl.

I hadn't thought about that moment until that... flash... that heat had coursed through my body. It had been terrifying, but what was worse was how much *more* I wanted. I wanted Beau's hand to go there, to rub right *there*, again, let the friction heat my skin because something...

... something had happened.

It shouldn't have happened. Sex - *desire* - was for procreation. To bring more souls into the world to follow the way of God's Chosen. And since... since...

Since I couldn't have children...

I licked my lips, forcing myself to remember. To think the thought I'd been running from ever since I found out the awful truth in that doctor's office as I bled and bled. *I can't have children... so I can't have... sex.*

I'd never wanted it before, but now?

Now I was sinning, and the worst part was that I was reveling in it.

I wasn't the one who had left the Chosen. They left me. They cut me loose and sent me out into the secular world. They couldn't expect me to hold myself to Chosen rules anymore, right?

Right?

I shut the door and sagged against it, that throbbing in between my legs reminding me of what I had cut short. My quiet house seemed to be waiting for me to do... something, but I couldn't take a full breath and that ache...

Mindlessly I reached down and laid my hand flat in between my thighs, then snatched it up and away when I felt how scalding hot I was down there. Was I feverish? Was I sick? But then why was the brush my hand trailing sparks across my skin? Why was I shivering now, unless I was sick?

I rushed to my bedroom and quickly stripped off my clothes, then opened the window to let the cool of the night into my bedroom. Pacing back and forth, I tried to burn off the energy that coursed through me. But when my nipples stiffened against the cold, it somehow only intensified the ache between my legs. Slipping under the sheets to escape the breeze was torture because even the brush of my skin across my clean sheets felt somehow sinful. The ache inside had become a throb, and I was suddenly aware of an... emptiness.

My only thought was to understand why I felt this way. But my tentative touch made me gasp as my fingers slid against slick, hot skin. The throbbing inside of me became a drumbeat.

"Ah, God!" The emptiness couldn't be filled by just my fingers alone. Frustrated, I sought the source of the ache, but the faster I rubbed, and my hands became Beau's hands, an echo of what he had done at the fire, the way his mouth had played across the tops of my breasts. I trailed my fingers across the path his lips had blazed, and arched into nothingness, wanting the warm hard bulk of him to press against again. The more I touched and explored the places that ached for him, the more agitated I became until - "Ah!"

It exploded out from nothingness, a scorching fire sending out sparks to alight in my limbs. I was shimmering, falling down in a shower of glittering light and the noises that came out of my mouth were like nothing I had ever heard from my lips before. My eyes shot open as the sparks settled into a warm, liquid glow.

Shocked and panting, I lay there naked, the sheets in a tangle from my bicycling feet, and stared at the ceiling. The ache was gone, it was true, but it had been replaced with the kind of all-consuming craving that should have terrified me.

But I wasn't terrified.

I blinked as I realized what had happened, and then blinked again when I realized, I wasn't afraid of what I had done.

I wanted to do it again.

And I wanted Beau to be the one to make it happen.

Chapter Sixteen

BEAU

"You look like your dog died." Claire looked up from her dinner and leaned her head into the living room. "Duke? You doin' okay dude?"

Our ancient Lab thumped his tail twice on the floor. Claire smiled. "Good." She turned back to me and when she saw I was still glaring down at my plate, she leaned over the kitchen island and poked me with her fork. "What gives?"

"Nothing." I was only picking at the stir-fry I'd helped make for my twin and her. I grabbed my dishes and scraped the leftovers into the trash, then dumped the plates in the sink, all the while ignoring my sister's laser-like glare.

"Is it about how Rachel didn't stay the night?"

"She wouldn't have!"

"I mean." Claire shrugged innocently and jammed a pile of rice into her mouth, then stabbed the air with her fork. "It sure looked like that was where things were headed."

"Shut up. And stop talking with your mouth full, you're gross."

"Bleeehhh!" She showed me a mouthful of chewed up food then swallowed. "Did she get all fundie-cult on you at the last minute? Is that why you're such a grouch?"

I shook my head. "I shouldn't have pushed her so hard."

My sister raised an eyebrow. "She didn't seem to be raising many objections."

"It wasn't right."

"I mean, she did say yes when you invited her."

I looked at my confident, bossy sister. It wasn't often I went to her for advice over, say, Jonah, but this was different. "Hey, you're a girl."

"Well done." She raised a snide eyebrow.

I rolled my eyes. "I just..." I sighed heavily. "Am I an asshole for wanting a girl like that?"

"A girl like what? A grown ass woman who's been making her own life and her own choices for two years now? Someone who left the only life and family she ever knew and struck out on her own with nothing but her own hustle?" Claire shook her head and softened her voice. "You're not an asshole, Beau. And she's not a child. As long as you stop when she asks you to—"

"Of course."

"Well then? What's the problem?"

I let out a long exhale. Claire was right, what *was* the problem? Except - "I have no idea what happened to her in there."

Claire lifted one shoulder. "So find out."

"How?"

"Jesus Christ you are such a hopeless man. Of all my brothers, I always thought you had the most sense and yet... here we are."

"Claire."

She opened her eyes wide and let her jaw go slack. "Duh! Ask her?"

I blinked. "It's not that easy."

"I assure you, it is."

"How do you know?"

She rolled her eyes. "I have twenty-three years of experience as a woman backing me up."

"Okay fine, but like... when?"

Her eyes gleamed in a way that I'd learned to be cautious around. "Beauregard Donovan King, I have never seen you so worked up about a girl before."

She had me there. But letting Claire think she was right about something was dangerous. "That's because you're not around much."

"Bullshit." She dismissed me with a wave. "Go get your girl and *ask her questions* about herself. Be her friend *then* her boyfriend or whatever. See how that works?"

I narrowed my eyes at her. "You know I'm right," she sing-songed. Then burst out laughing as I silently grabbed my keys and headed out the door.

Driving across town reminded me that Finn and I still hadn't nailed down our living arrangements. Right now, I could be across Crown Creek and out on the western border of the county in less than ten minutes, but when we moved out into the woods the way Finn wanted? Shit, I wondered if he even knew how much life would change, how much more of a project everything would be.

Did I want that change too?

I pushed the question aside once the college came into sight. Far from the leafy campus and stately edifices of your usual university, the campus of Crown Valley College looked like a federal prison. Apparently, the school founders saved on blueprints by just asking a penitentiary designer to just hit copy/paste. It was ugly with a capital U. Even the streaks of color from the setting sun couldn't make the box-like towers look beautiful. Crown Valley earned the nickname Frown Valley, and most of the students commuted rather than be surrounded by its hideousness twenty-four seven. This meant that the parking lots were huge and the bus shelter pretty much an afterthought. It was located in the remotest corner of the campus and to reach it, Rachel would have to cross acres of baking asphalt first.

I wished like hell I knew which direction she'd be coming from so I could save her the trip, but I didn't know her shifts very well. This was awkward as fuck, but Claire had said to be her friend, and a friend would pick her up from work, so she didn't have to waste an hour riding around on that broken down country bus that only showed up once in a blue moon. And a friend would ask questions about her day and listen in the hopes of finding out more about her.

Maybe a friend wouldn't sit there in his car, watching the bus stop until she came out, and maybe a friend wouldn't have startled the fuck out of her by leaping from his seat and shouting her name when he saw her, but at least I was trying, right?

"Beau!" She was still clutching her bag to her chest, but the terror in her face had finally quieted down to amused confusion by the time I crossed the road and met her at the bus stop. "What are you doing here?"

I swallowed. She didn't look exactly overjoyed to see me. Maybe my sister had been wrong. What *was* I doing here? "I thought you might like a ride?" It came out as a question. Fuck, this girl was reducing me to stammering and upspeak. I'd never felt this off-kilter before, not even when I was playing in front of twenty thousand screaming fans at Madison Square Garden. "It's getting kind of hot," I went on, looking both ways along the deserted, no-bus-in-sight road and gestured for her to follow. "I cranked the A/C for you." Then I caught myself. "Unless you like the windows down better? I can do that too. What do you like? Windows or A/C, I mean?" *Fuck, STOP TALKING.*

I forcibly clamped my mouth shut and waited for her to speak. After all, listening to her and finding out about her was the whole point of me coming way out here, right?

But she didn't speak. Not for a long, long moment. She must have been really hot, because the pink that had started on her cheeks was now spreading across her chest, right across those places that I had kissed last night. Or maybe it was just the fading pink sky that had her looking so beautiful.

Shit, I'm staring. I wrenched my eyes back up to meet hers. "I just wanted to be sure you're okay." I swallowed and looked down, and had to work really hard to force the words out. "If you're not okay with me being here, just tell me and I'll leave, Rachel. I promise."

"Don't leave."

I snapped my head back up so fast I almost gave myself whiplash. "Really?"

Her smile was like the sun peeking out from behind a cloud. First a small twinkle and then shining full strength. "Thanks for coming." She looked like she wanted to say something else, but caught herself and fell silent.

Feeling unreasonably proud of myself, I nearly sprinted across the road to open the door for her. She followed behind me, still quiet, and I had to catch myself to keep from running my mouth even more.

Rachel let out a small sigh of relief once she sat down. I'd run the air conditioning down to meat locker temperatures. You could almost see your breath. "It's early in the year for it to be this hot." Oh, awesome, I was making small talk about the weather. The back of my neck heated and I jammed my foot down on the accelerator in frustration. We lurched out into the road in the least graceful bit of driving I had ever done in my life, and I decided that I would count backward from three hundred before I was allowed to say anything else.

The silence in the car was thick and heavy, the silence of waiting, of held breath and furtive glances. It was not friendly silence and I was here trying to make friends with her, to get to know her.

I was only to eighty-three when I lost it. "How are voice lessons going?"

"Good." She answered quickly enough, and her voice didn't hold any traces of hostility toward me. Why was she so tense then? "Your sister is really nice."

I was about to disagree when I remembered that Claire's advice was why I was here with Rachel in the first place. "She's okay."

"She's teaching me a little more about music that's popular right now." She glanced at me from under thick lashes. "I've got a lot of catching up to do."

Here. Right here would be the place to ask her. But my tongue tripped over my question and I ended up asking the wrong one. "Can you sing something for me?"

She shook her head. "I don't think I'm ready yet."

"Are you sure?" I dared to nudge her with my arm. "You've done it before."

"With a few drinks in me, yeah."

"It doesn't have to be a popular song. How about that hymn you were singing before?"

A quick glance at her revealed that the blush was back again, and this time I had to wrench my eyes back up again before I drove us into a ditch. She was so fucking beautiful, the way she sat there poised and proud, yet shy and vulnerable too. There were so many angles to her, she could be a wholly different person depending on which direction you approached her from. "It's okay." I took a deep breath. "You're right, you're not the performer here. I am."

I cleared my throat and started to sing.

I didn't know the words much beyond the first verse. But I knew them well enough to startle Rachel. "How sweet the sound," I sang. "That saved a wretch like me."

I let the last line fall away as I pulled into her driveway and slid into park, then held my breath. "Rachel?" She was watching me with her lips slightly parted, the pink high in her cheeks, eyes glittering. In that moment she was the most beautiful thing I had ever seen and fuck being friends, I couldn't do it, not with her. "Rachel, I—"

She threw her arms around me and silenced my doubts with a kiss.

Chapter Seventeen

RACHEL

His voice reached inside of me and found all of those places his hands had not yet touched. When he sang, it was like he was kissing me with his words.

And then he was kissing me with his mouth.

"Beau." I was saying his name, again and again, because it was the only thing that made any sense. Everything I thought I knew about the world, about men and wickedness, was wrong because he existed. This generous, caring man - who made my body quiver with the expectation of something I'd never experienced but already knew I craved - was real and he was saying my name now.

It sounded just like a prayer.

His kiss was devouring. His tongue sought dominion over my mouth, sweeping away any hesitation as he nibbled, bit, and tasted. "You tell me," he breathed against my neck as his mouth wandered lower again. He tugged at the strap of my tank top, kissing and soothing the red line where my bra had chafed me before trailing his kiss down to the top of my breast. "You tell me if you want me to stop."

"I don't want you to stop." It was the truth and it had been for a while. And if I had known how much it would inflame him, I would have said it a lot sooner. His hazel eyes darkened to deep emerald before he hissed in a deep breath. "Stay there." The command in his voice made me shiver, but it was anticipation, not fear.

He opened his door and was at mine in a second. "Come here. Now." He lifted me from my seat and straight into his arms.

I wrapped my arms around his neck as he said my name against my lips. "Rachel. Say it again. Tell me you don't want me to stop because, angel, I don't know if I can."

"I don't want you to stop." I pressed my lips to his throat, feeling his pulse jumping under his smooth, warm skin. "Beau, I - last night—"

"I pushed you too hard, I know."

"You didn't. You made me feel." I cleared my throat. This was not a sin, no matter how much it felt like one. "You made me feel things I wasn't used to feeling but..." I lifted my chin and looked him in the eye, wanting to see his face when I said, “But I want you to make me feel them again."

His growl terrified and thrilled me in equal measure. He swept me up into his arms and somehow managed to unlock the door one-handed while the other hand held me tight. "I can do that," he was murmuring against my neck. "We've got all night, angel, and I want to show you all the ways I know to make you feel good." He set me on my feet just inside the doorway to my room and looked me full in the eyes. "I need to tell you something."

I held my breath. "What is it?"

He shook his head, looking both amused and exasperated at once. He lifted my fingers to his lips and kissed them firmly. "When I came out to pick you up, it was with the idea that I wanted to get to know you." The gleam in his eyes grew wicked enough to make me catch my breath. "I'm planning on doing just that."

"You are?"

"First question." The light brush of his lips against my earlobe had me shivering. "What do you sound like when you completely lose control?"

"I don't know."

He grinned. "Let's find out."

With an easy authority, he steered me back into my bedroom until the backs of my knees caught against the bed and I sat down. With my heart in my throat, I looked up as he lifted his shirt over his head and casually discarded it. He looked down, a smile curling his lips. "Do you want to touch me, Rachel?"

I wanted to do that more than anything I'd ever wanted in my life. My hands trembled as I lifted them to his naked stomach. When my fingers brushed his skin, his abdomen twitched and then tightened and when I looked up again, I could see that his breath was coming faster now.

Until now, I had never really known what it felt like to be powerful, but knowing that this man was just as affected by my touch as I was by his made me want to laugh in triumph. I looked up at him and slid my teeth across my bottom lip. "Oh shit, don't do that, Rachel," Beau growled.

"Do what?"

"That thing with your lip. You really have no idea how sexy you are, do you?"

"I don't think so."

"Here, let me show you."

He leaned over me, backing me up until I was flat on my bed looking up at him. He was so close to me that I could see the way his beard swirled around his jawline. When he lifted my tank top, I flinched, only a little, but he saw and took his hand away, leaving my breasts still hidden as he ran his hand over my skin and around my waist. Even being this exposed to him felt like a sin.

But if this was sin, then I was the best kind of sinner.

He exhaled and then lowered his lips. Even as he was kissing my navel, I felt that ache in between my legs. "Unf." I was making sounds and lifting my hips, aware that he was doing something that was disconnecting my mind from my body, but powerless to stop it. His mouth traced a line right to the very top of my waistband, and that was when he looked up with his eyebrows raised.

I heard his unasked question and exhaled. "I don't want you to stop."

He hummed his approval, thick fingers tugging at the waistband of my heavy work pants. It was only at the last second that I remembered

I was wearing my usual underwear - high waisted and generously cut - the kind of panties that Everly had laughed and called granny panties. I'd assimilated as best I could to the secular world, in every way but in my underwear. "Don't laugh at them." I put my hands down to cover up, suddenly ashamed.

He looked up at me and placed his hand over mine. "There's nothing to laugh at." He gently lifted my hand and then smiled. "Except maybe at the fact that you think these would stop me. Rachel, you could be wearing a clown costume right now and I'd still think you were the most beautiful woman in the world."

I believed him. That was the most surprising part, the part that made me allow him to tug my pants down over my hips. He was watching me intently as he peeled my socks from my skin, rubbing circles in the center of my heel until I sighed in pleasure, and then brushing his hand back up my calves. I believed him when he told me I was the most beautiful woman in the world, because there was nothing but truth on his face when he gently nudged my thighs apart. There was nothing but bliss on his face when he bent his lips again, and when I said his name, there was only worship in that sound he made.

I believed him. I believed *in* him.

It had been so long since I had something that made me feel like I belonged. I wanted to belong to Beau. I wanted to be his and let him care for me. I wanted to fall back and know that he'd be there to catch me. I wanted to trust in him. Could I trust in him?

He sighed again as if he could hear my racing thoughts. "Angel, I want to kiss you now."

"Yes." I tilted my head up to reach for his lips and he chuckled.

"Not there."

When his finger brushed against my panties, I inhaled sharply, embarrassed at how the cool fabric betrayed how soaked they'd gotten. Without me even realizing. But the noise Beau made was pure admiring approval. "Just like that," he murmured, and I realized I was arching against his hand. "This is gonna be the answer to my question, sweetheart." A choked sound escaped my lips when his finger brushed the epicenter of the ache. "How you sound when you lose control? I want to find out." He exhaled as he leaned over me, and his hazel eyes were the whole world. "Will you let me find out?"

My chest was so tight I could barely breathe. Just the thought of him kissing me... there... had my whole body on fire. I wanted it, but there was no way I could survive seeing it. I reached up to flick off my bedside lamp, and the darkness settled across us like the chaste dresses and underskirts I wore when I was one of the Chosen. Normal and claustrophobic at the same time. The second he disappeared from view, my thoughts started to turn around on themselves, settling into panic.

Beau reached over and flicked the light back on, and I was startled to see his face so close. "I want to see you."

I swallowed. Nodded. Because - I believed him. And I didn't want to feel like I was alone in the dark anymore.

He bent to brush my lips sweetly with his, and then pressed his hand between my legs. He sat up a little and my mouth fell open at the warmth and pressure. He stayed perfectly still, letting me get used to the feel of him there, the first time anyone had ever touched me in that place. The muscles in my thighs jumped and a strange clenching sensation wracked through my core. The ache became a pounding throb that pulsed through my whole body. I lifted my hands, letting my fingers brush up his arms and then across his chest.

I arched up to him. "I don't want you to stop."

Chapter Eighteen

BEAU

Her heat was nearly scalding me. It was pure torture to sit here, with only a millimeter of drenched cotton separating me from what had to be the most perfect pussy in the world.

But I needed her wanting. I needed her desperate. This was new to Rachel, her virginity was glaringly obvious from her nervous gestures, her awkward passivity. I wasn't going to push her. Even though every cell in my body was screaming at me to dive between her legs and make her come until she went blind from pleasure, I needed to hold back until I was certain she was certain.

And so I waited.

Rachel squirmed underneath me. A beautiful thing. With the light on, I could see that flush creeping across her chest. She was running her hands all over my skin - quite nice in its own right - but even better was the look of undisguised fascination in her eyes. Fascination and... hunger.

"I don't want you to stop."

She must have read my mind because she said it right as she arched herself into my hand. My fingers slipped along that heat. "Fuck." I brushed them back up again until I found that place that made her inhale sharply and squeeze her eyes shut, and then began to move them right... there. In slow, tight circles at first, while she pressed into me and then pulled away.

It had been years, nearly a solid decade, since this had been enough to get me off. Dry-humping a girl over her clothes? It shouldn't have been enough, but it was so much more than that with Rachel. With Rachel, just the sight of her bare tummy had me sweating. The way her hair had come loose from her braid in sweet tendrils had me completely undone.

I let her squirm and shiver until a low moan fell from her lips, surprising us both. "Right there, huh? Is that the spot?" I moved forward, needing to watch her face, and planted my hand by the side of my head, propping myself above her. "That's a beautiful thing, yes, just like that. God, you are so beautiful Rachel." I moved my fingers faster over that drenched cotton. The scent of her desire filled my nostrils. "You are so fucking beautiful." I was cursing now, starting to lose it. All the blood in my body was rushing to my dick, leaving nothing to think with.

Rachel moaned again, opening her mouth as if to scream and then swallowing it back down again. Frustration rose off of her and almost shimmered in the air. Immediately, I understood. That whisper of cotton was suddenly an insurmountable obstacle.

I leaned down to lick and suck at her neck as I shifted my hand. Slowly - testing her reaction the whole time - I slipped my fingers underneath that cotton barrier. When they found the slick skin hidden underneath, Rachel made a sound.

The sound.

The one I'd been wanting to hear.

The one she made when she lost control.

It surprised her. I could see it in the way her eyes flew open, like some part of her awareness was still too nervous to give in. But when my lips closed over the top of her breast, nipping through the fabric, that noise rose in pitch. High and keening, she gasped, and I leaned in to capture that sound with my mouth, my fingers working faster now, bringing her up and up until she went suddenly stiff, a gasping moan dying in her throat, replaced with...

A scream.

Rachel screamed against my mouth and it was the most beautiful sound I had ever heard. She came like nothing I'd ever seen before, shattering from the inside out. I pressed my lips to her neck and felt her pulse race under my tongue, and my own pulse beat a frantic tattoo in my ears. And when her scream fell away in a dying gasp, she inhaled sharply as her eyes flew open and she rasped out a guttural, "Fuck!"

I sat up and stared at her.

She clapped her hand over her mouth. "Oh no!"

I froze. This was it, this had to be her line. Rachel reacted to cursing like she did to loud noises, jumping nervously and staring in the direction of the offending sound. I'd pushed her too hard. I opened my mouth to apologize, but then her eyes went wide and mischievous. "Holy... shit!"

"Holy shit," I echoed, for different reasons. I leaned over to cover her mouth with mine before I accidentally professed my undying love for her. Because holy shit was right.

She threw her arms around my neck and pulled me to her with such enthusiasm that I nearly exploded right there. "Wow."

The scent of her arousal was still clinging to my fingers, driving me insane with the need to taste her. "I'm not done."

Her eyes went wider.

I grinned. "I told you I was going to kiss you too."

"You are."

"Not there."

Her chest hitched a little as I slid down the bed and yanked her panties down. My hands were almost trembling in my haste to see her, bare before me. She lifted her hips obligingly, trusting me, and that made me all the more frantic to put my face there and breathe deeply.

She smelled like every delicious thing I'd encountered, and she tasted like heaven on a plate. Her nervous gasping died away the second my tongue slid against her, and she and I both groaned in unison. I tried like hell to slow down and savor this, but the need to consume her, to devour her and claim her and make her come with my tongue was overpowering me now. I pressed my hands down on her thighs, holding her in place, the better to lick and suck and kiss. I could feel her muscles quivering under my hands, could feel her pussy clenching whenever my tongue slid inside, and I knew she was close, so close.

I spread my hands under her and lifted, kneeling upward so that her hips were off the bed. The view of her - her smooth skin, her hair splayed across the pillow in a wild tangle unlike anything I'd ever seen on her before - had me harder than I'd been in my life, and I set to work devouring her from this angle.

She arched, grinding herself against me, taking what she wanted, and I gave her all I had. When her legs splayed out in a sudden electric shock, I held her in place, not letting her shy away from the shockwaves that coursed through her body. And my reward was the music she made as she came on my tongue, and the way she shattered into a million pieces before opening her eyes and staring at me.

My heart thudded in my ears as I quickly shucked off my jeans. Her eyes went wider as she caught a glimpse of me, but when I pulled the condom from my wallet, they filled with sudden fear.

All at once, my heated blood cooled, as if ice had been suddenly dumped in my chest.

"Rachel."

"It's okay. I'm okay." She tried to smile. "I'm good. So good."

But there was still that panic in her eyes. Slowly, I leaned down and pulled my pants back up.

She sat up. "What are you doing?"

She was still flushed and beautiful. My lips still tasted of her, and my fingertips still burned with the feel of her skin under mine. Her cries were still echoing in my brain and there was nothing I wanted more than to make her scream while I was inside of her but...

I leaned down and kissed her once. "I'm good."

"Really?"

"Really."

She sighed a little, and I couldn't help but catch the relief in it before she smiled. "I don't think I could move."

"It's okay." I grabbed my keys.

She rolled over and reached for me. "Stay?"

I licked my lips. “I was hoping you'd say that."

I slid between her warm, soft, floppy body, wedging myself between her and the wall. When she sighed against me, molding herself to fit alongside me and pulling my arm over her, I knew I hadn't been lying just for her sake.

I was good. So good.

Really.

Chapter Nineteen

BEAU

Yes. Blue balls are real. The pain is real.

But the ache in my groin was all but drowned out by the sheer pleasure of having Rachel waking up in my arms.

The morning light was seeping in through the uncovered window and the sound of the creek was a constant babbling murmur outside. I shifted a little, feeling the stiffness from being jammed into a too-small bed for the night, but it was worth it when I looked over and saw her stirring.

She sniffed and made a small mewling noise of protest that had me shushing her and brushing back her hair in sleepy contentment.

She stretched and shifted. And then kicked out with her leg, catching me right in the shin. "Ow!" I was suddenly quite awake.

"Shit!" Rachel had apparently broken her own cussing taboo forever. She rolled over to face me, adorably covering her mouth. "I... forgot you were here."

"You sleep like a dead person." I yawned and reached down to rub my leg. "I checked a few times over the course of the night. Just to make sure you were breathing."

"I know." She glanced down sympathetically and put her hand over mine and we rubbed my leg in tandem. "Comes from growing up with nine brothers and sisters."

I froze. "Nine?" When she didn't correct me, I whistled, impressed. "And here I thought *I* had the surplus of siblings."

"It might be more now." She sat up, tugging her shirt back down over her stomach, much to my sadness.

"Yeah?" There was a story here. A clue to who she was, who she'd been and what she'd fled from. I held still, the way I would when I spotted a deer in the woods. Not wanting to spook her.

She was staring at some spot on the wall. It was probably sleep that made her eyes look so tired, but her sigh made me wonder if it was something more. "Chosen families are big," she said carefully. "We... they... believe in collecting souls. So not only do you have large biological families, but we... they... adopt kids out of foster care a lot too. I've been gone two years now. So that's plenty of time for my mother to have another baby and maybe even adopt one too." She sat up straighter and seemed like she was trying to shake the sadness off, but it settled back down around her shoulders like a shawl, making her slump. "My mother writes to me maybe once every couple months or so, but she doesn't tell me much that's important."

"Your mother writes to you?" This was news. This was definitely surprising news, and it banished that last bit of ache from me when I realized that this - her sleeping in the same bed as me, her confiding these secrets to me - was a far bigger step than her having sex with me. This mattered much much more. "I have to confess, that's surprising to hear. I thought you'd be—"

"Cut off completely?" She slid from the bed and looked at me, then exhaled something that might have been a laugh before looking down and twisting her bare toes on the floor. "My... leaving. It was... I wasn't kicked out if that's what you're thinking. And I didn't... run away in some kind of dramatic night escape."

She must have seen the surprise on my face because this time her laugh was more genuine. "I know. Sorry to disappoint you. But I left because..." Here her words tripped up like she was about to reveal something before she caught herself. "It was a kind of mutual decision. Because there really wasn't a..." She sighed heavily again and looked at the window. "Place for me," she finished hurriedly. "There wasn't a place for me there anymore."

A small, tight ball of worry suddenly knotted inside of my chest, though where it had come from I wasn't exactly sure. "Would you go back? I mean, if there was a place for you?"

"I don't know." There was nothing but truth in her voice and for some reason that broke my heart. "At this point, I'm not sure I really can." She glanced at me like she remembered I was there - and what we had done - all of a sudden. "I mean," she gestured between us with a glint in her eye that was much more reassuring than the wistful one that had been there a second ago.

I stood up and went to her. Putting my arms around her felt like the most natural thing in the world. "Right here. Right here is a good place for you," I said as I folded her against me.

She made a small noise that could have been a laugh or a sob, and I knew she needed the privacy to decide which it was so I just held her a moment.

She took a deep breath. "I need a shower," she said looking up at me. "If you're going to keep hugging me like this."

"Oh I am."

She smiled. Then licked her lips. She didn't say anything more, just padded over to the bathroom. But then she paused in the doorway and looked back at me before she stepped in.

Without shutting the door behind her.

"Well fuck me," I breathed. Was that an invitation?

I was just stepping forward to find out exactly that when a faint buzzing caught my attention. I nudged my toe against my jeans which were puddled on the floor next to Rachel's bed and felt the vibration of my cell phone on my foot. "Fuck." Only nine people in the whole world actually had my number which meant that if someone was calling, I needed to hear from them. I glanced at the caller ID and saw that it was the ninth person. Dale Fenwick of Silvergate Records. Our label rep. Returning my call.

I'd forgotten that I'd put in a call to him last night. Just to gauge if there was any interest in the reunion show. I'd meant to go immediately to my siblings and see how they felt about it, but then... Rachel.

Rachel had happened and made me forget everything but her.

Feeling guilty, I let it go to voicemail with a whispered, "Sorry Dale."

Then the water swished on and the thought of Rachel naked drove the guilt away.

Chapter Twenty

RACHEL

I could still hear him moving around out in my bedroom, which made me acutely aware of my nakedness as I stepped into the shower.

It had been pure boldness that led me to leave the door open. Was I insane?

Or maybe I was drunk.

Drunk with the power this man made me feel.

"He didn't try." I mouthed the words to my distorted reflection in the showerhead, seeing my own wide, shocked eyes reflected back to me.

What he'd done... what he'd done to me, I knew it had to be a foregone conclusion what came next. And though I'd never done... that, before, I still knew enough about men or thought I did anyway, to know that I couldn't expect him to give like that without taking something for himself.

I wasn't blind. I could see the hunger in his eyes, the way they'd gone almost black with need. I'd felt it too, the urgency pressing against my thighs, the long hard shape of him that was both thrilling and terrifying at once. And I'd felt an answering ache inside of me when it had brushed against me, like a hole had opened up inside of me and I needed him to fill it. I was terrified, it was true, but I was ready as I had ever been before but he'd just... stopped. And snuggled up beside me.

And held me until I'd fallen asleep.

And I finally, *finally* understood just how wrong I'd been about him.

And if I'd been wrong about him, what else had I missed about the secular world and the people in it?

Maybe I didn't need to be so frightened. I didn't want to be frightened.

So this bright, brand new morning had me doing the bravest thing I could think of in that moment.

I left the door open so Beau could shower too.

Shower with me.

When I heard his tread on the tile, I trembled. Just a little. Not out of fear though. I was done being afraid because I'd learned that, with Beau anyway...

There was nothing to be afraid of.

He was silhouetted by the shower curtain, allowing me to watch him as he slowly slid his boxers down his hips. I sucked in my breath at the first glimpse of him. Even in shadow, he was beautiful. Even though he was a man, the word still applied. He was beautiful in the way a creek in wintertime was beautiful, with lines written by nature obscuring hidden power.

"Rachel?" he said my name.

I looked down and realized I was covering my breasts. Boldly - bravely - I let my hands fall to my sides. "Hi there."

"Is it all right if I come in?"

I wasn't frightened. I was smiling. "Yes." And just in case he needed as much reassurance that this was okay as I did, I put my hand up and in one quick stroke, I pushed the curtain to the side.

Beau's mouth fell open when he saw me. I stood there, and I should have shivered, but the heat of his gaze defied the cool water of the shower. I was blushing, I could feel it, even as I looked down and took him in.

He was fully naked. And fully - fully... I could think this word, I could say this word - erect. Yes. There was no other word for the way his... cock - I could say that word too - stood away from his body at a rigid angle. My own mouth fell open as I forced - no it wasn't force - myself to gaze at him in the exact way he was gazing at me now. With my full, careful attention, I let my eyes slip along that impossibly smooth skin, noting how it went purplish as it neared the head. My hands twitched at my sides, greedy to touch it.

Beau saw. "You look good wet," was all he said as he stepped into the tub with me and shut the curtain behind him.

All at once the space felt tiny. No matter how I shifted, I brushed up against his skin, so there was nothing to do but go into his arms when he opened them. It made perfect sense. "Good morning," I spoke into his chest.

"Yes, it is." He let his hands slide up my back. "A very good morning."

That first kiss felt easy. Natural even. He kissed me like he'd been doing it forever, like there was nothing new or strange about standing with each other while fully naked. It was easy to be brave with Beau because he didn't call attention to the strangeness.

So I kissed him back. Naturally. Easily. His smile curled across my lips even as his tongue slipped into my mouth. Minty - he'd brushed his teeth, and that fact made me smile right back at him. This whole thing, what should have been so scary, was making me smile instead.

I was happy. When I was with him I was so - fucking - happy.

"Mmm, I like you all slippery like this." He slid his hand down my arm, his fingers brushing the side of my breast.

My nipples tightened just from that slight grazing touch, starting the ache that I never seemed to be without these days. It was the ache that guided my own hands, slipping down from his shoulders and sliding past his pecs. His stomach tightened, and he hissed in a breath as my fingers sought downward and then -

Yes.

Yes.

"Fuck." He drew in a sharp breath when my hand closed around his... cock. "Rachel. Goddamn. Sorry for cursing but—"

"Don't." I stood on my tiptoes and caught his lower lip between my teeth, wanting him to stop apologizing. A fleeting thought to be frightened of doing this flickered through my head as fast as a lightning flash, but it was gone before I could grab ahold of it.

Besides, I had ahold of something much better.

"Holy." His words were muffled against my mouth. I nipped down a little harder, making him hiss, as I began to move my hand. It was some instinct that hadn't shown itself until right now. Maybe it was bravery. Or maybe I knew because of the way he was moving his hips, thrusting into my palm so that I could feel that slick skin moving inside of my grip. He, in turn, must have had some kind of instinct that told him what to do. How else would he have known the ache this was causing me. "So beautiful," he rasped against my lips as he slid his hand between my thighs.

The second his fingers made contact with my overheated skin, it was like a bomb went off inside of me. I shrieked against his lips, going up onto my tiptoes when he slipped that finger inside of me. It was tight, painfully so, until it wasn't. Until it was perfect and I needed more.

And that's when Beau took over.

Some part of me was still trying to move my hand, still trying to be in control of what was happening, but he overrode me, spinning me around so that my back was against the cold shower wall. I yelped when he pushed me flat against the cool tile, then yelped again when he slipped another finger inside of me - "Oh! Oh..."

A quick, bright flash of pain melted away, leaving only warm, spreading pleasure in its wake. His thick fingers were thrusting in perfect time - fast enough to give me the delicious friction but slow enough so that I felt it every time. I wrapped my hands around his neck and then... and then I lifted my leg and wrapped it around his waist, pulling him closer to me. The head of his cock just brushed against me. So close, so close. "Ah fuck, that feels so fucking good, angel," Beau groaned as he pulled his fingers away. I watched, rapt and completely dumbfounded as he slid his slippery... cock... along the soft folds of my most private place. The delicious friction, the tantalizing slide of it, had my knees quivering in a moment. I clung to Beau, crying out as he lowered his forehead to mine. The way his eyes fixed on me sent me right over the edge and suddenly I was shaking and quivering and then crying out. "Fuck, yes. Fuck, yes." Beau kept up a litany of quiet, strangled whispers, urging me to fall, and fall I did because I knew he would catch me.

When I blinked back up at him, the water had gone lukewarm, but there was... there was still something.

I closed my hand around him.

"You don't have to," he rasped out, but I was already moving my hand again. His cock felt even more slippery in my hands and I realized with a start that it was from me - that was my slickness. "I want to," I reminded him, and I did. "I want to see you - uh - I want to watch..."

My words faded into a blush, but Beau understood. "You want me to come for you, angel?"

I nodded, licking my lips.

"Here." He put his hand over mine, making me grip tighter. "Like that," he urged, guiding me to grip right up to that silky head. "You have to look at me. I want to see your face. Oh, fuck, Rachel." His lips fell open. I gasped when his cock twitched and somehow got even harder. "Rachel, I—"

His words were lost in a strangled cry. He jerked his hips back with a long, low groan, but I didn't avert my eyes the way he probably thought I would. I watched as he sagged against the wall and gasped with his strong shoulders heaving with each ragged breath.

"Rachel," he finally whispered. He straightened up and then caught my mouth with his.

The water had gone completely cold by then. But I barely noticed.

Chapter Twenty-One

RACHEL

I shivered over my coffee and took another warming sip. "Better?" Beau asked.

I looked up at him and smiled. Or, actually, I smiled wider, because I hadn't actually stopped smiling yet today. "Getting there." It was kind of adorable how freaked out he was by my shivering. "I'll warm up soon enough."

"We should have gotten out before the water got so cold but..." He trailed off and raised an eyebrow that did a much better job of warming me up than my cup of coffee.

"But," I echoed with an even wider smile. I felt like my face was going to split wide open.

He topped off my mug and then sat down at my battered kitchen table. "You sure you don't have to go in today?"

I nodded. "I'm not on the schedule. I double checked."

He leaned forward, and I was momentarily too distracted by the nice way his forearm muscle bunched and flexed as he rested his elbows on the table to hear what he was saying. "What?"

He grinned and set his mug down. "Today. You want to go there today?"

"Go where?"

Beau didn't get mad when he had to repeat himself. Which was nice because I always seemed to be distracted when I was around him.

"The Summer Kick-off Festival is this weekend." He leaned back in his chair and looked out the window. The ever-present burble of the creek floated in on the breeze, along with the screech of blue jays and the buzz of red-winged blackbirds. It was already hot in the kitchen and the last chill of the shower faded away as I sat in the sunbeam and watched Beau think. "I always wanted to go, but we always missed it. Touring and summer festivals and stuff. It was this big huge thing for the town and this is literally the first year I can make it." He looked at me. "You've been, right?"

I ducked my head and took a sip of my coffee. "As a spectator. No." I set down my mug, the better to twist my fingers nervously in my lap as I recalled. "When I was really little, they kept me away. You know, there's a lot of bad influences there." Beau raised his eyebrows in surprise at this, which made me laugh. "The sight of women wearing short shorts and holding hands with men and kissing in public and all. That kind of bad influence." Beau's eyebrows went back down again as he blew out a rueful sigh. "But when I was older though, I worked it."

He leaned forward again. "Right, that's right. The Chosen have a booth I heard."

I nodded. "We sell a few spring vegetables and some honey, but mostly it's baked goods."

"Like the potato bread you made me?" He looked suddenly hungry.

"We'd be up all week beforehand just so we could bake enough, but we always ran out." I shrugged. "So my whole experience of the festival is from the back of a tent. We'd roll the community truck right to the back of it, the better to discourage us from walking around and... seeing things." I went to take another sip of my coffee but then set it back down again. The acid in my stomach was already acting up just from remembering.

"Do you not want to go?" Beau's voice was soft and gentle.

God, he was so sweet. I leaned in and covered his hand with mine. "I think it would be different now, don't you?"

It's different now. That's what I told myself as we parked along the street a few blocks from the center of town. The road blocks were set up and the tents crowded the streets and tumbled out onto the bridge that crossed the creek. Above us blazed a bright blue, high-summer sky and the air was full of the smells of cotton candy and kettle corn.

I felt my breath catch in my chest. In the past weeks, I'd engaged in a million little rebellions, but this was a big one. Made even bigger when Beau reached for my hand.

It felt good to be linked to him like this. It felt good to walk down the middle of the street, unconcerned that others might see me touching him. It felt so... good.

I stopped suddenly and spun around. Beau laughed in surprise when I went up on my tiptoes to kiss him, but he caught me up in his arms readily and kissed me back. Right there in the middle of the street. It was wild. It was crazy.

It was amazing.

"I could get used to this," he murmured against my mouth. When I looked up at him, his hazel eyes twinkled. "Is that all right? 'Cause I really want to get used to this."

Pleasurable heat spread up my face. "That'd be okay with me," I mumbled as I looked down at my toes. Then grinned to myself as he slung his arm over my shoulder.

We wandered that way through the stalls, weaving our way from vendor to vendor and always with some part touching. He brushed his hand on my arm to call my attention to a set of windchimes he thought would hang nicely on my porch. I ducked under his arm to admire some earrings he immediately bought for me. He slid his hand around my waist and held me close as he ordered us both some of the kettle corn that had been driving us crazy with its delicious smells. I rested my head on his shoulder as we sat on the curb and devoured it across the street from the Crown Tavern.

"Hey." He nudged me and pointed to the chalked sign in the middle of the sidewalk in front of the bar. "You see that?"

"Open mic?" I read. "Yeah?"

"You should do that."

"Me?" I looked at him in confusion.

He grinned and popped a piece of kettle corn into my mouth. "Dare you." There was mischief in his hazel eyes.

"Seriously?" I looked at the sign again. "No way."

"I'll play the piano for you." When I looked at him again, he shrugged. "Or you can do it alone, whichever you prefer."

"No way!" I laughed and nudged my shoulder into his. But then paused and thought for a second. "Do you really think I should do it?" A small bud of pride was starting to bloom in my chest.

"Absolutely. You have a fucking beautiful voice." When he caught me gaping at him, he shrugged again. "What? You swore in front of me last night, I thought we were past that."

I laughed and stole the rest of his popcorn. "Fuck you." I grinned gleefully, which made him burst out laughing.

"I'm going to sign us up." He got up and wiped his hands on his jeans. "You're not going to try to stop me?"

I took a deep breath and then let it out. The last bit of worry about the sin of pride. "No."

He held out his hand and then hauled me to my feet. We crossed the road and went over to the tattered piece of paper hanging on the corkboard just inside of the bar. Inside, Taylor was desultorily wiping down the bar, but even his fierce scowl couldn't dampen my wild spirits. I signed my name and then flung myself at Beau, kissing him with everything I had, right there inside of the doorway to Crown Creek's only bar. He lifted me and then let his lips trail down past my jaw. I opened my eyes in shock when he nibbled my neck and that's when I saw the group of women staring.

"Rebecca." My mouth was suddenly as dry as a desert.

Confused, Beau pulled away and looked in the direction I was staring.

A girl dressed in pale blue homespun stepped forward. She was taller than when I last saw her, and her face had lost some of its roundness.

But I'd recognize my sister anywhere.

Chapter Twenty-Two

BEAU

She dropped my hand like it had scalded her. Her whole body was stiff as she stared at the Chosen woman who had stepped away from the group.

Same dark hair. Same pale skin. Same heart-shaped face, but her lips were different.

"Is that your sister?" I whispered, needlessly.

The girl she had called Rebecca was white as a ghost, but as she stared at Rachel, and then me, and then back to Rachel, her face went as red as a beet.

"Hi." I didn't like how small Rachel's voice sounded.

"What are you doing?" her sister hissed.

"What do you care?"

"You're right. I shouldn't care. Because obviously, you don't!"

"Rebecca!" Rachel's voice broke in a sob.

With a swish of long skirts, Rebecca turned her back and started to stomp the rest of the way to their booth. A few of the women looked back at Rachel. Some looked sympathetic, but most looked downright titillated. Whispers and shocked giggles carried all the way over to where we were standing.

I looked back at my angel and blinked. "Are you okay?" Another needless question, because she was clearly not. When I was a little boy, I was briefly into survivalism and studied up on all the various ways you could get into trouble in the wilderness. There had been a whole chapter in my favorite book regarding snakebites, with vivid illustrations of what to look for in the victim.

Rachel could have been the illustration for shock.

"Hey." I slung my arm around her again, trying not to wince at how stiff she was. "Can I help you? Tell me what you need."

She stepped a little to the side, effectively sidestepping my embrace. She flipped her long braid back over her shoulder and lifted her chin. "It's okay."

"Clearly it isn't."

The robotic way she turned her head chilled me right down to my shoes. "I'm fine, Beau. I mean, I left, right?" She shook her head. "It doesn't matter." Color was rising back up into her face. "I left for a reason," she said with her voice getting tighter, angrier. "I'm out in the real world now." She reached down and grabbed my hand and squeezed, hard. "And I'm doing just fine."

"Yes, you are." I wanted to argue, but it seemed foolhardy to argue in the face of such determination.

"Although," she faltered. "I could actually really use a drink."

"Well, we're right here, so that works out well." My lame attempt at a joke was completely ignored. She wasn't even looking at me. She was looking across the road, staring even.

I looked where she was looking and spotted the drab, flapping skirts of the Chosen women as they set out their wares at their booth. Rachel didn't move until the one in pale blue - her sister - stopped setting out the wrapped packets of bread and looked back out across the street.

It was only when Rachel was sure that her sister was watching her that she turned and went right into the bar.

I followed her. Of course. And I tried like hell to ignore how the ground suddenly felt so uneven under my feet. Like a rift had popped up where none had been before.

Chapter Twenty-Three

BEAU

"How many is that?" I asked Rachel, even though I knew damn well it had been too much already. "Definitely time for some water, right?"

"I'm fine." It was all she'd been saying the past hour. Variations on a litany that I knew wasn't true.

The festival had dumped a load of strangers into the bar. We were pressed in at all sides and my worry about Rachel had me on edge enough to actually snap at a guy who got too close. "Hey, you mind?" For the first time, I was starting to understand Finn's longing for the woods. Being alone - only surrounded by the people I cared about - sounded pretty appealing right now.

Rachel tried to take another deep swallow of her mixed drink, but I gently tugged the glass from her hand. She looked at me, shocked, and more than a little pissed then sighed heavily when I shoved the water glass into her hand. "Drink. Remember what I told you? You're going to feel like shit in the morning if you don't stay hydrated, especially since it's so damn hot in here." I shot a significant look at Taylor who went on wiping his glass aggressively.

I nodded when she sighed and took a long swallow. When she let it fall back down to the bar, I took it back before she spilled. "Do you want to go see the rest of the booths now?" We'd been inside this dark bar for way too long.

She bit her lip and shook her head.

"Because your sister is out there?"

"That doesn't matter."

"It clearly does," I said, as gently as I could. "Do you miss your family?"

She looked at me like I'd asked her if she showered naked. It was obvious. "Of course."

"So why did you leave?" Again, I said it as gently as I could. "Believe me, I know how obnoxious family can get, I'm like the poster child for it. But something is obviously bothering you." I handed her the water again and prodded her to take another drink, which she did begrudgingly. "And it's killing me," I said truthfully.

Her eyes went bright for a second before she collected herself and set the water glass back down again, a bit more steadily this time. "I told you. I left because there was no place for me there."

"Right, but I don't know what that means."

She opened her mouth as if she was about to explain and I held my breath.

Then she grinned and leaned forward. "It's okay." She nuzzled my neck and then slid off the bar stool and into my lap. "I'm okay, especially because I have you." She wiggled a little and started kissing me. Hard.

Instantly I was hard for her, just like I'd been since the day I met her. But her kiss was wrong. Desperate. As she shoved her tongue into my mouth, I could taste the alcohol that clung to her lips. "Jesus, Rachel," I panted because she was really getting me worked up. "Angel, you know I want you, but not like this. You're too drunk."

"I am not," she slurred.

"Right. That's it." I scooped her up. "Thanks, Taylor!" I sang out sunnily to the glowering bartender.

Rachel burst into tears.

"Okay," I promised as I hurriedly ducked out of the back entrance to the Crown Tavern, and around the parking lot, out of sight of the Chosen tent. My car was on the other side of the bridge, and there was no helping how many people saw me hustling my sodden drunk girlfriend through the crowds. If Rachel were in any shape to notice, she would hate this, I felt that acutely.

I finally bundled her into my car, where she slumped in a teary pile. Her quiet crying was far more disturbing than the angry front she'd put up for me and even more worrisome than the faux seduction she'd tried to spin out to distract me.

When I finally had her home and in bed, I stood there for a moment. Part of me wanted desperately to climb back in there with her. But it wouldn't be right.

I yanked the grubby bar receipt out of my pocket and scrawled a quick note to her. *Call me when you wake up.* Then I paused with the nub of pencil hovering in the air, unsure as to how to sign my name. *XO Beau? From, Beau...*

Love, Beau?

I glanced at her one more time, feeling a strange ache in my chest. If I thought it would do her any good at all, I wouldn't hesitate to march right into the Chosen compound and demand to know what the hell they were playing at. But I knew that would do nothing for Rachel, and what's more, she would probably end up pissed at me for interfering.

I hated not being able to help.

I hated not even knowing *how* to help.

I scrawled my first initial on the piece of receipt with no sign-off. Just 'B.' Then left her house, locking the door behind me.

Claire's Jeep wasn't in the driveway. She was probably out with her trio of best friends and for that I was grateful. I couldn't deal with my sister's penetrating questions tonight. Not when I had no answers.

"You okay?" my mom asked immediately upon seeing me.

"Sure."

"Well, you sure don't look it."

"I'm just tired." That wasn't a complete lie. Wedging my six foot three frame into Rachel's bed hadn't made for a very restful night's sleep.

My mother narrowed her librarian-eyes, looking like she'd like to pick up her glasses just so she could peer over the top of them at me. "Rachel seems like a nice girl," she finally said.

"Yup."

"You're not spending the night over there again tonight?"

"You don't miss anything, do you?"

"Not where my kids are concerned. Which is why I wanted to ask you." She lowered her voice and glanced toward the stairs. "Any idea what's up with Finn?"

I pressed my lips together. I'd been spending so much time wrapped up in Rachel that I was forgetting to keep an eye on my brother. "Not sure, exactly."

"You're keeping close watch on him, right?"

The anxious note in her voice jolted me right out of my Rachel reverie. "Yeah, of course." This was a lie, as of this moment. But it didn't need to be. "That's why I came home, to spend some time with him," I decided suddenly.

"Good." My mom sat back down and picked up the thick book she'd had in front of her when I arrived back home. I watched her a moment and couldn't help but notice that her eyes weren't moving across the page at all. She was just sitting there. Worried.

My skin was crawling with the need to fix something - anything. I hadn't figured out how to fix things for Rachel yet, but I was pretty sure I knew how to fix my brother.

I took the stairs up to Finn's room two at a time.

His light was on, a good or bad sign, depending on how you looked at it. On one hand, it was good that he wasn't spending all of his time sleeping like he used to. But on the other hand, that meant he was sitting alone in his room and had been for hours. I knocked. "Can I come in?"

There was a shuffle and the sound of blankets falling. "Yeah," Finn grunted.

I opened the door and tried not to wince at the smell of stale air. Purposefully leaving the door open behind me, I went over and settled on the bed next to him, kicking away the pile of blankets that lay knotted on the floor. "You been downstairs at all today?"

"Yeah." Finn was flicking through his phone without looking at me. He'd probably been doing that for hours now, but I didn't want to ask.

"Hey, uh, so about the house."

His eyes flickered with interest.

"I really want to make a move on it." The smell of stale air and my brother stagnating with it put some urgency in my voice. I tried to slow down, not rush him, but it was hard. "I think you're really going to like it."

Finn rolled over onto his back. "Yeah?" If there was interest in his voice, it was buried under a layer of sadness.

"It's exactly what you want. I mean, cabins in the middle of state parks don't come up for sale every so often."

"I just want to be away from everybody." Finn finally let his phone fall to the side. "You say it's good?"

"I haven't toured inside yet but yeah." I clapped my hand on his knee. "It's pretty perfect."

I held my breath as I waited for him to respond. My heart was pounding with the need for him to get excited. Be happy. Look forward to this.

Finally, he let out a sigh. "I trust you." He let out a breath that could have been a laugh but didn't sound much like one. "I trust you more than I trust myself, honestly."

Those words were like an icy knife slipping just under my ribs. "What do you mean?"

"Not like that, Beau."

I tried to rearrange my face into neutral lines, but it was too late. The panic had already set in. "Not like that?" I asked, my throat dry.

Finn sighed and sat up straighter and I hated that I needed him to be the one to reassure me. That wasn't how this was supposed to work. "How many times do I have to promise that I won't do that again?"

I tried like hell to smile. "Maybe one more time."

"I'm not going to try to off myself again, Beau." I winced at the flippant tone he used.

"You know I hate it when you use that phrase."

He spread his hands. "Fine. Kill myself. Commit suicide. Whatever. I'm not going to do it, Beau."

He reached out. That was what convinced me. Not his words but the fact that he clapped his hand on my shoulder. I wanted to believe that if Finn was really unreachable again, then he wouldn't reach out to me. "Those were bad days, Beau."

"I know." Twelve years wasn't long enough to dull the pain of remembering that day. I was ten years old and scared like hell as I watched the ambulance doors shut with my twin brother unconscious inside. I wanted to go with him, we'd never been separated before. I wanted to pitch a fit, to throw the mother of all tantrums until they allowed me to go with him. But then I saw my mother's grim, tear-streaked face and my childish indignation fell away. And right then, at ten years old, I understood perfectly that it was more important that I take care of others than it was to be taken care of myself. I went to my mother and put my hand on her shoulder much the same way Finn had his hand on mine now. "I'll take care of him, Mom," I'd promised. "I'll watch out for him."

And that's what I'd always done, ever since. Take care of him. "What would you say about playing music together again?" I asked him.

Finn let his hand fall back. A spark of interest flared in his eyes and then died away. "The band broke up."

"The label wants the band together again." I shifted, feeling the excitement bubbling inside of me. With any luck, that weird twin-connection meant that he'd feel it too. "Just one performance, but it'll be enough to buy the house outright." Finn was tilting his head with interest, so I put the cherry on top of the sundae with a promise I hoped like hell I could keep. "Just one performance and then you can have all the seclusion you want."

It worked. He was chuckling. "All I want, huh? But won't you still be there?"

The heaviness slid from my shoulders. "Well yeah, idiot. You're never actually going to be rid of me." I gaped at him, rolling my eyes comically.

"Really?" Some of the sourness crept back into his voice. "Not even when it comes to this chick?"

My blood heated. "She's not just 'some chick.'"

"I didn't say she was."

"Don't, Finn."

"What? You're gonna go be with her at some point though, right? That's where you're headed, I can tell." He tapped the side of his temple. "I know things."

I opened my mouth to tell him he was wrong, then shut it because I'd be lying. I did want to see where things were going with Rachel. But I also knew I'd made a promise to my mother. "Nah, man." I clapped him on the shoulder a little harder than I meant to, making him wince and stare at me. My throat felt tight, but I forced the words around the lump that was forming. "We're a team for life."

Chapter Twenty-Four

RACHEL

The clouds were gathering on the horizon. Huge, thunderheads boiling upward in the west, black with the promise of ranges and tinged with the greenish threat of hail too. It was up to me to get the cows in from the pasture. I slid off the fence rail with sudden purpose but was distracted by the swish of my skirts around my ankles.

My skirts. How strange that I should notice them like this? They were a part of me, and yet they felt so heavy around my hips, like the hems were weighted down. I glanced down to find that the reason was I had dragged them through the mud. I did not remember this, but that didn't concern me now.

A gusting wind picked up, sharp enough to send my braid swinging. The clouds were closer now - much closer than they should have been. Time seemed to be speeding up, but when I tried to move, it was as if I was knee deep in heavy snow. I could barely move my feet.

It was my skirts. My mud-caked skirts were dragging me down, so heavy I had to sink to my knees. Panic choked my throat closed as the first boom of thunder sounded over my head and I looked up in horror as the spooked cows started racing to the barn for safety. Their sharp hooves bit the earth, I could feel the vibrations under my hands. I pushed up. I tried to move. I needed to get out of the way before they trampled me, but my skirts - my skirts were so heavy. I couldn't move out of the way of the stampede bearing down on me. I was going to be crushed and the thunder was so loud that no matter how loud I cried out, no one could hear me scream. But I screamed anyway. I screamed, and I screamed as the thunder boomed overhead and -

I screamed and suddenly I was no longer there in the pastures that ringed the Chosen compound anymore. I was in my bed, with the sheets twisted tightly around my legs.

I kicked them free in a blind panic and that's when I heard the rumble of thunder that had made its way into my dreams.

My nightmare.

I kicked the blankets straight onto the floor and only then - with my legs free and unencumbered - did my heart rate start to slow. "Beau?" My voice was sleep-thickened, and my throat was raw. "Are you here?"

The house was silent and the space next to me was cold. I rolled over to look for his shoes by the bed but was halted by a slice of pain knifing through my head. I blinked and dug the heel of my hand into my eyeball. "What the hell?"

And that's when I saw the glass of water and three white aspirin on my bedside table.

So he had been here. I reached for the water and guzzled it, suddenly parched, then remembered at the last moment to save a few sips to swallow down with the pills. Then I let my head flop back down onto the pillow.

I had gotten drunk yesterday. Why? Because I had seen Rebecca - the memory came back with such clarity that doubled over, curling into the fetal position as I clutched my belly. My sister had seen me with Beau. I blinked at the empty water glass. Anger was heating my blood, anger at Rebecca and the rest of the Chosen. My family. Who'd cut me off. What did they care if I was acting secular now? I was happy, happier than I'd been in a long time. Happy because I had a man who took me home and tucked me in and left me water and aspirin for when I woke up hurting after seeing the people who, once upon a time, had warned me not to trust people like him. Musicians were evil, rock musicians were Satan's envoys to earth, but when I was with Beau, I felt closer to heaven than I'd ever felt wearing the skirts of a Chosen woman. He was nothing like I had been taught he was. He was wholly himself and what he was, was a wonderful man. I didn't belong to the Chosen anymore.

I wanted to belong to him.

I reached for my phone, so eager to hear his voice that I didn't even sit up.

He picked up on the first ring. "Hey."

"Hey." The last bits of my headache vanished as soon as I heard his voice. I rolled back onto my pillow again and smiled up at the ceiling. "I missed you this morning."

"I missed you too." He sounded like he had just woken up too. "How are you feeling?"

"The water helped. The aspirin helped more."

"Are you okay?" He wasn't just asking about my headache, I could tell.

The remnants of my dream were still swimming in my head. The horror of the oncoming stampede, my complete inability to move when the danger was bearing down on me. I squeezed my eyes shut. "I'll be all right. If I can see you soon."

"You can." I loved the slow honey in his voice. The ache for him - the one that never quite died away - clenched my core and held tight. "And besides," he added playfully. "We have to rehearse for open mic."

I had forgotten about our plan. That blissful moment turned ugly when Rebecca had spotted us. I swallowed down the bitter bile that flooded my mouth, but my nightmare was still nipping around the edges of my consciousness. Rebecca's ugly words were still ringing in my ears. "Of course," I said to drown them out. "You want to rehearse, huh? That's how you want to spend our time together."

His chuckle melted the ice in my veins. "We can do a lot of things together, I'll pick you up soon?"

"Yes." I exhaled and hung up, then stared at the ceiling. When the nightmare demanded I remember it, I sat up and then pushed out of bed. The act of moving seemed to be enough to keep ahead of the stampede, and while I'd been hampered by my skirts in the dream, in real-life, I could still move freely.

Right?

I'd taken a quick shower and was just pinning my hair up to the nape of my neck in order to let what little breeze there was in the humid soup of the morning play about my neck when I heard the distinct sound of Beau's car on the gravel of my driveway.

Just the sound of it. That was all it took, and my body almost vibrated with the need to see him, to be held by him.

To be loved by him.

I closed my eyes, but it was still right there. The word. Four letters. It hadn't quite taken form yet, but I could feel it. What this was.

I loved him.

"Shit," I muttered.

And then grinned.

I flew out of the house so fast that my braid came unpinned and uncoiled down my back. I didn't care, especially not when Beau caught me mid-leap and spun me around, then wrapped my braid in his fist so he could guide me to kiss him deeper.

"Good morning," he murmured against my lips as I smiled and kissed him again. "Wanna hear something funny?"

"What's that?" There was an outside world, I was fairly sure of it, but the only thing I cared to notice was the way his hazel eyes looked green today.

"It felt weird waking up without you in my arms." He tucked a stray strand of hair behind my ear. "I don't want to do that again. Do you?"

My heart felt like it was too big for my chest. Like someone had inflated it like a balloon. "No." I smiled at the idea. "I think we should never do that again."

Beau opened his mouth to agree with me. At least that's what he probably meant to do before he was interrupted.

"Hey there!" another voice rang out. "You coming?"

I blinked in confusion and Beau sighed. "I'm sorry. They insisted on coming."

I looked over at the car to see Claire's bright smiling face and Finn's gloomy one. "Oh." The balloon in my chest deflated so fast I sagged inward. "Okay, sure."

"I'm really sorry," Beau whispered, tucking my hair back again. "But maybe you can let me make it up to you later?"

I inflated again. "Sounds like a plan." I followed him around the side of his car and grinned when he opened the door for me. "What's the plan?"

"They got the house!" Claire interrupted before either of the brothers could speak. She grabbed my shoulder, shaking me with her excitement. "It was my idea the way they ended up working it out. See, it's like a rent-to-own thing—"

"I'll let Claire do the talking," Beau sighed under her chatter, making me giggle. He backed the car out of the driveway as Claire went on explaining that the owner agreed to a closing date a few months from now, with the guys renting it until that time. "They've still got to put down a deposit, which I told them was pretty stupid since they're going to be the owners in the end, so what damages are they putting down a security for—"

"Remind me whose house this is going to be?" Finn asked the heavens with a mighty eyeroll.

Claire smacked him. "You needed me." She wagged her finger under his nose. "I understand how things are done in Crown Creek. You all left so you have no idea."

A weird tension hung in the air. I glanced at Beau who may have shaken his head imperceptibly, or maybe he hadn't at all. I turned and looked out the window, eager to see the house the brothers had decided on. I planned on spending a lot of time there.

Beau reached out and squeezed my hand, then lifted it to his lips. "You okay?" he asked. I blinked at him, confused until I realized which road we had turned down.

I sucked air in through my teeth before I could collect myself. "I'm fine."

"You want me to turn around? We can take the long way."

I glanced back at Finn and Claire. They were both listening intently. Finn seemed confused, but Claire's sharp eyes saw everything. Including how my hands twisted in my lap. I consciously set them down. "No. It's fine."

We dipped down the slight hill that led into the broad valley. The valley I knew by heart.

The ominous clouds were still gathered on the horizon, but overhead, the sun pierced through the gray in shafts of light all around us. Lighting the places I knew best.

We were driving past the Chosen compound. "Slow down," I asked Beau.

He hesitated, but then did what I asked, slowing and pulling over to the shoulder. Gravel crunched under the wheels as I looked at the place that had been my home for twenty years.

"I don't..." I cleared my throat around the catch in it. I didn't want to get upset. I wasn't upset. "It's weird looking at it from this angle."

"Why?" Claire was pasted against her window, staring at the buildings like she could see through the walls.

"There's a back entrance. Down by the creek. It goes through the pastures and it keeps the eyes off us." It was strange how easily I slipped into the patterns of Chosen speech, even after two years away. I pointed. "See down that way, the gray building? That's the main meeting house, I guess you'd call it the church maybe? That's where most everything happens in the community. There's a reason it's the farthest from the road." If I closed my eyes, I could perfectly picture the dusty road down to the meeting house, but I couldn't see it from here. I was on the outside, looking in. Which was strange, but wasn't that how I felt in the secular world too?

Where did I belong?

"What about the houses up here?" Claire pointed at the cluster of tired looking but still proud houses barely visible through the trees.

"That one," I pointed and held my finger steady, so they couldn't see it trembling. "That's my family's. See the broken window by the cellar? My brother Jesse did that with a rock. I guess they still haven't gotten the money together to fix it." A strange tug pulled at my heart. I should send the money, I thought, out of nowhere. I cleared my throat. "All the houses are together like this because we're - they're"—I corrected when Finn looked at me—"a community. I could go to any house and ask for a snack or join meals." I was starting to smile in spite of myself. "I never really did, because I was a homebody, but my sister Rebecca—"

"The one I met?" Beau asked. He sounded like he was trying to keep careful control of his voice.

"Yeah, she's always been like that." Now I was grinning. "She's the polar opposite of me. Sometimes I envied her, and then I felt bad about it and tried even harder to be good to her." I shook my head. "She doesn't make it easy." I leaned up against the glass. I knew it was silly to try to spot people from the road. Keeping out of sight of secular eyes was one of the first things any Chosen child was taught. We could walk into their world and observe them, but we never let them see us when we were in ours. But unlike secular eyes, mine knew where to look. I searched the rooftops for scrambling children, then down around the roots of the conifers for kids collecting pine cones. I watched the backs of the houses for women doing the home-gardening and getting the wash from the lines. But there was no one out. A sudden memory hit me, and I glanced at the clock in the car.

Noon. Of course. It was time for the breaking of bread. Everyone would be down at the meeting house. My cheeks heated. How could I have forgotten?

A faint sound caught my attention. I looked up to see that Beau, Claire, and Finn had all been watching me. I blinked. How long had I been staring longingly out the window?

"It looks like a really nice place to grow up," Claire said, tactfully interrupting the awkward silence.

I lifted my chin. "It was." For some reason, I felt close to tears.

"Must be weird," Finn piped up.

I licked my lips. I'd purposefully avoided coming down this road, but now that I had, I was glad. I was here in the car with them, but I didn't belong here. But I didn't belong there either. "A little," I finally said.

Beau exhaled sharply and then suddenly his hand was in my hair. With fire in his eyes, he pulled me to him, pressing his forehead to mine for one moment before slanting his mouth down to mine.

I inhaled sharply as the tears that had been threatening to fall suddenly burned away. A small sound escaped my mouth, but he swallowed it with his sudden, desperate onslaught. My hands trembled as they moved to cup his face, but once my fingers found his skin, they stilled. Even as my heart rate sped up, a kind of peace washed through me. Maybe I had no idea where I belonged, but when I was with Beau, it didn't seem to matter.

Maybe I belonged with him.

"Ah..." Claire coughed from the back seat. I reluctantly pulled back from Beau and shot her an apologetic grin.

"Let's go," Beau said, pulling away. I glanced in the side mirror, wanting to see the compound behind me, but we'd kicked up so much dust that it was blocked from my view.

Chapter Twenty-Five

BEAU

I'd been planning it forever, but now that it was here, it felt like it was happening too fast.

I walked the perimeter of my childhood bedroom one more time, but I knew I wouldn't find anything I'd missed. The boxes that lined the walls were already filled with all my possessions. What was left behind, what I kept picking up and putting back down again were the things that belonged to my parents, but that I had always thought of as mine. The crazy quilt my great-grandmother had made which had covered my bed since I'd commandeered it at age six. It felt like mine, but it belonged to my mother - an heirloom that she deserved to keep. It belonged to her, not me. Just like I'd always belonged at this house.

But now it was time to move on.

My phone buzzed in my pocket. I smiled a little, even though I didn't check the text messages that were blowing it up. I knew who it was. My oldest brother Jonah had been texting me plans all morning. The idea of getting the band back together had him ecstatic. Of course, being Jonah, he was busy trying to tell me what to do. I knew my text messages would be full of his advice and musings. I'd have time to read through them all later. In my new house.

If Gabe's PA called me back though, then I'd answer. Gabe was somewhere in Asia shooting his reality show, and the time difference meant it was hard to connect. I'd sent him an email, but I never really expected him to write back. Gabe wasn't one for sitting down and methodically committing his thoughts to paper. Finn had jokingly suggested we hire a skywriter to catch his attention, and I'd actually given it some serious thought.

Finn wasn't saying it aloud, but I could see that spark of excitement in his eyes when I talked about it.

And then there was my sister.

At first, I thought I'd need to clear it with my brothers first. Then I'd dismissed it as unnecessary. The idea of shutting Claire out of the band was not ours. In fact, we'd fought our old manager when he'd declared us the King *Brothers* and left our sister out of it. I'd always felt like we should have fought him harder, given how things ended up.

Now that my future was in my own hands, I had no problem asking Claire to join us. The only problem had been the ringing in my ears that persisted long after she'd finished shrieking, "Yes!"

The house. The tour. It was all falling into place. Careful thought and planning had gotten me here.

Of course, Rachel hadn't been part of the plan.

At this, I smiled and stopped fiddling with the hem of the crazy quilt. I stood up and smoothed my hand over it, leaving my bed made for my mother to find for probably the first time ever. No, Rachel hadn't been part of the plan, but she was something I wanted to start planning around. I didn't know what the future looked like past the concert, but I knew I wanted her in it.

It hit me like a punch to the gut. I actually doubled over and had to lean against the wall. I wanted a future. With her in it. I wanted to wake up next to her and be there when she unbraided her hair at night. I wanted to fall asleep listening to the sounds of her breathing. I could see one night stretching into thousands. I wanted her smiling at me, and singing her pretty hymns as we cooked side by side in the kitchen. I wanted her desperate kisses and the way she leaped into my arms every chance I could get them.

Oh my God. I loved her.

I straightened up. Already a plan was forming. A new plan. I needed everything perfect. I needed soft music. Candlelight. I needed to tell her.

And then I needed to show her. I'd make love to her slowly. So achingly slowly that we'd both go wild. And then I'd rest by her side, with her hair tickling my face.

And then I'd do it again.

The thought had my heart racing. I grinned. With one final pat of the old, familiar wall, I grabbed a box and headed down to the moving truck. Yeah. Everything was definitely falling into place.

Chapter Twenty-Six

RACHEL

"Here it is." Beau could barely suppress his proud smile as he unlocked the door to his new house.

I stepped through the door and inhaled the scent of fresh paint. The windows were all open and the faint buzz of bees was the only sound outside but for the whisper of the wind through the pines. I turned in a slow circle, taking in the exposed wooden beams, the clean white walls and the deep, river stone hearth at the other end. The only furniture was a few scattered chairs and an out of place rug. "Wow," I said, and my voice echoed off the empty walls. "It's so big!"

"Lots of room for guests," Beau said as he pressed his hand gently to my lower back. "Let me show you the deck."

I let him lead me through the huge, high-ceilinged room and out through a sliding glass door. Out on the wide deck, the sun was beating down on us until Beau grinned and set a rusty wheel on the wall to creaking. A faded awning unfurled from its hiding place along the front of the house. "That's handy," I said and turned to look out over the front lawn. It swooped down to a reed-choked fishing pond. Behind that, tall woods rose up to scrape the blue sky. The sun was dipping lower now. "You've got a west view," I realized.

Beau came over and slid his hand around my waist. I sighed against him, resting my head on his shoulder. I could feel his voice rumbling in his chest before he spoke. "We can watch a lot of sunsets here," he said, turning to press a kiss to the top of my head.

"You and Finn?"

"You and me." He pulled me around so I was facing him. I rested my cheek against his chest and listened to the slow thump of his heart. "You're going to be over here a lot."

"I am?" The thought thrilled me down to my toes.

"Rachel." He leaned down and pressed his forehead to mine. The way I loved, where his eyes were everything that mattered. "I've been thinking a lot."

"Me too."

"No, I wanted to tell you that—"

"I'm heading out now, k?"

I jumped back when the door creaked. I hadn't even known that Finn was still here and by the expression on his face, neither had Beau. "Yeah sure," he answered through gritted teeth. He looked so crestfallen that a traitorous laugh bubbled up from my stomach and escaped out the side of my mouth with a snort.

Beau grinned and looked back at me. "Are you—"

"I'm not laughing at you. I'm just—"

"What?" He twirled me around so my back was to the warm outside wall of the house. I heard the glass door swish closed as Finn made his escape, but Beau didn't even glance away. He kept his eyes on me.

I licked my lips. "You made a funny face."

"I make you laugh?" He brushed his lips against mine. "I'm glad," he said against my neck. "But I'd rather be making you scream."

I gasped when he slid the door open and then swept me into his arms. "Beau?"

"I had a new bed delivered already." His grin made my heart beat faster. "It's all ready for—"

"For?" I was panting. I couldn't say it. I needed him to.

He knew it. He knew me. As I tumbled backward onto his wide bed, he asked me. "You, Rachel." He kissed me. Long and slow until I was gasping and arching up into him. "Are you ready?"

There was no more thought. No more worry. No. I loved him, and I wanted to show it. "I'm ready."

"I'm going to be so good to you, angel."

"I know." I did know. "I trust you, Beau."

I wanted to say more, but it was swallowed in a moan. Somehow, in the past few moments, he'd lifted my shirt over my head and tossed it away, unfastened my bra with the same deft quickness and now his lips were on my breast. "Oh my God," I groaned as the warmth of his tongue slipped over my nipple. The warmth spread out, melting me into a puddle, and then he nipped lightly with his teeth. The jolt sparked across my skin, making me sizzle.

"Are you good?" He wound my braid around his fist and used it to tug my head to the side, exposing my neck.

"Do that again."

He chuckled. "This?" He nibbled at my earlobe.

"No at my..." I swallowed and steeled myself to say the word. "My breast."

"Your tit?"

I turned and saw he was grinning evilly. I licked my lips. "Bite my left tit, Beau," I commanded, relishing the strange taste of the word in my mouth. "Fucking bite it."

His eyes went wide. "Fuck me," he murmured and bent to do exactly what I'd asked.

The sharp pain melted into the most delicious heat. I moaned again. "Other one."

"You're killing me." The strain in his voice made me shiver and then I yelped when he nipped and sucked at my right... tit. "God, Rachel. Tell me you're ready. Tell me again."

"I'm ready." I swallowed and then grinned. "Beau."

"Yes. Yes angel, yes."

The words came out with no hesitation. "Fuck me, Beau."

It was like a tether stretched to its limit suddenly snapped. Like a dam filled to capacity suddenly burst. Three words holding everything back suddenly giving way. I felt the strangest sliding inside of me, like I was being fundamentally rearranged from the inside out. I wondered if I was even me anymore because I didn't recognize the biting, sucking, kissing woman who was tearing at Beau's closed like she was possessed by Satan himself. I barely knew who I was as I yanked his jeans down below his hips and nearly swallowed his cock whole. I didn't know who it was that laid back and spread my legs and let Beau bury his face between my legs.

But I liked her.

I liked being her.

Beau grunted as his tongue found my center, my... pussy. "You're so wet already," he groaned, almost like it pained him. "God, Rachel, you taste so..."

"I want to know."

He drew back and looked at me. Me, it was me who said those words. Neither one of us could believe it. "Kiss me," Beau ordered.

I sat up and pressed my lips to his. "Is that what I taste like?" I asked.

"So sweet." He slipped his hand between my legs and rubbed until he had me gasping, then brought his fingers to my lips. "Lick, right here." His eyes went wide when I did. "You're fucking amazing." His voice broke in a rasping growl. He seized my braid again and held it tight in his fist while the other hand returned to the place between my legs. "Angel, I don't want to hurt you," he said, watching me carefully. "So I want you to come for me. Can you do that for me? Can you come right on my fingers.? Yes. Right like that, oh my God I love how you watch me. Keep your eyes right here, angel."

I could feel him moving, but whatever he was doing was lost in the waves of sensation that were coursing through me from his fast moving fingers.

"Right like that."

I gasped, my chest hitched.

"Right, just like that, just like that, come for me, Rachel, oh God. You're coming, you are, oh fuck, I can feel you!"

I screamed and the world shattered right as a hot, bright burst of pain flashed and then melted away.

I looked down and saw that Beau was inside of me. "Oh my God."

"Shh," he murmured, stroking my hair. "I'm right here. This is as far as I'm going to go," he soothed as I gritted my teeth against the impossible fullness. "Even though I have to tell you it's killing me. You feel so good, angel."

"I do?" The thought emboldened me, and I was filled with the urge to start moving. I arched my hips, gasping when he sank into me even deeper and his eyes went wide and then narrowed. "Is that good too?" I wondered.

My answer was his growl. He cradled me backward until I was on my back and he was over me, and even though I was vulnerable to him now, I felt so much power when I saw the way his face contorted in pleasure.

"Only just..." he gasped as he moved, the tiniest of strokes.

I inhaled sharply and he sank all the way inside of me, right up to the hilt.

"Fuuuck." His eyelids fluttered, beautiful dark lashes shadowing the hazel. "I want to fuck you right like this, Rachel." His hips jerked as his muscles quivered with the strain of holding back. "But baby girl, if I do, it's going to be too much for you. I want you to be on top of me."

I gasped as he bent down and rolled us as one and suddenly I was the one looking down on him. I froze in place, hardly believing the position I was in. Chosen women weren't in charge. That wasn't how we were raised. We were raised to be helpful and provide solace to our husbands and -

"Ride me," Beau said with a gasp. His hands brushed up to my waist and then down to cup my buttocks. He lifted me once, just to show me what to do. And I suddenly remembered.

I wasn't a Chosen woman anymore.

I was Beau's woman.

Chapter Twenty-Seven

BEAU

She knelt upward, long hair tumbling free of her braid in a wild tangle. Her eyes met mine for one second and then she closed them in bliss as she slid down, taking me in completely.

I struggled to let her take her time. Because she felt so fucking good. Had it felt this amazing before? I couldn't even remember a time before Rachel, and I didn't want to either. I wanted to be right here, with her, watching as she found her rhythm and her mouth fell open as it started to feel amazing for her too.

"Fuck." She started grinding herself into my pubic bone. Her short, shallow strokes were driving me crazy, but then there was the way she kept cursing. "Oh shit, Beau. Oh... shit!" and that was more than enough to make me lose my mind.

"God, I love it when you cuss," I encouraged her, gripping her by the hips and guiding her higher. The rough slap of her skin on mine was almost as amazing as the sound of her fumbling and stuttering when she realized how much she was losing it. "Say all the filthy words, Rachel. Look at my cock. Your greedy little cunt is swallowing it right up."

She turned even redder at my coarseness, but it turned her on too. Leaning back, she began to ride me in earnest. I was mesmerized by the way her perfect tits bounced, the way her hair swung like a pendulum, tickling my thighs. "Beau, it's, oh it's close, I feel it."

"Yes." I moved my hand, positioning one behind her ass, giving her the leverage she needed to slam herself down, while with the other, I slipped to the front and pressed my thumb right to her clit.

Her eyes flew open. "Oh! Fuck!" Her hips bucked wildly, and she ground herself frantically against my fingers, using the friction to get herself off.

And then it happened.

Rachel fell apart.

A shattering moan raked up from deep within her and I felt her clench me tightly from within.

"Oh fuck," I groaned, not even worried about whether I was making sense anymore. 'Shit, shit, shit."

She came with a cry, tossing her head forward and falling against my chest. I sat up to meet her, hugging her tight to me as I drove myself into her from below, cursing mindlessly as I felt her cling to me. We rocked as one for only a moment before my own control shattered and I buried myself in her with a guttural roar.

I might have blacked out. At the very least my sight dimmed, tunneling down to a pinpoint to focus only on a freckle on her skin. I stared at that freckle as my heart thudded to quiet, mind empty of everything but three words. "Rachel—"

"Oh my God, Beau." She sagged and then fell in a heap to the side before I could catch her, and then giggled as her eyes closed. "I feel like I'm drunk."

I grinned even though the moment to tell her had slipped right through my fingers. "Just call me Long Island Iced Tea," I teased her as I leaned in for a kiss.

She huffed out a scandalized gasp and then socked me lightly on the shoulder, then fell back again. "Hitting you took all my energy. I need a nap now."

I kissed her sleepy eyes and slipped from the bed. Quietly I knotted off the condom and slipped it under the tissues in the trash. Then I looked for my washcloths, discovered that I hadn't unpacked them yet and ended up wadded some tissue and running it under warm water. "Here, for you to..."

I stopped in the doorway. Rachel - naked and beautiful, with her hair tumbling around her like a blanket - was fast asleep in my brand new bed.

Chapter Twenty-Eight

RACHEL

Beau's house was still empty, but my heart was so... fucking full.

I finally understood why the Chosen elders warned us so strenuously about the dangers of sex. Because now that I'd had it, it was all that I wanted.

I'd woken in the late evening to find that Beau was watching me sleep. It had been gentler that time, Beau acutely aware of how sore I had to be, but I'd flipped him onto his back and showed him I was doing just fine.

He seemed to like that.

He also liked it when he finally folded himself around me and I'd fallen asleep in his arms, but he liked it even better when he woke up with my hand around the erection that had started pressing into my lower back. That time we'd both been too exhausted for much athleticism, but we made up for it in tenderness.

Now I was awake in this strange, empty house, rifling through the few small boxes he'd brought over in the car yesterday as if what was his was also mine. "There's gotta be a mug in here somewhere." I tried to catch my yawn before it split my face open, but Beau chose that moment to wander bare-chested into the kitchen and laugh at me.

"Tired?"

"Someone kept me up all night," I grumbled.

He puffed up proudly. "Someone didn't seem to mind it so much while it was happening." He reached past me and pulled out the big blue mug of his that I liked the best. "I'd say we broke in the new bed pretty well. I slept like a baby."

I smiled down at the coffee he was pouring for me. He must have slipped out of bed this morning to make sure it was brewing. If I hadn't been sure about loving him before, now I was certain. "No, you didn't. I've never heard a baby snore like that before."

He froze, making me burst out laughing, but he looked terrified. "I snore?"

I reached out and touched the tip of his nose. "No. And even if you did, that'd be okay. I can sleep through anything. My house was always noisy growing up."

Beau's expression took on that one of wary eagerness. I'd noticed it whenever I made passing mention of where I grew up. It was like he desperately wanted to ask me about it but was afraid of what he'd find out. I cleared my throat. "My sister Rebecca - you met her, you remember." Beau grimaced. "She snores like crazy, but would never admit it. 'It's the walls creaking,' she'd say. Or, 'I was just going to wake you up, I can't sleep through your snoring.'" I shook my head. Rebecca was slippery that way, never letting herself get pinned down, always ducking and deflecting. I knew that was how she was, but her words were still playing in the back of my brain on repeat. *"Why should I care? Because obviously you don't!"*

Beau's voice brought me back to myself. "Did you have to share a room with her?"

"Of course. There were four of us in the room and whatever baby had been born most recently."

Beau blinked, but then just nodded. "I shared a room with my brothers a lot when we were on tour. I never could figure out who the snorer was. It seemed to change every night."

I opened my mouth to tell him that sharing a hotel room was nothing like how it'd been for me but then paused. He was trying to reach out to me. Even though we'd grown up so differently, there were still so many things that were the same.

I went up on my tiptoes and kissed his nose. "Shower?" I asked.

That seemed to pique his interest.

After we'd run the water cold and shivered into our clothes, Beau took me on a tour of the property. We ducked under the boughs of the conifers and blinked in the patches of sunlight that filtered down through the green. On the other side of that stand of trees rose a field of waist-high grasses with a huge granite boulder rising in the center like a stone ship in a sea of green. We lay there watching the clouds, letting the sun-warmed rock make us sleepy, then Beau heard my stomach growl and yanked me to my feet. "I had an idea."

His idea turned out to be - fishing.

Ripples were studding the weed-choked pond at the bottom of his lawn. Mayflies and midge danced crazy circles on the surface, and every so often the buzzing silence was broken by the might splash of a fish nabbing itself dinner. Beau strode down the lawn with the swagger of someone who already looked at this place as *his*. I swelled with happy pride for him.

Right up until the moment he handed me the pole with a condescending smile. "Have you ever been fishing before?"

I stared at him incredulously. "Are you really asking that?"

He raised an eyebrow and I let out a disbelieving laugh. "Beau, the Chosen are taught from a young age how to be self-sufficient." I cast out my line with an expert flick.

"Well okay then." He took a respectful step back. "Should I just shut up and let you do your thing?"

"Fish do like it better when it's quiet," I teased, softening my words with a smile. He grinned, running his tongue over his teeth in a way that made me excited about how much trouble I was getting myself into.

But then my rod dipped, and the bobber disappeared with a loud *gloop* sound. "I've got one!"

Beau shifted like he wanted to help me reel it in, then took another step back. "You good?"

"I'm good." The fish fought hard, but I'd landed much bigger ones. I'd helped pull newborn calves into the world. I wielded a mop and a twenty-gallon bucket whenever there was a spill at work. The fish really never had a chance.

A rainbow trout flopped onto the grassy banks. "Oh God," I groaned. "I hate watching them flop."

"I know." Beau looked a little green.

"Where's your knife?"

He blinked at me, stunned, but when I put my hand out, he knelt down and pulled it from the tackle box. I quickly put the fish out of its gasping misery.

Beau gaped. "Jesus," he muttered. "Where did I find you?"

I laughed, feeling light and proud. So many of my skills didn't translate into the secular world. I barely understood my smartphone and I'd never sent an email until Everly helped me set up my account. But this was something I knew. Something I was good at. I quickly set to work gutting our lunch.

Beau went back to the house to fire up the little charcoal grill he'd bought from the outdoor store yesterday. I hummed to myself as I filleted the fish, tossing the guts back into the pond for the other fish to feast on. When Beau came back with a plate, I deposited two beautiful fillets onto it for him.

Beau looked down, then without warning, he yanked me to him. "I smell like fish guts!" I protested as he peppered my forehead and cheeks with adoring kisses.

"Don't care," he mumbled, turning me around and backing me toward the house.

The coals had gone out by the time we got to them, meaning Beau had to light the grill again. That was the only thing that went wrong on that otherwise perfect day.

That night, after we'd showered and before he fell asleep, Beau wound his hand into my braid and used it to pull me closer for a kiss. He fell asleep with a smile on his face and his fingers in my hair.

Chapter Twenty-Nine

BEAU

It was moving day.

My mother wiped her eyes surreptitiously on the hem of her blouse as she went through the cupboards one more time. "You sure you don't want the mug you gave me for Mother's Day?" she asked, holding up the battered white ceramic piece I'd festooned with Finn's and my handprints at age nine.

I went over to her and kissed the top of her head while simultaneously taking the mug from her and gently setting it on the counter. "Okay, first thing? I gave that to you, so it belongs to you. Second?" I laughed as I leaned down and pawed through the box she'd been filling. "We already have this stuff, Mom. You don't need to give us your..." I paused and pulled out a strange tine studded implement. "What the heck is this anyway?"

"A pastry cutter." She took it and put it back into the box.

I reached in and took it back out again. "Mom." I tried to keep any exasperation out of my voice. Her eyes were already shining with tears. If they started to fall in earnest, I would lose it. "I'm never going to use a pastry cutter."

"But Rachel might." She took it out of my hand and put it back in the box with a look like she was daring me to defy her one more time. "She's a very good baker, she'd probably appreciate having a nice piece of equipment like that." Her nostrils flared. "It is a very nice pastry cutter, Beauregard."

My full name. Shit. I threw up my hands in surrender. "Fine." A faint beeping that had been in the background suddenly got louder and I heard my brother's shout. "That's Finn with the moving truck anyway." I kissed her on the head again. "I gotta go help him load up."

Three strong brothers should have made short work of the boxes, but when you threw in a bossy sister and a father who considers his packing skills to be one of the most impressive things about him, it meant that loading the moving truck took a lot longer than it should have. Rather than stick around and mediate the spats between Jonah and my father about where the best place to stash my upright piano (I was leaving the grand at my parents' since it had been my grandfather's) I decided to head over to the house and do one last spot clean. Because with Finn as my roommate, it might be the last time the place was ever cleaned again.

When I got to the house, I stood in the driveway for a moment, taking a deep breath. This was going to work. I scanned the lawn, wondering why it looked so empty, until I remembered that all growing up I was used to seeing our lawn spread out with our various projects and all the discarded bikes and bats and balls we always dragged out whenever we were home from a tour. I wasn't used to things being so... sterile. Even the air smelled faintly of bleach.

Then I sniffed again and realized that smell was coming from the house. The doors and windows were all opened. I definitely had not left them that way when I'd locked up last night.

"What the hell?" I called out as I nudged the door the rest of the way open.

Faint music wafted out from the kitchen. The sound of an angel singing. "Rachel?"

"Oh!" She dropped the sponge she'd been scrubbing with and

jumped when she heard my voice. "You're here! I didn't hear the truck!"

"What are you doing here?" Yellow rubber gloves flopped open at her elbows. She looked like she was wearing some kind of pillowcase trimmed with lace at the collar. "What are you wearing?"

She looked down at her garb and pressed her lips together. "I was going to change before you got here," she said, looking abashed as she fingered the white fabric that billowed around her. "Chosen undergarments. I only wear them when I clean now."

I shook my head. "But why are you here? And aren't you working today?"

She grinned shyly. "I switched hours. I could either clean for other people. or I could come over and clean for you." She struck a proud pose. "One thing is for sure. I know how to clean. It's my job after all."

I looked at her, hunger thudding in my veins. With her hair pinned up in a halo around the crown of her head and that billowing white garment wafting around her, she had never looked more like an angel. "What?" she asked with a sly grin when she saw my expression.

In two steps she was in my arms and in ten more we were in the bed. "I don't know"—I groaned into her neck as she tore my shirt over my head—"how long we have. The truck could be here at any minute."

"So hurry," she whispered as she guided me inside of her.

I was so worked up it took an embarrassingly short time. Rachel's cries were just dying away when we both froze at the sound of truck tires on the long gravel driveway. Rachel started giggling into my shoulder. "That was excellent timing."

I kissed her fiercely. "I'll make it up to you later," I promised as I pulled back and tossed her the shirt she'd brought to change into. We hurriedly changed into our clothes and were out on the deck to greet my family before they had even turned off the engine.

My brothers tumbled from the truck, shouting about who could carry more boxes in one go. Claire followed behind them, crowing about how she'd been the one to find this house in the first place, and my father slung his arm around my mother's shoulder and whispered something into her ear that made her laugh and then dab at her eyes again.

"I like your family," Rachel whispered.

I put my arm around her in an echo of my dad, then waved down at them, feeling Gabe's absence acutely. My family was all here, at my house, and I had my girl in my arms to make it even better. I pulled her close, smelling the bleach in her hair before kissing her. Everyone I cared about under the same roof, all of my family spilling out into the lawn and calling out to each other.

The only thing that could make this better would be if there were some kids running around.

I stiffened a little and felt my grip on Rachel tighten. I could picture them. Right now. A boy and a girl, maybe twins. One that looked like Finn and one that looked like Rachel. In between my family's shouted questions and whoops of discovery, I could almost hear their giggles as they chased each other around the yard.

"You happy or something?" Rachel tipped her head to beam up at me. "You always hold me tighter when you're happy."

"Yeah." Emotion choked out the rest of what I wanted to tell her, but it didn't matter. With her background, coming from a huge family like she did, she'd understand, right? "I'm just thinking."

"Hey, Beau? You gonna maybe help?" Claire was standing in the doorway with her hand planted on her hip. She rolled her eyes and stomped away.

I sighed and grinned at Rachel, then moved to follow, but she stopped me with a tug on my hand. "Hey. what were you thinking about? Just then?"

I took a deep breath. "This is going to sound random, but, do you ever think about what it'd be like to have kids?"

All the color drained from Rachel's face. She glanced over at the spot where Claire had been and dropped my hand.

"Oh shit. Sorry." I shot her a sheepish grin. Rachel was a pretty private person. She definitely didn't want to have this discussion with my parents and my siblings within earshot. "Bad timing. Come on."

She was quiet as she went through the door first and I cursed my carelessness. Rachel was right, this was definitely not the right time to be discussing this. But I needed to hear from her exactly how she felt about it. I'd always wanted to be a dad. It was important to me.

Maybe some time this week, when the stress of moving had died down, I'd take her out to dinner and we could have a real talk about it. It was okay to take our time. After all, I planned on spending a lot more time with Rachel Walker.

Chapter Thirty

RACHEL

"I don't think I have ever been more tired," I complained as I flopped onto Beau's bed.

All around us, stacks of boxes loomed in corners. Wadded paper towels littered the floor and the clashing smells of different cleansers hung in the air. Beau hadn't figured out all of the light switches, so his north facing bedroom was succumbing to the gloom. I closed my eyes and listened to the unfamiliar creaks and clangs of the house settling. I hadn't noticed them my first night here. My attention had been... elsewhere. But tonight I knew there was no chance in hell of us succumbing to the same kinds of distraction. For one thing, I was exhausted. For another, I was sweaty and in need of a shower. The shower would have been a priority a week ago, but I was becoming very comfortable with Beau, and that meant I was more concerned with closing my eyes than with how I smelled.

The house was quiet. Finn was down by the pond with a beer, watching the sunset. Yesterday was the solstice and red still clung to the clouds even though it was close to ten pm. "It's still light out and you're ready for bed?" Beau teased as he flopped down next to me.

My head was buzzing with the day and being in the middle of Beau's wild family. I hadn't laughed like that in years, and Mrs. King had thanked me profusely for helping and made me feel like I was part of the family.

It had all been so nice that I was able to push the hurt of Beau's question way back down inside. It was innocent, after all. Just one of those random things. I was pretty sure he wasn't serious. Chosen men got married almost as young as Chosen women, but out here in the secular world, I rarely saw men his age actually want children. Especially not men his age who were talking to their old label about restarting their rock and roll career.

No, it had been a fluke, so I ignored the raw ache inside of me that his question had re-opened and lifted my chin at him. "Today wore me out," I told him.

He raised an eyebrow. "I'd like to wear you out too."

His eyes darkened for a moment, and then he was overcome with a cheek-splitting yawn that made me burst out laughing. "Ha! You're tired too."

"This is pathetic," he grumbled, rolling onto his back and yawning again. "I'm getting old."

I leaned up on my elbow. "Yes, you are." I poked him in the chest with my finger. He snatched it up and brought it to his lips. I gasped when he kissed and then bit at it. "Hey!" I protested. "How would you like it if I bit you like that?" I bent over and nipped him in the neck.

He groaned. "I'd like it very much," he confessed, turning to catch my lips with his. At the touch of his lips, I felt sparks in my bloodstream and my thudding heart sped faster as he rolled over, crushing me beneath his weight.

We moved slowly, and languidly, stripping each other out of our clothes and kissing the salt-kissed skin underneath. He used his fingers and lips to bring me to a lazy orgasm, and then unrolled the condom along his length.

And then swore. "Shit."

"What's wrong?" I blinked up at him, feeling like my head was stuffed with clouds. My body was still singing with what he'd done to me, but my grin faded when I saw his expression as he looked down.

"This is my last one too," he grumbled and pointed.

There was a tiny tear at the tip. I held my breath, not entirely sure what this meant, but Beau cleared it up for me immediately. "Shit, we need a back-up, angel. I know you're not on the pill or anything right?"

My blood turned to ice. "No."

Beau shook his head, glowering at the torn condom as he ripped it free. He hurled it to the trashcan and then took a deep, steadying breath. "Would you mind going on it? I'd totally pay for it, I know it's expensive." He turned with a pleading look on his face. "I hate asking you to take it all on yourself, but we don't want you getting pregnant before we're ready, you know?"

My heart thudded sickeningly in my chest. One beat. Two beats. The tears were stinging my eyes, but if I just concentrated on my heartbeat, I could keep them from falling.

"Rach?" Beau sat down next to me and put his arm around me, pulling me close. "Angel, I know. It sucks. I know that's not how you were brought up, I just don't know any other way."

He was being kind. If he had been callous or dismissive, I might have had a prayer of keeping myself together. But the gentle hum of his concern sent me over the edge. The first tear splashed down onto his bare leg. He looked at it and then back up at me, then let out a shocked gasp. "Baby, why are you crying?"

I clenched my fists and pressed my lips together, but I couldn't hold it back anymore. I looked at Beau and knew I needed to tell him the truth.

"I don't need to go on the pill."

He narrowed his eyes, still not understanding. "I'll definitely keep wearing condoms, of course. But I don't want another scare like that—"

"It won't be a problem," I said dully.

He stared at me.

"Beau. I had a complete hysterectomy three years ago. It saved my life." I swallowed past the lump in my throat. Looking at him was too hard, so I looked down. "But I'll never be able to have kids."

Chapter Thirty-One

BEAU

Rachel was in pain and all I wanted to do was reach out and hold her, but I couldn't move. I was frozen in place, horror turning my blood into ice water as I listened to her slowly, haltingly, tell her story.

"I used to faint with every period." She twisted the sheet in her hands as she stared fixedly at a point on the wall. "Every month it got worse. They told me - they told me it was the curse of womanhood and I needed to pray harder, to lift my burden up. But the bleeding only got heavier, and then I started to bleed even when it wasn't my period." She looked down at her hands, her cheeks red with anger and shame. "I used to stuff old undergarments under my skirts to catch the blood before going out into the fields to work, but they'd be soaked by midmorning."

An involuntary growl escaped my throat. She glanced at me and then pressed her lips together. "Since God wasn't answering my prayers, it was clear to the rest of the community that I was an unredeemable sinner. I started losing my friends. My parents lost their friends. We were isolated, but my mother," her voice caught. "My mother was brave. She defied the Elders and snuck me out of the community. I'd never been to a hospital before. From the way the Chosen kids all gossiped, I was sure it had to be either the gateway to hell or some kind of mystical fairyland. I almost wish I'd been conscious enough to see it."

She fell silent. I unfroze enough to be able to reach out and take her long braid into my hands. I twisted the curl at the end around my finger twice before trailing it up to rub her scalp. She hummed quietly and closed her eyes, ducking to let me knead the tension away around her temples and smooth the wrinkles in her brow. I focused solely on that, letting my sight go all tunnel vision because I was afraid that if I turned my head, I would see the two perfect children - the boy with my brother's face and the girl with hers - running far off and out of my reach.

"Come here," I grated out. I pulled her to me and wrapped her in my arms. The sob she'd been holding back broke loose and she started to cry against my chest. Great, heaving sobs, the sound of the pain she'd been through. My stomach twisted. She was in so much pain. I loved her so much and there was nothing I could do to help it and that was like a knife to the gut.

"I - I lived." She laughed ruefully and pulled back from me, wiping her eyes. "I mean, obviously. But the fibroids were throughout my uterus." She didn't even color at the frank word. "The only way to stop the hemorrhaging was to take the whole thing."

"How old were you?" My voice was little more than a croak.

"Twenty. I went back to the Chosen afterward. I mean, of course I did, it was all that I had ever known but..." Her voice caught again, and I pulled her to me until she could catch her breath enough to continue. "Word got out. And, and the men I'd grown up with, the ones I expected to be matched with and marry, they - they didn't want me. What good is a wife who can't bear children?" Anger crept into her voice. "Who would want such damaged goods?"

"No."

"They didn't say it to my face," she spat. "But they didn't need to. I knew when the Elders came to me and told me I had a new calling in life. 'Go out and make my way in the wide world and bring the message to the secular.'" She snorted. "Right. That's not how it works. No one has ever been given that kind of task. I wasn't being sent forth," her voice rose into hysteria. "I was being discarded!"

"Rachel!" I cupped her face between my hands as her eyes darted wildly. "Rachel, look at me." Her chest hitched, but her eyes found mine somehow. "I'm right here, okay? You got through it and you're doing so—" My voice broke. "So well." Emotion welled up in my chest, robbing me of the rest of my words, so I tried to pour everything I was feeling into a kiss.

She gasped, and then sighed, then sagged against me. I gently lowered her back down to the bed and touched her face, her tears were still flowing freely, but she was no longer sobbing. "I never cried about it," she whispered, sounding surprised. "This whole time, I never cried. I never... mourned what I lost. My family, they told me to be grateful that I had my life."

I licked my lips. The little boy and girl who'd been running around in my brain, the ones that laughed and ran for me and called me Daddy, they had disappeared over a horizon and for a second, I mourned too. Then I pushed them to the side. "I'm grateful you're *in* my life," I told her, lying down and fitting myself around her. I leaned up and whispered into her ear. "I need you to know that."

She made a small sound and then nodded. I wrapped my arms around her and held her until her tears subsided. I wound her braid into my hand and held it tightly, as much for me as for her. And when her breathing relaxed into the slow, careful sips of breath she took when she'd fallen asleep, I closed my eyes against my own tears, catching them before they could fall.

Chapter Thirty-Two

RACHEL

In the morning, Beau smiled at me like nothing had changed.

He must have thought I didn't know him.

But I knew him.

His sadness was hidden in the slope of his shoulders as he waited for the coffee maker to finish brewing. Rather than let me see it, he went behind the door of the pantry and heaved a sigh that I felt right down to my toes. He didn't notice me behind him in the bathroom until he lifted his bowed head and his eyes refocused from whatever faraway place he'd gone to in his head and I could see the deep worry lines that marred his smooth forehead. Maybe he thought his beard hid his frown. It didn't.

When he saw me there, he kissed me like I hadn't ruined everything last night.

But I knew.

"I wish you didn't have to work today," he told me as he grabbed his keys. I had only just tugged my shirt down over my head. Was he hurrying me out the door? "Hope it's not too rough of a day."

"I hope I don't have to yell at too many people today," I said, trying on a smile.

Beau blinked at me and then recognition flooded his eyes. "Yeah me too. Save your voice for tonight."

He probably thought I didn't notice that, either. That he had forgotten tonight was the open mic night we had signed up for. That hurt settled into my stomach to join the other hurts that were crouching there. "But I don't need to be at work yet?" I came out as a question. *Are you trying to get rid of me now?* I didn't ask. Because I wasn't certain I'd like the answer.

"I know." Beau was halfway out the door already. "But Gabe's calling the house in a few minutes."

"Your parents' house?"

"Right. It's tricky with the time zones, so I need to be there right on time and..." He trailed off when he saw my skeptical expression and tried for a big grin. "You'll be bored."

"I don't think I will." I was pushing hard. The same way I had when the Elders had come to me and told me my new mission. "But why?" I had demanded back then. I wanted to hear them say it. I wanted them to admit that I was damaged goods and that's why they were doing what they were doing. Because I had no future with the Chosen.

Did I have no future with Beau, either?

I lifted my chin and kept pressing. "I don't even think I have my keys on me," I said, patting my pants and then dramatically pawing through my purse. "We could stop by my house first."

"Yeah, okay." Beau still seemed distracted. My shoulders slumped as the fight went out of me, and I silently followed him to the car.

The ride back to my house was silent and awkward. My stomach felt heavy like I had eaten something that sat wrong with me. And when he kissed me goodbye, tears came unbidden to my eyes. It was a goodbye kiss, but I no longer felt the promise of 'see you soon.'

Was he giving up? My family had discarded me for being damaged. Was Beau ready to do the same?

I walked into my house, feeling like a zombie. I wandered through, picking up things that had always belonged to me and staring at them like I had no idea how they'd gotten there. I carried things from one room to another and back again, with no idea of what I was trying to accomplish. The windows had been shut the whole time I'd been at Beau's place, and the heat was sticky and oppressive. I yanked open the windows, proud of finding *something* that had actually needed to be done and then I cursed. "Fuck it."

Being here, alone, was driving me nuts. I needed to go for a walk. I grabbed my keys out of my purse and went to the door.

I locked the door behind me and was just stepping off the porch when I saw the figure, her skirts billowing around her ankles as she stomped toward me with her head down, eyes on her shoes. I squinted, unable to make what I was seeing make sense. My sister? Here?

"Rebecca?"

She looked up from her boots and sneered. Her face was bright red with exertion and heat.

"Did you... walk here?" The Chosen compound was—

"Seven miles," she finished for me. And then sat down at the edge of my porch and hiked up her skirts. Then looked at me and remembered I was "secular" now and yanked them back down again.

I stared at her. The dissonance of having my sister, here, in my space, left me so disoriented that I fell back onto years of training. "Can I get you something to drink?" I asked robotically.

Rebecca looked like she wanted to decline but thought better of it. "Yes," she said, equally robotically. Then, "Thank you."

I nodded and turned back to go into the house. I knew better than to invite her in. She wouldn't come. I ran some water from the tap and then just paused, staring out the window over the sink out to the creek. Emotions - anger, confusion, a desperate loneliness, a strange hopefulness - all competed for dominance, clawing over one another to be the first to rise to the surface. Leaving me feeling nothing at all. Numbness made my limbs heavy and even the glass of water seemed to weigh too much. I had to use both hands to carry it back out onto the porch.

My sister took it without saying anything and drank it down. Then she set the glass carefully at the edge of the porch and took a deep breath. She was staring so hard at one place in my driveway that I turned to look at it too. There was nothing there.

The silence stretched out for so long that my curiosity got the better of me. "I didn't know you knew where I was living." Why was I laughing?

"Everyone knows." She stared harder at that point in the driveway and I realized with a start that she was looking at it so she wouldn't have to look at me.

Anger finally rose to the surface, pushing down the other emotions and taking control. I jumped down off the porch and moved right into her line of sight.

"Everyone knows?" I repeated. "Seriously? Everyone knows, but I've been left to fend for myself for two years now? Completely alone?"

"You don't make it easy!" Rebecca shouted. She forgot herself and glared at me, then reddened and looked down.

I gaped at her. "I don't make it easy? What the *fuck* are you talking about?"

I cursed to rattle her, and it worked. She jerked like I'd held a match to her foot and leaped from the porch to stand before me. "The way you carry on," she hissed. "With your *secular* friends and that... that... *man* you're carrying on with. In *public."*

"What do you care?" I threw up my hands, and Rebecca flinched, which only made me angrier that she thought I'd ever hurt her. "You cut me off!"

"You were to go out into the world and bring souls back to us! That was the mission the Elders charged you with!"

"Oh please. They were trying to get rid of me. There was no mission! That's bullshit and you know it!"

Rebecca reddened. She leaned in close enough that I could see the faint lines around her eyes. They hadn't been there two years ago. When I last saw her this close. "There was a mission and you failed," she hissed, enunciating each word like a stab to my heart. "And I don't care what you do with your life, I can only pray for your soul." The corner of her lip curled in disgust. Then twitched as her eyes filled with tears. "But what you're doing is ruining the lives of your family. Don't you care about that at all?"

I folded my arms, closing myself off to her words, but not quickly enough. "How the fuck do you figure?" I snarled through the wrenching pain in my chest.

"You're Fallen."

I inhaled sharply and took a step back. "I am not," I whispered in a high, reedy voice I didn't recognize as my own. "I was sent away, I never left on my—"

"The Elders have declared you Fallen and you know what that means."

"No."

Rebecca shook her head. "We're shunned. Mom risked *everything* to get you medical treatment." Her voice broke. "You owe her. You owe all of us. Because now that you're Fallen, none of the kids will play with Lydia and she cries every night. None of the women will bake with Mother or help with the washing. None of the men will consider me." She blinked hard and looked away and I had to resist the urge to reach out to her, to comfort my sister whose main goal in life was to be a wife and a mother. "Father was shamed at last service," she continued once she'd collected herself. "It was the smallest thing, something that would have been overlooked before you started carrying on this way. But because of you, he was called up."

"No." My hand was over my mouth. I shut my eyes as tight as I could, but I could still see it, my proud father, the grandnephew of the prophet, called before the congregation and flogged... I shook my head. It was too horrible to even consider.

But Rebecca nodded. "Yes. At Meeting yesterday. And I knew..." She took a deep breath and stepped forward.

I looked down in shock when I saw her hands slip over mine. My sister squeezed my hand, just like she'd always done. Whenever we'd shared a secret or made a pact. I blinked, but the tears fell anyway. It had been so long. She glanced up at my face and I found myself looking into eyes the same shade of brown as mine. "You belong with us, Rachel."

I looked down and away. Rebecca let go of my hand and stepped back. "You know that Joel's birthday is coming up."

I blinked up at her. There had always been talk of my older brother stepping in as spiritual leader. Once he was of age. "I didn't forget. He's going to be twenty-five finally."

Rebecca shook her head and glared at me like she was trying to reduce me to ashes. "How can the Chosen be led by a spiritual leader whose own sister has Fallen?"

I gasped. "They can't. No. Joel's been groomed for that since he was a child."

"He has a challenger now." She blinked slowly. "Because of you."

I tried to take a breath, but panic was stealing it away. Rebecca lunged forward, grabbing me by the shoulders. "You belong with us," she repeated. And then turned and started back up the driveway without a word.

As she trudged away, I wanted to call out to her. To yell that I wasn't a Chosen woman anymore. I was Beau's woman.

But the words tripped on my tongue. I wanted a future with Beau. He was a good man, he'd stay for a while even in spite of my infertility. But eventually, there would be someone else. Someone who could have his babies and give him everything he ever wanted.

"Rebecca!" I shouted.

My sister stopped and turned, those heavy skirts flowing around her ankles like currents in the water. Did I want to go with her? It would be so easy. There was no future for me out here. I'd been discarded by the Chosen. But that had already happened, and I had survived.

If Beau discarded me, I wasn't sure I'd make it.

I needed to think. "Here," I called to my sister. "At least let me give you bus fare."

Chapter Thirty-Three

BEAU

"You there?" Jonah yelled, way too loudly. Finn grumbled and clapped his hands over his ears.

The connection fizzed and crackled and then suddenly Gabe's voice blared through the speaker. "—talking about this, I say fuck yeah!" he yelled as loud as if he were right there in the room with us.

Which he would be in twenty-four hours.

Shooting had wrapped early for his show. He and Everly would be flying home soon and meet us in New York City.

Us. All of us.

I looked around at the kitchen table. Jonah, Finn, Claire, and I had all sat down in our normal spots. Even though it would have made more sense for us to crowd around the laptop at the head of the table, we'd all instinctually gravitated to the spots where we'd sat as kids.

We were almost all back together again. This morning with Rachel had been weird, but I knew I'd have time to deal with that tonight at the open mic. Right now, I was too caught up in the excitement of my siblings as we all shouted into the computer.

"Do you even remember how to play?" Finn teased Gabe. "You've been off doing this daredevil bullshit for so long."

"I'm fucking fine," my hotheaded older brother growled. "Do you remember how to play bass? Wait, do hermits even play bass?"

Claire laughed, but Finn remained serene. "You're just jealous."

Jonah looked at Gabe and somehow even with the lag time, they still managed to shake their heads no in perfect unison.

"Can we focus, please!" Claire clapped her hands together like a schoolteacher and Jonah snapped to attention. Probably because his fiancée was a schoolteacher. "Can we all take a look at the itineraries?" She tapped the printouts she'd put out on the table and we'd all ignored. "I have a few questions about Day 2."

I looked over at Finn who rolled his eyes. "I'm going to need to move even deeper into the woods after all of this," he complained. I grinned at him. He still sounded gloomy as hell, but I could tell he was excited. He talked when he was excited, and he was asking questions and giving out shit left and right.

I leaned back in my chair. That was good. The whole reason I'd started planning this reunion was for Finn and it was working. Sure, I'd have to go to New York for a few days, but maybe Rachel might want to come with me?

I tapped my fingers on the table as Jonah and Claire jockeyed for who would be the point of contact with the studio down in New Jersey and let my mind wander back to this morning. If I wanted her to come with me, I was definitely going to have to apologize for my reaction. I steepled my fingers and pressed them to my lips as plans whirled around the table. I'd just been surprised. Shocked, even. I hadn't meant to be distant, but now that I sat here and thought about it, I realized I'd fucked up. She probably thought her inability to have kids would be a problem.

It wasn't. I loved her. We'd figure something out.

Maybe we'd figure it out when I took her to New York with me.

"So that's it, then?" Claire looked startled. "Is this seriously happening?"

"It looks like a good plan to me," came Gabe's garbled voice.

Jonah cleared his throat and coughed. "It's going to be good to be on stage with you guys again," he said, looking down at his hands.

"Uh oh, he's getting sappy!" Claire crowed. She leaned in and rested her head on his shoulder. "Awww, I'm telling Ruby you're gonna cry!"

"Shut up," Jonah grumbled even as Finn leaped from his chair and tackled him from the other side. "Group hug!"

"Ha!" I leaped up and belly-flopped on top of Finn, sending Jonah's chair toppling over to the side. "Oh my God, get off!" Claire's muffled voice begged from the bottom of the pile.

"Hey!" Gabe yelled. "What the fuck just happened? Where did you all go?"

Finn turned and grinned at me and I nodded. Then I reached onto the table. "Group hug!" I shouted and hugged the laptop.

"What the fuck?" Gabe's voice was muffled and tinny against my chest.

"Gabe! Help!" my sister choked.

Gabe laughed. I put the laptop back up on the table, then stepped over the pile of bodies. "One, two, three!" I grabbed Claire's wrists and hauled her out from under the pile.

"I think you assholes punctured a lung," she groaned, rubbing her side. Finn immediately started giving her shit about being a delicate flower, so she sucker punched him in the stomach. Jonah laughed and then held up his hands to ward them both off when they turned on him, reminding them that he was the singer, and to watch the throat. Gabe was shouting encouragement from the laptop, telling Claire to go for Jonah's 'stupid hair.'

I sagged against the wall I was laughing so hard. This was so normal to me. My big, crazy family.

How could I not want one of my own?

I loved her. I needed to tell her that and then we'd go from there.

Right before I stood up and went to save Jonah from being poked to death, I resolved to fix this with Rachel. Tonight.

Chapter Thirty-Four

BEAU

There were only a few scattered people at the Crown that night. A far cry from the tens of thousands who used to cram into the stadiums to hear the King Brothers play.

But this was fine. They weren't here to listen to me play. They were here to listen to Rachel sing. *I* was here to listen to Rachel sing. To remind her that even though I had fucked up royally this morning, I was still here for her. And after tonight was over, I would confess that I loved her and ask her what kind of future we could have together.

I was strangely nervous. Maybe it was Rachel's nerves rubbing off on me. The soft breeze that wafted in through the open door sent the papers tacked up on the community bulletin board to ruffling, which made her jump. It made *me* jump. I tried to laugh it off and reached out to rub her shoulder. "How are you?" I asked her for what felt like the millionth time.

And for the millionth time, she just gave me that wan nod and the faint smile that barely even reached her eyes. She'd been quiet on the ride over and had gone even quieter once we'd reached the Crown.

Nerves were a bitch. I tried to reassure her. "You have an amazing voice and we've practiced this song at least one hundred times. In fact," I teased her. "I'm almost sure I heard you singing it in your sleep the other night. So I know you know it. You don't have to worry about that."

Her smile brightened for a millisecond but then faded again.

"Okay, I get it." I patted her shoulder. "I'll shut up and leave you alone."

I kept my promise and busied myself with helping Taylor with the speakers and microphones. My sister, there to see her prized student in her debut, bossed us both mightily, but when Taylor got grumpy, she finally rolled her eyes and found a seat in the front row. I was taping down one of the cables when I noticed the crowd starting to fill out, taking their seats in the semi-circle of folding chairs that surrounded the battered little raised platform that served as the stage.

I quickly miked up my piano and nodded to Taylor. The last thing Rachel needed was a restless, antsy crowd the night of her big debut. We needed to make sure we started promptly.

Taylor nodded back and went to the main mic. I quickly ducked behind him and made a beeline for Rachel, who had been sitting in the deep windowsill underneath the neon signs advertising Genesee beer. "Showtime!" I whispered, feeling that giddy spark in my veins again. I thought I had lost it after all those years of trudging from city to city and playing the same stale songs. But tonight, I was excited again.

For her.

I reached out and squeezed her hands with mine. "You're going to be awesome." I leaned in for a kiss.

She shied back immediately and glared at me, her eyebrows knitted together. I pulled away and looked at her, feeling like she'd just slapped me in the face.

She pressed her lips together and then gave me a smile that was more worrisome than the look of death she'd just given me. "Can you... can you give me some space, please?"

Stung, I stepped back. Stage fright did weird things to people. It didn't mean it hurt any less, but I at least understood. I went over to the piano and sat down.

"Thanks for coming out tonight!" Taylor said into the mic. You could only tell he was smiling because his eyes were crinkled because his mouth was completely covered by his enormous, man-of-the-woods beard. Which reminded me about how careful I'd been about trimming mine since things started getting serious with Rachel. Beards are great, but unobstructed kisses are even better. "We've got a new face with us this evening, which is awesome! Give it up for Rachel Walker!" He stepped back to join in the smattering of applause. I looked at Rachel and gestured for her to stand up and wave, but she was staring past the crowd with a ferocious look on her face. Her game face, maybe? "And"—Taylor went on when it became clear that Rachel was intent on ignoring everyone—"a very familiar face too. Give it up for Beau King of the King Brothers on piano!"

I waved and pointed at each audience member in turn to make up for Rachel's distance. It was okay that she didn't know how to handle an audience, she wasn't used to it the way I was. She just had to sing, I could handle the rest of it. Claire was standing up, shrieking and hollering like we were the Beatles on Ed McMahon. "Thanks," I mouthed to my sister, then turned to see if Rachel was ready. I waved at her again and nodded.

She jerked like a puppet on a string, then lurched to the microphone like she was fighting a strong wind. Confused, I turned to the keys.

We'd rehearsed far more than I needed. I played the first few notes of the Ed Sheeran song she'd chosen, the one she had sung to me that first time I heard her sing. It had a long intro, and as I built to the crescendo, I turned and nodded to her.

She didn't move. There was a pause in the music. Her cue.

"Go!" I mouthed.

Rachel opened her mouth automatically.

Nothing came out.

Stage fright. It had to be stage fright. Claire leaned forward, her fingers pressed to her lips in concern. Out of the corner of my eye, I could see Taylor shaking his head darkly.

Okay. No big deal.

I played around her cue, improvising some variations on the melody. "Four, three, two, one," I murmured, then looked up to nod at her next cue.

Rachel wasn't even looking at me. She stood there, wide-eyed and panicked, staring out at the crowd.

There was a cough and then a titter of nervous laughter. Rachel's head whipped around. "What are you staring at?" she demanded of the guy in the front row.

I leaped up. In every show I'd ever played, we had one mantra. 'The show must go on.' No matter what happened, we were professionals and we kept our promises.

My training kicked in like muscle memory. "Hey, sorry." Stepping in front of Rachel, I gave the guy a sheepish smile. "Nerves, right? Anyone else get stage fright?" I nodded hard, inviting them to nod with me. *The show must go on.* "Can you all give it up for my girl here? Round of applause for Rachel, right?" I clapped until they clapped along with me, then turned to grip Rachel's shoulders. "It's okay," I reassured her. "We can try again, okay?"

She blinked and then nodded.

I hurried over to the piano and started again. This time Rachel looked down at the floor, and then up at Claire. Claire was nodding along with the beat and Rachel started to tap her toes. I felt the tension in my chest start to release. Okay. Here we go. I reached her cue.

Rachel opened her mouth and the first note came out in a terrible, off-key squeak. Claire winced visibly, and Rachel noticed. Her face reddened again.

I smiled at her even though inside I was a mass of worry. What the fuck was going on? Where was her beautiful voice? "From the top?" I asked her, not knowing what else to do. *The show must go on.*

"Fine." She huffed into the microphone, setting off a blast of feedback that made the crowd groan. I was so rattled that I plunked my fingers down on the wrong keys. "Fuck," I breathed and then took a deep breath.

I've choked before. Where one failure becomes two and then a cascade, and then an entire avalanche bearing down on you as you scramble in vain to regain your composure. Choking in front of a crowd was to be expected and I was okay with it as a general job hazard when I was with my brothers or on my own. But not with

Rachel. I pulled myself together and played the intro for what seemed like the millionth time. Rachel turned and looked at me and I nodded at her again, a smile stretching across my face. There it was. I could feel it with a performer's sixth sense. This take would stick. We'd found our groove. Rachel hit her cue perfectly stepping up to the mic to belt out the first words of the first verse...

And then stopped. And trailed off.

"Oh no," I heard Claire moan.

Rachel's mouth was wide open. "I forgot the words," she whispered and looked around wildly like someone might hold up a cue card with the rest of the verse printed on it. "Psst!" I hissed at her, ready to prompt her, knowing she could keep going if she just got past this.

But Rachel's head whipped around and she stared at me like I was a stranger. For a moment she looked just like a wild animal that had been cornered.

And then she turned and ran right out the front door.

I leaped to my feet. "I got her," I told Claire, who had jumped up to help. "I'm sorry everyone!" I shouted and ran after her.

Chapter Thirty-Five

BEAU

The last thing I saw before I burst out into the night was my sister raising her phone to her ear, and I felt a strange twinge of resentment that she could take a call when everything was going so wrong. But I shoved that thought to the side and concentrated on finding Rachel.

"Where are you?" I bellowed, turning a circle in the middle of the parking lot. It was all shadows out here, the streetlights had yet to wink on. I heard footsteps and rushed off in the direction. "Rachel? Where the fuck are you? Are you... are you hiding from me?"

My answer was silence. I stopped and turned another frantic circle, savagely raking the hair back from my eyes.

And then I heard a voice calling my name. A female voice.

But it wasn't Rachel.

"Beau!" Claire was rushing across the parking lot right as the lights winked on, leaving her eyes in deep shadows that gave me chills for some reason.

The reason was clear the second she reached me, out of breath and panicked. "Finn!" she gasped. "Something's wrong with Finn!"

"What?" My head was still spinning with the need to find Rachel.

Claire reached out and tugged me toward the car. "We have to get home, come on!"

And just for a second, I thought it might be possible to do both. I believed I could split myself in half and somehow be there for both the woman I loved and the brother who needed me. It seemed like something I could absolutely manage. For a moment, I had split into two people, able to do two things simultaneously. I put one foot down to follow after Claire as she tugged me to the car, then spun forty-five degrees to put down another foot toward Rachel.

"Beau!" Claire shrieked.

The two me's converged and I snapped back to being just myself. A man who had to make a decision. Rachel was hurting, but Finn might actually be physically hurt. I picked up my foot and deliberately turned myself toward the car. I could make up with Rachel in the morning, but Finn needed me right now.

Claire left her Jeep and jumped into the passenger seat of my car and I gunned it, peeling out of the parking lot and speeding across the dark roads to my parents' house. "You sure he's here?"

"That's what Mom said." Claire stared at her phone like it might have answers. "What the hell happened? He was doing so good?"

I shook my head, unwilling to even say it, and nudged the accelerator even higher. My tires squealed as we turned down our road and rocketed up to the front of the house. I threw it into park and Claire was out and running before I'd even turned off the engine.

I caught up with her and then overtook her, throwing the front door open. "Mom!"

"Up here!" came my mom's strangled reply. I took the stairs two at a time and then stopped before I tripped over her as she crouched there in the hall.

"Oh God, what happened?" Claire choked from behind me.

Finn was stretched out across my mom's lap. His boots stretched into the bathroom, but she had his head in her hands as she shook him again and again, "Wake up, baby boy. Wake up."

"Did he take pills?" Claire sobbed.

"I don't know! Wake up, Finnegan!" My mother slapped him lightly on the cheek.

I sagged down to my knees. "Goddamnit, Finn!" I shook my brother. His head lolled to the side and I checked his pulse, then lifted his wrists. "No sign of cutting. Finn!" I smacked him so hard my mom gasped. "Goddamnit, wake the fuck up!"

This was my fault. I had no idea what happened. I had no idea if he took pills or not because I wasn't fucking here. "Finn!" I roared, yanking him out of my mother's arms and shaking my brother. "I get it, okay? I fucking get it, I should have been here to take care of you, but don't you fucking do this!" I jammed the heel of my hand into my eye to wipe back the tears. Anger ran red hot in my veins. "Finn, wake up! Did you fucking take something?"

Helpless with rage, I did the only thing I could think to do.

I wiped my hand on my pant leg and then jammed my fingers right down his throat.

My mother yelped. "What are you doing to him?" and tugged at my hand, but I barely even noticed her. "Get it out," I growled. "Come on you fucking bastard, get it out."

"Beau, stop it!" Claire moaned as Finn retched and gagged. I ignored her and jammed my fingers farther. "Come on!" I shouted.

Finn choked, and then vomited in one huge stream, splashing me with vomit from my shirt right down to my shoes. Frantically, I searched the foul-smelling remnants.

There were no pills.

I choked back the vomit that rose to my own throat, but I couldn't hold back the rage that closed around my throat. "Goddamnit!" I shouted, smacking Finn in the shoulder. He grunted and his eyelids fluttered. He was coming around and that only made me angrier. The delicate thread that had always held me back suddenly snapped. "You fucking asshole!" I raged, shaking him until his teeth clicked. "What the fuck, Finn? What the fuck!"

"Beau!" my mother pleaded, trying to hold back my blows, but I couldn't stop. I shook and hit my brother again and again. "Beau!" Claire shouted, and she and my mother hauled me off of him.

The minute they pulled me back, I snapped out of the unhinged rage. "Oh shit," I groaned, burying my face in my hands. The smell on my fingers was enough to make me retch again. "Oh shit, oh shit."

My mother pulled me to her, and I buried my head against her shoulder while she shushed me. Claire clung to us both and wept.

"Mmm-- what the hell?" Finn's groggy, slurring voice broke the spell. All three of us froze and looked at him.

He pushed himself up on his elbows and took stock of the vomit that had soaked through his shirt. Then he looked over to the three of us and took in Claire's tears, my mother's frantic rocking, and my clenched fists. He blinked once and then understanding swept over him. "What the -- oh. Oh God. You thought -- seriously?" He yanked his shirt off over his head and tossed it away in disgust, then raked his hands through his hair before staring at us in disbelief. Staring at me. "I said," he breathed. "I would never do it again and *I meant it.* Yeah, I guess I might have had too much to drink and passed out, I get that." He glared right at me. "But I was fucking *celebrating* because I'm *happy* the band is going to play together again!"

At my sharp inhale, he burst out into a rueful laugh. "Yeah, bro! That's it!" He knelt up, his knees wobbly and sniffed in disgust at the mess on the carpet. "Well, I guess you saved me a hell of a headache tomorrow so cheers for that." He turned and looked back at me and for a moment we were kids again, each other's best friends, a brain shared between two bodies. So even as he was saying something, I swore I heard another meaning to his words. "You have to stop hovering over me, man." His voice cracked, and he looked away. "I can stand on my own two feet."

"Can you?"

"Yes!"

I paused and let that hang there. Because the next question was the more important one. "Do you *want* to?"

He pushed himself up to his feet and for a second, he looked more scared and lost than I had ever seen him. But then he rearranged his face into its usual skeptical lines. "Uh, yeah? You've got a chick now. I'm not planning on being some sad third wheel in your life." He blinked and then looked at Mom and Claire as if he suddenly realized they were watching. He sighed heavily. "I'll go get the mop."

"I'll get it." My mom sprang to her feet. She hurried down the stairs. Claire hovered another moment before following after her and leaving me with my brother. "You mean that?" I asked. Poking at the wound. I had to. "You think me being with Rachel makes you a third wheel?"

Finn shrugged and wouldn't meet my eyes. "You got her, you don't need me," he mumbled.

"Oh fuck you!" I spat. Shame and anger warred inside of me. Never in my life had I lost it like this. And never when it came to my brother. Guilt made me shout. "You know I fucking chose you over her tonight?" Panic suddenly coursed through me. "Christ, she ran off in the middle of our set and instead of following her and figuring out what was wrong, I came here to deal with your bullshit! Ah, fuck!" I shouted as I realized just what I'd done. "Fuck!"

"I never asked you to," Finn mumbled. "You didn't have to."

But I barely heard him as I pounded down the stairs and back out the door. I needed to get away from him and this feeling of losing control. I ran out to my car and screeched out of the driveway. Heading to Rachel. Praying I still had time to fix everything.

Chapter Thirty-Six

BEAU

The clock on the dash read a quarter past midnight. I had no idea how it was still that early. This night had already stretched on for weeks. I tugged at my beard, wondering if it had gone as white as Father Time's.

I was pulling into Rachel's driveway when I remembered I was still covered in Finn's vomit. "Fuck it," I growled, smacking the heel of my hand into the steering wheel. I'd take a shower at her place. I'd kiss her, find out what was wrong, beg her forgiveness for not putting her first, and then hop in the shower before taking her to bed.

I was so wrapped up in these plans that it took me a second to figure out what was wrong with Rachel's house.

It was dark.

Okay. It's past midnight. Maybe she's gone to sleep, I thought to myself, ignoring the way the hair on my arms had started to stand up.

I vaulted up the rickety stairs to the sunken porch and banged on the door. "Rachel! I'm so sorry. Can I come in?" I paused and listened for any sounds of movement. "I know it's late, but I'm here now." I waited. "Rachel?"

The only sound was the soft burble of the creek. Even the wind had gone silent, all the night creatures fast asleep. An eerie feeling swept over me again.

I moved over to the side of the porch and jumped down. "Rachel?" The kitchen was dark, of course. I walked around the side of the cabin, my feet crunching in the gravel the landlord had thrown down in lieu of doing any kind of landscaping. If that was the kitchen window, then over here was Everly's bedroom, shut up and dark, that was no surprise. The bathroom window was also dark, not even the nightlight Rachel left on in the outlet to cast its weak light out into the darkness.

For some reason, this made me even more frantic than before. I sprinted to her window and sighed with relief when I saw it was left open. "Rachel?" I whispered. "I'm sorry, I know this is creepy. I just need to know you're okay. Go back to sleep."

The wind slipped by in a sigh that sounded just like the ones she made while sleeping and for a moment I thought it was her and that I'd done it. I'd taken care of Finn and now I was here making things right with her. I'd done it.

Then the wind kicked up at the same pitch. When I realized that was what I'd heard, I went up on my tiptoes and looked in through her window.

By the light of the moon, I could see her bed.

It was empty.

I could feel each heartbeat thud loudly in my ears. *Thump.... Thump.... Thump...* as the realization hit me in waves. She wasn't in bed. She wasn't in bed.

Where the fuck was she?

I yanked my phone out of my pocket so fast I almost dropped it. With fumbling fingers, I found her number and pressed 'call,' trying to get my panicked breathing under control. As it rang in my ear, I heard a faint sound from her bedroom.

Horrified, I let my hand fall to my side. The ringing continued. Her phone was lit up on her nightstand, the blue light illuminating the bed, the room, the house... and me.

Everything she'd run away from.

Everything she'd left behind.

I was too late.

Chapter Thirty-Seven

RACHEL

Morning broke, as it always did, with the smell of cows drifting through my open window. That meant they were being driven out to pasture in the watery early morning light and I gave a silent prayer of thanks that I'd been exempted from that chore and was allowed to stay in bed.

Then I sat up in abject panic. "What the fuck!?" Morning shouldn't break with the smell of cows, it broke with the smell of coffee seconds before Beau brought it to me while I was still in bed.

This was not my bedroom with the window that faced the creek. This was...

This was *my bedroom.*

My limbs moved with a heavy slowness like I was underwater. Deep underwater, with the pressure bearing down on my chest. I struggled to take a full breath, but the sodden humidity was already oppressive, even this early in the day. Squeezing my eyes shut, I forced myself to take deep, regular breaths. And *think.*

It came back to me slowly and then all at once. Rushing from the Crown Tavern and into the night. I ran for my life like I was being pursued by predators, in a blind sprint.

I was a full mile out of town before I realized where my feet were headed.

My mother looked terrified when she opened the door. But then she saw me and her face melted with love. "Come in," she urged.

I'd stepped over that threshold and looked around. "I'm home."

"I'm glad." She embraced me once again and then held me out at arm's length. Her lip twitched. She didn't mean for me to see it, but I did. "I have some clothes you can wear in the front bedroom."

I looked down, instantly aware of the way my filmy blouse clung to my shape. I was wearing jeans. A *woman*. In *pants*. "Hurry," she urged, patting me once more. "Before Father wakes up."

I found the sleeping garments just where my mother said they'd be. When I was a child, they had felt like the softest silk, but now I was only aware of the way they billowed around me. I pushed the door open to the back bedroom, where the girls slept. There were a few snorts. Miriam mumbled something and rolled over and Lydia opened her eyes. "Hi," I said, until I realized she was sleeping with her eyes open. She hadn't outgrown it yet. For some reason this made me feel... relieved.

The bed at the far corner was stacked with old blankets in need of mending but was otherwise unoccupied. It was, after all, *my* bed.

I'd thought there would be no way I would be able to fall asleep, but a six mile run through the darkness meant my body sank into that bed like it was a cloud of softness.

Now though, I could feel every rough spun nub.

As I sat there in my old bed, trying to make my surroundings make sense, I heard the rustling of my siblings as they began to wake. First to rise completely was Rebecca. I braced myself as she rubbed her eyes and blinked sleepily. Then she looked up.

"Rachel."

Immediately, everyone was awake and staring. I swallowed. "Hi."

Rebecca pressed her lips together. Then she nodded once and then yelled at Miriam to pick up the mess she'd left in the middle of the floor.

And the spell was broken.

My sisters tumbled out of bed, going through their morning

routine like everything was normal. I went downstairs to help Mother with the breakfast, working side by side with her in the kitchen just like always.

"Amos is walking now?" I marveled, as the fat baby I remembered toddled into the kitchen on his fat little legs then stopped short when he saw me.

"Amos!" I cried, kneeling down to embrace him.

He screwed up his little face until it turned red and then burst out in angry tears. Lydia swooped in from the front room and scooped him up, glaring at me before she hustled him into the other room, shushing like the little mother she'd always been. I stood back up again. "He doesn't remember me."

My mother smiled up from the mound of eggs she was cracking into a bowl. "He will."

"And Lydia definitely hates me."

Mother winced at the ugly word and mouthed a silent prayer. I felt heat rise up on my neck. I was out of practice. "She does not. She is wary."

I nodded. Being wary of those in the secular world was something deeply ingrained. But I wasn't part of the secular world. I belonged here, right?

A bearded man appeared in the doorway and my heart skipped a beat to think that Beau had followed me here. Until I blinked and realized he looked nothing like the man I loved.

Had loved.

I never told him. And then I just... left. What must he be thinking right now?

"Rachel!" My father's booming voice brought me back to the present. He gruffly pulled me into a hug, and when he pulled back again, I caught him wiping at his eyes. "Will you come to Meeting today?"

My tongue knotted in my mouth. Meeting - with all of the eyes of the community on me, watching for signs of corruption - seemed far beyond anything I could handle now.

But then I looked at my mother's hopeful face and watched my little sister hoist my baby brother higher on her hip. I looked at my father and remembered how he'd been shamed at Meeting because of me. Guilt overwhelmed me, and I ducked my head. "Of course. I'm looking forward to it."

He nodded his pleasure and then shouted for my brothers to follow him out to the fields. I fell into step with Rebecca as we took our buckets down to the water pump. Everyone in the community had to fill their buckets for their animals here, which meant that everyone who was there saw that I had returned. The news spread like wildfire and by noontime, the whole place was straining to catch a glimpse of me. I saw recognition on faces I'd forgotten about, and smiles of welcome along with wary, terse expressions of disapproval. I ducked my head down and went about all the chores I could do in my sleep. Like I'd never even left.

Like the last two years of my life had never happened at all.

I belonged here, I reminded myself. And even if it didn't feel like that yet, I needed to force myself to push on.

For my family's sake.

Chapter Thirty-Eight

RACHEL

Most outsiders would not recognize a Chosen Meeting House as a church. Rather than under lofty spires reaching heavenward, we met under tin roofs, in a corrugated metal box that was freezing in the wintertime and boiling in the summer. Our surroundings were meant to keep us humble and serve as a reminder of how impermanent life was here on Earth.

Already, the metal shed had started rusting in the corners. I took my place in the uncomfortable metal chairs donated by a secular man before he renounced everything to join us. I had never wondered about him until this moment, always assuming that he'd done it to redeem his sin-stained soul. But now I found myself wondering his name. What kind of life did he have before he'd joined the Chosen. And what had he left behind?

The smell of rust hung in the humid air, as did the smells of the bodies around me as the rest of the community filed in. I tried to take shallow breaths. Were we always packed in this closely - like sardines in a can - or had I just never noticed until now? I looked over to the other row of chairs, trying to remember how many rows in total we used to pack in here. Was it always eleven? I could have sworn it was nine last I counted.

I felt a jolt when I saw a man with dark brown hair and a beard slip into the last row, then hated myself for even looking for Beau here in this sacred place. I wrenched my eyes away from the bearded man and tried to focus on anything else.

Sarah Hayes had a new baby, the one I remembered was now playing hide-and-seek with her skirts. I tried to take an interest in that, but it only made me feel wistful. People had been born since I had gone. And people had died too. Life had gone on without me. It didn't seem fair.

"Have you finished your prayers?" my mother whispered, prodding me in the shoulder.

Hastily, I turned and bowed my head, knitting my fingers together in my lap. My mother sniffed and then closed her eyes again. The irritation smoothed out of her face and was replaced by complete serenity as her lips began to move soundlessly.

I screwed my eyes shut and tried to reach my own bliss. But I couldn't hear the sound of my prayers over the noise of the people around me. The stifled coughs seemed as loud as gunshots, and every rumbling tummy felt like an earthquake. I shifted and tried harder, determined to believe again. But instead of peace, I was filled with frustration.

At last, one of the Elders, a young man I didn't recognize, maybe sent in from one of the other communities, called for bread breaking. We passed the fragrant loaves to one another and smiled our greetings, but my stomach roiled and I could barely swallow it down. I grimaced up at Rebecca, who was watching me closely. Like she was checking to see if I spontaneously caught fire the second the bread touched my lips.

She seemed disappointed that I didn't.

There was a rustle and the sound of shifting bodies and I remembered at the last moment that now was the time to stand. I smoothed the heavy skirts that were now clinging to my legs and wiped my forehead before tucking my white cap snugly back down onto my head. For one moment, I crouched to reach for the water bottle I had always carried out in the secular world. But there was no water to be had during Meeting. The deprivation of being thirsty was supposed to remind us of our mortality.

I swallowed. I could really use a drink. In all senses of the word.

Then Widow Reed's high, warbling voice rang out making my hair stand on end when everyone joined in. My throat went dry.

"Amazing Grace, how sweet the sound..."

It was the hymn I'd sung for Beau. The one he swore made me sound like an angel. I squeezed my eyes shut against the tears that were suddenly gathering. My mother, thinking I was overcome with the emotion of being "lost then found," reached down to squeeze my hand, and I wanted to yank it away and run from her, but I stilled myself and whisper-sang along. My voice definitely wasn't that of an angel. I sounded like the hiss of air from a leaking balloon.

One hymn slid into another as the spirit moved various Chosen to sing praises. It was a game of "who is most pious," and it could go on for hours. When the last song died out with no one suggesting a new one, I breathed a sigh of relief.

But only for a moment.

Because I knew what came next.

"Brothers and Sisters!" the new Elder boomed. "When one of us sins, it brings shame to all of us. We are all responsible to keep pure, both within our hearts and within this sacred community..."

My heart thudded so loudly in my ears that it drowned out the rest of his words, but I didn't need to hear him. I gripped the bottom of my chair, forcing myself to stay in my seat and not run screaming from the room.

It was time for the Shaming.

The Chosen believed if you sin you must ask forgiveness from both God and the community by standing in the front of the Meeting and confessing. Confessing was bad enough, especially when your sin was something private or worse, something you hadn't even known was a sin in the first place, like when Gloriana Hastings was shamed for wearing revealing clothes only because she had grown so fast that her skirts had risen above the ankle without her realizing.

Or when you didn't know your sin was a sin because you had only been in the community a few days and still did not understand the rules.

With a violent jerk, my mind wrenched back to that meeting all those years ago when my sister Miriam had first been adopted into our family at the age of eight. Sweet and shy, she'd endured things I couldn't even imagine within the foster system. We were eager to show her a peaceful life, and to give her the love and affection she'd lacked for so long.

Right off the bat, her black skin had made her a target of whispers. She was watched far more closely than any other small girl in the community, and not even a full week had gone by before she'd transgressed. It was for the simple sin of going outside to collect the wash wearing only her undergarments. But she'd been seen and branded immodest. When her name was said at during Shaming, I had leaped to my feet to defend her, but my mother had yanked me back down again. I watched in horror as an innocent little girl, already so scarred by the life she'd led before coming to us, was forced to lift her skirts until the tops of her thighs were bared. She hadn't made a sound when the rod struck her tender flesh, I knew she'd learned to stay silent in the foster home she'd been in before coming to us.

And that made it so very much worse.

"There are those among you who clutch your sins close to you, letting them weigh you down. Brothers and sisters, how will you rise into Heaven on Judgment Day if your sins are an anchor around your neck? Confess your sins and when you are finished, call upon your neighbor to confess theirs, so they might be free from the weight as well."

I heard a rush of breath like everyone was readying themselves to speak at once. And I realized, with dull, numb horror, that nearly all of the heads were turned in my direction.

I knew that was how it had to be. If I truly wanted to belong again, I needed to accept my punishment for leaving. I needed to confess all that I had done wrong while out from under their watchful eyes.

But what if I didn't believe I had done anything wrong?

My mother reached out and pressed her hand on my shoulder. As if she wanted to keep me sitting in case someone said my name. "No," I whispered, not daring to move my lips. "I won't do it."

"Then," the Elder continued, sounding slightly disappointed, "I'd like to call on Sister Rachel Walker."

I jerked my head up, ready to run if he so much as came near me...

But he was raising his hand. "We welcome you," he blessed me as the rest of the congregation stretched out their hands. "We are grateful that you have returned to us, and we ask the Lord for His Almighty blessing on you, Sister Rachel, as you begin again to walk the path of God's Chosen."

I looked around, awestruck, at all the hands reaching out to bless me. "You belong here," my mother said as she squeezed my arm. "You belong here, with us."

I squeezed my eyes shut again and nodded and hoped that everyone believed that the tears that were now falling were tears of joy at having finally come home. I hoped I could believe it too.

Chapter Thirty-Nine

BEAU

I picked up my phone and double checked that the ringer was on. Just in case. There were still no voicemails - from anyone. Not that I could have missed a call, the way I'd been checking every phantom vibration. But I checked again. Nothing from the police. Nothing from the private investigator I'd hired, and then fired, and then thought about hiring again.

Nothing from Rachel.

I deliberately set my phone and walked towards the window and looked out to the surrounding trees without seeing a thing. I was blind. And numb. I felt nothing except the need to check my phone again.

The ringer was on. No one had called in the ten seconds since I last looked.

"Where the fuck are you?" My silent house had no replay. Just like me, it had no idea where Rachel had disappeared that night. I sank down into a chair and raked my hands through my hair. I hadn't trimmed my beard in days and it was sticking out all wild-man crazy, which suited me. I had already gone through the shock and worry stage of grief.

Now I was angry.

Finn's head bobbed past the side window, out on his morning walk.

We'd flipped roles. While I had been a basket case these past four days, Finn was happier than I'd seen him in forever, spending his days tramping around the fifteen acres that came with this house. He spent a lot of time throwing rocks into the pond and watching the ripples as they formed rings on the surface. He was in nature, and finally at peace.

And I fucking hated him for it.

We'd barely spoken since the night he'd drank so much I thought he'd overdosed on pills. He knew that I blamed him for Rachel disappearing. Last night he'd stood in the doorway to my bedroom and watched me as I talked to the detective on the missing person's case, and when I hung up, frustrated, he'd actually looked abashed.

"Look man, I know you're hurting. But I didn't ask you to come take care of me. You did that on your own."

Which was as close as I was going to get to an apology from Finn.

"I know," I'd said, running my hand through my hair again. "And that's the worst fucking part." I'd chosen my brother over the woman I loved and as a result I'd fucking lost her. I had no right to be angry at Finn for Rachel's disappearance.

But I still was.

And that was bad, because we were about to be spending even *more* time together.

I grabbed my suitcase. "Yo!" I shouted out of the window, but Finn wasn't on the side lawn anymore. I stomped out onto the deck to see my where the hell my nature-loving Zen-monk of a brother had wandered off to and spotted him down the sloped lawn at the edge of the fishing pond. Memory assaulted me yet again, as that golden moment when Rachel surprised me with her fishing skills invaded my head. Grief washed over me and right after it came a wave of rage worse than what I'd felt the night of Finn's "overdose." I checked my phone one more time just to feel the way my heart sank when I saw she hadn't called me to explain, and then tucked it into my pocket and leaned over the deck railing to glare down at him. "We gotta go!"

"Van's not here yet!" he hollered back serenely. I didn't even realize you *could* holler serenely and that just made me even more agitated. I checked my phone again.

And it started ringing in my hand.

I was so startled my hand jerked, momentarily loosening my grip. My phone slipped from my hand and rang again as it seemed to hang there in space.

"Fuck!" I cried as my phone fell over the railing. "Fuck!!"

At that moment, the limo-van crunched and swayed its way up the driveway, but I was only half aware of its arrival. Desperate, I leaned over the railing, praying the impact hadn't shattered it, but there it was, lying in the grass face-up.

It rang again.

I had half a mind to jump right over the railing after it, but the twelve-foot drop was too high. I growled out a curse and sprinted to the side stairs.

The doors to the van slammed. "Hey! You guys aren't even ready!" Claire called out. "Come on!"

"Shut up!" I barked savagely. My feet hit the grass and I was already running to the spot where I'd last seen my phone. "Shit, where are you? Shit!"

"You lose something?" Finn floated back up the lawn with the relaxed gait of a man who hadn't lost everything.

"Phone!" I turned in helpless circles in the grass.

Claire was watching all of this with pursed lips. "You guys, we really need to go, New York City is not exactly close to here. Aren't you even a little excited? Come on!" she whined. "Today's the day, dammit!"

I ignored her and kept walking with my head down. Everything - the ride to New York, the upcoming reunion show, all of it - could wait until I found out who had called. "I think Rachel called," I managed to choke through my frustration. "And right as it started ringing, I dropped my *fucking* phone over the railing because somebody"—I glared at Finn— "wasn't here at the house and waiting like he should have been."

"Hey!" Finn held up his hands to ward me off. "This isn't *my* fault. You're the keyboardist, you shouldn't have such clumsy fingers."

I was about to tackle him to the ground when Jonah - who'd come up behind me without saying anything - suddenly called out, "Is that it?"

I spun and then dove when I saw the glinting metal. Finn stared at me like I'd gone completely mad, which I very well might have. Claire still looked confused, but Jonah - who'd fallen in love with a sweet, strong girl who'd changed him completely - seemed to understand.

"I hope it's her." He gave me a solemn nod. I took a deep breath and looked at the miraculously uncracked screen.

My heart sank. "It's not her number." I looked again and my heart squeezed even tighter. "I think it's the detective on the missing person's case."

"Well, call him back!" Claire exploded.

I had already hit callback. "Jenkins," came the brusque voice on the other end of the line. I recognized the bored, skeptical tone of the detective I'd spoken to that frantic night she'd first gone missing.

"Yes, hi." I cleared my throat and tried to sound more in control, then shoved that aside as useless. I was completely and totally out of control. "This is Beauregard King, I think you'd just called me in regard to Rachel Walker?"

Three of my siblings were staring at me with wide eyes. Claire had her hands over her mouth. Jonah was watching me with his hands shoved in his pocket. And Finn was staring at his boots. But all three of them were here, and that made me feel a tiny bit better.

Detective Jenkins inhaled sharply. "We've located the subject in question."

I gave a whoop of relief and cupped my hand over the mouthpiece. "They found her!" Claire clapped and launched herself at me for a hug, but Jenkins was still talking, "...does not wish to be contacted."

I pulled back from Claire. "I'm sorry, what was that?"

Jenkins sighed. "Rachel Walker does not wish to be contacted."

It felt like he'd sunk a knife right under my ribcage. "She's.... Why?"

He gave a dismissive chuckle, "Oh you know how it is down at that compound. Calling you Satan and all that nonsense. It's all pretty shady if you ask me, and I was looking forward to finding some evidence of lawbreaking when you gave me this case, but she turned up safe and sound, wearing all those heavy skirts and telling me that she was there of her own free will. Wasn't much I could do after that."

My hand dropped away from my ear. Numbly, I stared past my siblings. She'd gone back? After what she told me, she'd gone back?

"What did he say?" Claire begged.

I blinked, and with the greatest effort, I hauled the phone back up to my ear. "Thank you for telling me," I said mechanically, then ended the call.

"What happened? Where is she?" Claire's voice was rising.

I looked around. Everything seemed wrong. Even the colors were strange. "This makes no sense," I muttered, frustrating my sister. "I love her."

And then, with a jolt, I realized I'd never told her.

And now I'd never be able to.

"Let's get out of here," I begged.

My brother, who had found a peace in this place he'd never had before, took a deep breath. Then he slung his arm around my shoulder. "Yeah. Let's get out of here," he agreed.

Chapter Forty

RACHEL

"Are you okay, Rachel?"

I took a deep, shuddering breath and then smoothed my hands down the front of my skirts as the detective made a U-turn in the dirt and drove away in a cloud of dirt. I wanted to scream and run after him, fling myself at his non-descript car and cling on to the bumper as he took me away from this place.

But my sister was watching me. Little Miriam with her wary expression and her big brown eyes. She gave me a tentative smile and I forced myself to smile back. "Of course."

She grabbed my hand. "Good. Because Mother told me to come fetch you." She tugged at my arm.

"Really?" I hoped she would forgive my mud-stained skirts and stained overdress. The sudden rain this morning had left the fields a rutted mess, and the lingering humidity had me feeling sodden and short of breath even before Detective Jenkins had rattled me so badly. Mother had been watching me very closely ever since my return and I didn't want her to see me looking anything but serene. "Do you know why?"

Miriam was almost bursting with the importance of her task. "You have a caller."

"A caller?" I gasped as I let her tug me back down the muddy central path that ran between all of the Chosen houses. It wasn't a road. More like a trail beaten down by the women's feet walking from house to house to borrow a set of needles or offer potatoes from storage. It was the pathway of our lives, our day to day existence. It used to seem so long to me.

Now I realized it was less than a quarter of a mile long.

Was I really okay with my world being this small?

My sister's hand in mine brought me back to myself. I followed her up the steps to the rarely used front door of our house, and then stopped when she shooed me to one side. "Mother said I am to let her know when you get back," she announced primly, clearly relishing the responsibility.

I obliged her by demurely stepping off to the side of the porch and as I did, I caught the sight of movement through the window. My mother scurried by, clearly agitated about something, and when Miriam politely caught her attention, she startled, throwing up her hands in frustration. Curious, I leaned in to see what could possibly be bothering her so much, but Miriam must have told her I was back from meeting with the detective because she turned and looked straight through the window, right at me. I couldn't read her expression, and that bothered me. My mother was usually an open book, but right now she was closed up tight.

The low rumble of far off thunder made me jump. Something was wrong. "Rachel!" My mother's voice was bright and falsely cheerful. "There you are!"

"Yes, I was speaking to the detective, Mother. Of course I told him that everything was fine and—"

"Yes, good, but come inside the house, we can't keep them waiting any longer."

"Them?" I echoed as I trailed behind her.

Inside the house, the humidity was even worse. This morning's storm had soaked the laundry that had been hanging on the line to dry, which meant that every spare surface was draped with damp clothing, which only added to the feeling of closeness. As I looked around, I realized that all this laundry would need to be rewashed, since the heavy rain had splashed up droplets of mud all over it. Which meant I'd be spending today doing chores I'd already spent all day yesterday doing.

My fingers twitched as I tried to fold them demurely in front of me, but I ended up clenching my fists instead. "Rachel?" my mother called from the front room. "Come join us."

"I have all these chores still to do, I don't have time!" I wanted to say. But I didn't. I ducked my head in apology and headed to obey my mother.

She was sitting in the front room, which was odd. Usually this was men's space, but when I looked again, I saw that my father was seated silently, with his head bowed in prayer. In the folding chair next to him sat a woman I vaguely recognized. She was short and squarely built and her light brown hair was streaked with gray. Her equally square husband was seated closest to me. In between them sat a reed-thin young man I didn't remember at first, then wracked my brain. "Levi?" I asked.

He looked up at me with a flash of desperation in his eyes that he quickly masked before looking back down at his feet again. His father gave him a rough sort of nudge. "Hi Rachel," Levi said tonelessly.

"We should give glory on this blessed day," my mother trilled. She folded her hands. "Father we thank you for revealing your plan to us, your faithful servants."

I ducked my head and squeezed my hands together, miming piety even as my head was racing. What was going on? What was the plan she was referring to? And why was my own father allowing my mother to lead the prayer? That was usually a man's role. "We know you have chosen us to walk a narrow path, but we know it will lead only to glory."

Murmured amens didn't do anything to clarify what was happening. Levi's mother mouthed a few more silent words of blessing and then opened her eyes. "We believe it is a good match. Levi has assented and we have prayed on it."

"So have we," my mother nodded quickly.

I looked between them both. "What is going on?"

My mother looked at me with her hand clasped to her heart, her eyes half-lidded in rapture. "It's Providence. God's holy will." She gestured to the red-faced young man with the blue eyes. "Rachel! Levi has agreed to marry you!"

Chapter Forty-One

RACHEL

"No!"

I leaped to my feet, shouting before I could stop myself. No. I couldn't marry Levi. I didn't love Levi. I loved....

"No," I repeated. I looked at Levi. "I can't marry you."

Tears swam in my eyes and in the watery haze, I swore I could see Beau's hazel eyes filled with pain. What had I done to him? I loved him, but I never even told him.

And now I never would.

"Rachel?" my mother hissed through her smile. "You're overwrought, I know. It's a surprise. You didn't mean to be so rude."

I blinked. Everyone in the room was watching me with varying degrees of horror on their face. I blinked again, remembering Rebecca's accusations. How my family had suffered because of me. "I'm sorry," I said, keeping my voice low so it wouldn't shake. I gripped my skirts in my hands. "I was just surprised because..." I seized on a glimmer of hope. "Mother, have you told Levi about how... how it's not possible for me to—"

"Providence has smiled upon us," she repeated with a wild gleam in her eye.

Baffled, I stood up and looked at the man who refused to even look at me in return.

"Levi?" He jerked when I said his name. I tried to smile. He must have been as freaked out as I was. "May I speak with you?" I looked around at the room. "If we are to be married and all."

"I will allow it," Levi's father said.

My own father glowered. "Ten minutes."

I nodded and ducked my head. Levi looked around as if he wanted someone to object, then glumly followed after me,

I rushed out of the sticky, humid house and into the marginally less sticky, humid outdoors, then tried to take a deep breath. Without meaning to, I looked again toward the place where the detective had turned around. Even from way over here, I could see the deep ruts his tires had carved into the mud as he left this place. If I followed his tire tracks, they would take me back to Beau.

And then I remembered that Beau wasn't in Crown Creek anymore. He'd left to go record with Claire and his brothers... was it today? Time had swirled together so I could barely recall how many days it had been since I left. Was it today that he was going to New York City? Yes, it was.

Hope that I hadn't even realized had flared in my chest like a candle lighting the gloom inside of me suddenly snuffed out. Beau was gone too, and I didn't even know how long it would be until he came back. And what would I do when he finally did come? Explain that I had chosen obligation to my family over my love for him?

The family that was trying to marry me off to a man I had never met?

"Rachel?" Levi's voice was higher than I had expected. I turned to see that he was as tall as I was, with a noticeable stoop to his shoulders.

But none of that mattered right now. "You really want to marry me?" I demanded.

He looked taken aback at the direct question, but I didn't care. "Is this really what you want?" I pressed.

"It's God's plan."

I blinked at the desperation in his voice. "You really think so?"

"I've prayed on it," he said, even more desperately. Like he was trying to convince himself as much as he was trying to convince me.

"Right but..." Heat rose to my cheeks, but this was not the time to let shame get the best of me. "You know I'm barren, right?"

I expected him to rear back. Having children was the most important calling of a Chosen wife. But he only closed, then opened his eyes. "It does not matter to me."

"How?" I demanded.

"I was one of the fosters," he went on in that same dispassionate voice. "I feel a great calling to raise children like me."

"Oh." All the pieces clicked into place. If we raised fosters together, then my infertility wouldn't be an issue. In fact, we'd be greatly admired in the community. There would be a place for me. A future for me. This should have been a relief. "Then I guess it all makes sense then?"

"Yes, it does," Levi said firmly. He reached out his hand. "Shall we go for a walk?"

I looked down at his hand, stunned that he'd even consider it until he rolled his eyes.

"You are my intended. It is allowed."

"Right." I let his hand close around mine, feeling like I was committing a terrible betrayal. The simple slide of skin against skin made me ache for Beau, that hollow place that only he could fill opening wide inside of me again.

Levi led us on an aimless walk around the fronts and then the backs of the houses along the main row. I wondered what he was doing until I realized. He was making sure we were seen.

And we were. Up and down we walked in front of everyone, making it public. I looked and saw that my younger siblings were out now, playing with other kids and not being shunned. My parents were inside entertaining Levi's parents, and later Levi's mother would most likely help my mother prepare a meal while the men talked. When I returned, I restored my family's good name. Marrying Levi would cement it.

I *had* to do it.

The weight of it settled on my shoulders. Once our allotted ten minutes was up, we returned to my house. At the bottom of the front stairs, Levi let my hand fall. Without that touch, my hand felt cold and I grieved the loss of contact. Something to hold on to. "Levi?"

He turned. I thought he might kiss me. I *wanted* him to kiss me. I was lonely and heartbroken and I *missed* being kissed.

"We'd better go in," my future husband said. And he turned his back on me and walked away.

Chapter Forty-Two

BEAU

Twenty-four hours ago, I was living in the country and in love with a girl I hoped would come back to me any minute.

Now I was in the middle of a noisy, clanging city - though I couldn't hear any of the noise because I'd been locked in a soundproof studio with my four siblings since early this morning - and the girl I loved was lost to me. It didn't seem possible that everything could have changed so completely and I could somehow still be the same person.

But I was. I was still Beau King, the keyboardist for the world-famous King Brothers, now just called The Kings because Claire was currently trying to fit her harmonies into our old songs.

It wasn't going well.

"Guys!" The tech flicked on the PA and then noticed Claire glaring at him. "And girls," he amended. "We're way behind schedule here. Should we take five?"

The soundproofed studio was cramped and small and smelled like coffee. Every inhale reminded me of Rachel and her love of the once-forbidden-to-her drink. For all of what we'd seen of the city that never sleeps, we may as well have stayed in the shed on my parents' property, in the studio we'd recorded in as kids. This was ridiculous and I opened my mouth to agree that yeah, we should take five, and maybe more.

But my brothers beat me. "No!" Jonah and Gabe barked in unison, then looked at each other. Jonah lifted his chin. "We're gonna get it, just..." He rubbed his hand from the back of his head to the front and then back again. "Just, give us a few more minutes to come up with something, okay?"

The tech looked skeptical but obliged by leaning back in his chair and resuming looking bored. I sighed and stared down at the white keys on my keyboard and wished it was a grand piano.

We'd asked for the rehearsals to be recorded, with the idea that we might get some footage for a possible DVD release in the future. But so far, all we'd gotten was footage of us bickering like a bunch of children.

"I don't know what the problem is," my sister sighed as she picked at her nail in that bad habit of hers she got when she was anxious.

"I know what it is. You're flat." Jonah sighed heavily.

"I am not!" Claire was immediately defensive. "This song is in the weirdest fucking key!"

"She's not wrong," Gabe pointed out, waving away her shouts of "See! See!" to go on, "We were all singing this shit back before our balls dropped. I can't hit these fucking notes anymore." He dragged his hand down his suntanned face. His jetlag was showing. He'd met up with us late last night - still on Vietnam time - and was now going on his thirtieth hour without sleep.

"But it's a fucking reunion show," Jonah said through gritted teeth.

"We're all older. We've all gone and done different things with our lives in the past two and a half years." Finn's temper was flaring. "I know I'm not the same fucking person I was two years ago and if these people show up expecting to see us staying exactly the same, they're fucking crazy. We're not going to be able to sound the same. We're just not." He glared at our oldest brother. "And no amount of you yelling at us is going to change that."

It was a testament to just how right he was about us changing that Jonah listened to all of this without getting defensive. "Look, I'm trying not to be a micromanager like before," Jonah said as he glanced at Gabe. It was a testament to how much Gabe had changed when he just nodded warily, acknowledging the bad old days between them without bringing them up again. "But the people that show up for this, they're going to expect to hear the old hits," Jonah went on.

"That's true." Gabe rolled his eyes. "And you know how much it pains me to admit that." Jonah scratched his nose with his middle finger, which made Gabe tackle him. And that's how I knew things hadn't really changed that much at all.

The familiar sight of my two older brothers wrestling on the ground should have made me laugh like usual. But I sat there at my keyboard and watched them, and couldn't feel a damn thing. Not happiness, not gratitude for the second chance we'd been given, not even irritation that they were wasting the little time we had to rehearse together. The only thing I felt was lost.

Lost. Never to be found.

Gabe's flailing leg hit my stool right as the lyric sucker punched me in the gut. "Wait!" I shouted over the grunting din. "I have an idea!"

Finn looked at me, already sensing what was coming to me. "New song?"

Gabe slipped out of Jonah's headlock and sat up. "Whaddya got?" he asked.

The snatches of vocals flitted through my head. Amazing Grace, as sung by Rachel, her high, pure voice singing words of grace and healing. It hurt like nothing had ever hurt before to see her sweet face in my mind's eye as she turned her face toward that sunbeam in my living room as I played the piano for her that first day she sang for me. But that hurt was a feeling, unlike the numbness that had weighed me down ever since I'd hung up on Detective Jenkins. "Paper," I said, reaching out my hand.

"Is this how he gets?" Claire asked as Finn put a piece of paper and a stub of pencil in my hand.

"Sometimes." Finn sounded excited. "And whenever he gets this way, the shit that comes out is pure fucking gold."

Gabe leaned over my shoulder, watching as I scrawled a few couplets, then savagely erased them. He wrote the music, then handed it over to Jonah who added the hooky beats and soaring bridges. Jonah then handed it back to Finn who figured out the harmonies around the melody that Gabe had already worked out. This was the way it had always been, and Claire watched with wide eyes as the four of us became one brain. "Open with the chorus?" "Yeah and then the—" "Beat drop, right here." "Fuck, that's sick but wouldn't we—" "Shoot the load too quick, nah man, transpose the key in the last verse." "Doesn't that sound—" "Right, it's got that eighties power ballad feel and—" "Shit, yeah that's fucking gold, what's the hook?"

"Claire!" Jonah shouted way too loudly. He shoved a piece of paper at her and then plunked out a melody on his guitar. "Sing that. We need a solo female vocal right there." He raised a challenging eyebrow. "You can hit *that* note, right?"

She scanned the paper quickly and then scoffed. "Stand back, boys." And then my sister belted out an updated version of Rachel's hymn. "Lost and found / how sweet the sound." The sound tech leaned forward, flicking on the cameras as we fell into a rough take.

Claire glanced at me as she sang the words I'd written, understanding in her eyes. Sympathy too. I had to look away as I played the chords that my heart had chosen. Watching her sing those lyrics that seconds ago I'd barely allowed myself to acknowledge felt too private. I'd written it for Rachel, but it hurt to hear it sung aloud. Because what I'd written?

It sounded a lot like I was saying goodbye.

I didn't want to say goodbye. I wasn't ready to say goodbye.

When the song was over, I squeezed my eyes shut. My siblings were respectfully silent.

Then the PA clicked on again. "There it is," the tech declared.

I opened my eyes to see my siblings all nodding. The tech was right. As heartbreaking as it was to play that song, it was also perfect. It sounded like a continuation of the songs we used to sing. Like we'd grown up but were still the same people. It sounded like the Kings.

"Guys...and girl." This new voice belonged to a label rep. "Listen, I know you said you just wanted to record some new material for a special reunion download, but this is fucking gold. You make a whole album like this? And we're in business again."

He switched off the mic as the five of us looked at each other in amazement. A new album? Getting back together for real?

Then he switched the mic back on and said my name. "Beau?"

"Yeah?" I snapped out of my stupefied reverie. "What's up?"

"One thing. If we're gonna take you on again, you gotta ditch the lumberjack look."

My siblings burst out laughing.

That night in the hotel room, I shaved off my beard. As I watched the hair swirl in the drain, it felt like I was watching the past two years drain away. Like they had never happened. Seeing the naked face in the mirror, I could almost believe it.

But when I fell into bed, exhausted and sad but happy at the same time, my hand reached out to twine into a braid that wasn't there next to me. And I knew that, as much as I wanted to pretend, those years had happened. And that the song I'd written wasn't a goodbye song. It was a "come-back-to-me" song. As sleep overtook me, I could almost hear her sweet voice singing it in my ear.

Chapter Forty-Three

RACHEL

The smell of rust hung heavy in the humid air inside the meeting house. I breathed shallowly, but the smell made me nauseous. As did the lack of windows and the way Levi's shoulder pressed into mine.

I was seated on the left side of the aisle with his family rather than with mine. Since the announcement of our betrothal, I'd felt myself being slowly absorbed into his family, forced to spend time in the kitchen with his mother, and awkward dinners with his foster siblings who all ignored me and passed food over my head, forcing me to duck. Nights I still spent with my own family, but most of that was spent sleeping like the dead with exhaustion after Levi's mother ran me ragged all day doing chores for her, so I rarely saw them. I'd returned for their sake. But this wasn't how I'd envisioned it.

The silence of prayers spread out, seemingly forever. I closed my eyes and tried to find peace. I squeezed my eyes shut and begged whoever was listening to make this feel right. To show me that I had made the right choice. "Give me a sign," I soundlessly begged.

I opened my eyes again and stole a glance at the man who was to be my husband, opening my heart to the idea of him. He seemed decent, almost too polite with me. He had blue eyes that were watery first thing in the morning. I had told him an allergy pill would help him, and then remembered that those were forbidden.

I always seemed to make those mistakes around him. Laughing too loudly, trying too hard to talk. Levi seemed to prefer me silent...and in a different room. But I vowed I would keep trying, desperate to find something to cling on to - a stray compliment, an admiring glance - that would make me feel...

Feel good again.

Levi finished his prayers with a sigh and looked upward again. I smiled at him. A small flutter of hope that this was it, the moment where we connected. He looked back at me with his watery blue eyes, holding my gaze...

And then his gaze slid right past me and back up to the front of the meeting house once more.

My stomach sank like a rock. No. That couldn't be my sign. I'd just have to keep looking.

The Elder at the front called for hymns. I stood with the rest of the Chosen, and then my heart skipped when the first strains of "Amazing Grace" began. We had sung it my first day back. Was that really only a week ago? It felt like a lifetime. I closed my eyes against the tears that seemed like they were always close to falling and wondered if Beau felt the same way when he heard it. I hoped he wasn't too angry that he couldn't hear the beauty in the words. I hoped he'd found some kind of grace inside of himself that made my betrayal not sting so much.

I hoped he knew I missed him more than I ever thought possible.

As the congregation sang, I raised my own voice. Closing my eyes, I let the melody lift me up, certain that this was the sign I had prayed for. My voice rose as I tried to drown out the sadness, and soon I was belting out the sweet words just like Claire had taught me. Just like I hadn't been able to that night at the Crown. I sang with all the hope I'd had and the grief I'd felt. I sang my love, lifting it up and then letting it go. The melody wrapped me up in its embrace and I sang as loud as I could.

And then stopped. Because the music had stopped.

And everyone was staring.

"Sister Walker." The Elder's nose was wrinkled like I had done something disgusting. "Vanity is a deadly sin."

My mouth fell open. "I wasn't... I'm not being vain, I just really like the song—"

"You put yourself above others, calling attention to yourself. Come forward."

I stuttered and looked around in horror. "To be Shamed? You can't be serious." Shocked gasps echoed off the metal walls and now I knew I would be Shamed for subordination as well as vanity, but I didn't care. This was insanity. I was only singing.

I looked to Levi in desperation. "Tell them! I was just singing the hymn! You're supposed to be my future husband, tell them this is crazy!"

"Vanity is a sin," he echoed in that same toneless voice he'd spoke in the night we met. I narrowed my eyes at him and then looked over to my own family. Rebecca and Joel were both looking down, not willing to meet my eyes. Miriam and Lydia were both staring at me with terror on their little faces. But my mother.

My mother was looking at me with such anger that it made me step back as if she'd reached out and struck me.

"Come forward," the Elder intoned again.

I tore my hopeful gaze away from my mother. She wouldn't help me. No one would. This was normal to them. Vanity was a sin, and those who sinned were punished in front of everyone to keep the rest of the congregation in line. Sinners had to submit and receive their punishment before they would be accepted back into the community.

But I would not submit.

"This is crazy." I held my head high as I shoved past Levi and his family. "All of this, it's nuts." I broke free of the crush and sprinted for the back entrance. My skirts tangled in my legs, slowing me down, making it easy for the Elders in the back to grab me. "What is wrong with you?" I shouted to my mother as they dragged me back up to the front, to the Elder waiting with the stick in hand. "Do something!" I begged as they lifted my skirts and bared my thighs.

My family, my future husband, my whole community, they all just sat there and watched as the Elder brought the slender reed down on my naked skin. I flinched and gritted my teeth to keep from crying out, then gave in and screamed.

I screamed after each one of the seven lashes. I let them hear my pain. I hoped like hell they felt it too.

But I did not let them see me cry.

Chapter Forty-Four

RACHEL

I slumped woozily when they stood me back up again. Everything was hazy through the cloud of pain. It took a small shove from the Elder on my left to get me moving.

I shuffled automatically down the aisle and then stopped short.

On one side sat my family. On the other side sat the man I was supposed to marry.

I stood there wavering in place. I did not belong with either of them.

"Sit down," my father ordered.

Humiliated, I shoved my way back to my seat, deliberately knocking into Levi with my elbow. Then I turned and lifted my chin as high as I could before sinking down slowly, hissing through my teeth. The raw, red lash marks that striped my thighs made sitting unbearable. I scooted down until I was at the very edge of my chair and kept my eyes shut through the rest of the meeting. When it was over and everyone rose, I stayed seated, refusing to move.

"Rachel."

I heard my father say my name, but I kept my eyes shut, hoping he would believe I was deep in prayer.

"Rachel!" my mother snapped.

I let my eyes flutter open but didn't turn to look at her. The meeting house had cleared out. Only my parents and Levi's parents remained, and all four of them were watching me as if they were considering an exorcism.

"We were under the impression," my father began. "That your time in the secular world was spent spreading God's word."

"Why would you think that? You never once told me that's what you wanted. You never even checked in to see if I was doing okay..." I started to say.

But my father spoke right over me like I hadn't even said a word. "We did not want to believe that you had fallen into secular ways. But your vanity and the stubborn pride you exhibited today show that you have."

"Seriously?

He ignored that too. I may as well have not even been in the room, because he turned to Levi's father with an obsequious smile that made my blood run cold. "We are grateful that, in spite of this, you are still willing to go through with this. We believe that it's probably best for Rachel's eternal soul if we hold this wedding soon."

"We agree," Levi's father said, glaring at Levi for some reason. "How about tomorrow?"

"Tomorrow?" I echoed. The word clunked in my head like a prison door sliding into place. "You want me to marry Levi... tomorrow?" I stared at the man in question, who looked just as blindsided as I was. Desperately, I appealed to my father with my eyes. I had returned to make their lives better, but now? Now they seemed intent on ruining mine completely. But he wasn't even looking at me. His gaze was fixed at some place in the distance, as if he was peering off into a future that only he could see. I wracked my brain for something, anything that would stall this. "Can I take a moment? To uh... pray on it?"

Levi seemed to seize on this idea. "My wife is right," he said with the most fervor I'd ever heard him be able to muster up. "I'd like to take a walk and pray on this." He glanced at me and seemed to understand my unsaid entreaty. "In solitude of course. To better hear God's plan revealed to me."

I nodded fiercely, then winced as the motion made my injured thighs brush against my seat. A burst of white-hot hate propelled me to my feet. I had to buy myself time. For what, I didn't know yet but I knew I just... needed... time. "You understand, of course," I said, all sweetness and smiles.

My mother inhaled sharply and then looked at my glowering father. "Come now. Don't you remember how nervous I was the day before our wedding? I think solitary prayer would be a wise action."

I breathed a silent thank you for her sudden compassion. "Thank you," I said quickly before my father could change his mind, and fled from the meeting house.

Outside in the heavy, soupy air, I gulped in a breath, but it didn't clear my head. My heavy braid seemed to be tugging insistently on my head, weighing me down. Stumbling on my injured legs, my only thought was to get as far away from the meeting house as I could. I winced in pain as I hurried away, my tears blinding me, so I had no idea where I was headed. I just knew I need to run, and so that's what I did, looping around down to the creek. Once under the trees and away from the prying eyes of the rest of the community, I slowed with my heart hammering in my ears.

The trickle of the creek reminded me so sharply of my little house with Everly that I started crying harder. Sobbing blindly, I rushed away from the memory of what I'd had and thrown away and ran full tilt toward the pastures and into the shadow of the big gray barn. Gasping, I sagged against the cool walls and dug my fists into my eyes, angrily wiping away the tears. "Goddammit," I raged. "Fuck! Fucking shit!" I cursed as loud as I dared. But it came out in only a whisper because I knew someone had to be watching. Listening.

In the next breath, my fears were confirmed. I heard the mutter of voices and then a thud as if something had hit the wall.

Then the unmistakable noise of a passionate gasp.

Slowly I rose up onto my tiptoes and peered into the gloom of the barn.

Two men were inside wrestling.

No. Not wrestling.

Kissing.

I held my breath, hardly daring to move a muscle as I watched the two men clutch and strain, grasping and tearing at each other's clothes in a rough embrace. Snatches of words, of desperate promises, floated out through the cracks in the barn walls. I heard "...tomorrow." I heard. "...doesn't change anything." I knelt down - slowly - to listen at the crack because there was something about that voice that sounded familiar.

Then the other voice, a different voice spoke so clearly it may have well have been right in my ear. "No, Levi. It's too dangerous."

I clapped my hand over my mouth to stifle my shocked gasp. Then I heard my future husband's wretched, pleading, "No!"

"This has to be the last time," the other voice intoned, and then his words were swallowed by the sound of another desperate, ragged kiss.

All the strength left my body and I slumped heavily against the side of the barn as it suddenly became crystal clear to me why Levi had wanted to marry me. I would be a human shield for his love, which was expressly forbidden by the Chosen. Levi was gay, and I was the perfect cover. Years could go by and no one would question what happened in our bedroom. No one would whisper and wonder if we had consummated the marriage.

After all, no one would ever expect a broken woman like me to get pregnant.

Horror punched me in the gut. Not because Levi was gay. But because I was facing down a life of never being touched. Never being loved.

Never being allowed to sing more loudly than a whisper.

I'd resigned myself to coming back to the Chosen. But I couldn't face a life without any chance of love.

I stood up. I wasn't going to do it.

I was going to find Beau. And then I was going to get down on my knees and beg for his forgiveness. If I had to go all the way to New York City, so be it.

I finally knew where I belonged.

Chapter Forty-Five

BEAU

The bright lights of the TV studio were like the blazing sun overhead.

It was the fifth day of our whirlwind New York City tour. After four productive days in the studio, the label's publicity machine had kicked in and we found ourselves getting primped and powdered for interviews.

Just like the old days.

Except this time, we had an overexcited Claire in tow. My sister, drunk on the limelight she was so jealous not to share with us all those years ago, was tripping all over herself trying to get a word in edgewise during the morning talk show appearance.

Unfortunately for her, Jonah-the-overachiever was in full-schmooze-mode. He could charm talk show hosts with one hand tied behind his back, and these two were no different from the rest of them.

Poor Claire. You could almost see the frustrated steam rising off her head. I almost burst out laughing.

And then they started asking about our love lives.

"Tell us about what's changed most for everyone during the hiatus. Jonah, I hear you're engaged?"

My older brother's fake smile faded and a real one took its place.

"That's right. Ruby wants a fall wedding, so we're looking at next September. Before the school year starts though."

"Oh!" This seemed to surprise the female host. "Is she a student?"

"A teacher." Jonah beamed with pride. "Kindergarten, actually. Which is good, because she's teaching me some tricks on dealing with this lot." He glared at us and gave an exaggerated eyeroll.

So many things had changed. But Jonah's exasperated schtick during interviews never did.

"And my girl is a nurse," Gabe interjected. "So when I inevitably beat up Jonah for saying things like that." He glared back pointedly. "She can stitch him back up, good as new."

"That's right." The male host turned to Gabe. "You're dating the woman who served as your nurse during your recovery, correct?"

"Everly." Gabe nodded, suddenly all serious. "She's the best thing that ever happened to me." He looked far away for a second, and then remembered himself and where he was. "This band being a distant second."

Both hosts chuckled. I chuckled right along with them, the years of practice kicking in to keep my face neutral, even as inside I wanted to run screaming from the room.

Because I knew the question would come to me soon. And what would I say?

The feeling that nothing had changed, that the last two years never happened, kept forcing me to remember that they *had* happened. And I was a fool. A stupid, cowardly fool for not demanding that the limo bus stop at the Chosen compound before we left town. I should have found Rachel and demanded to hear her tell me it was over to my face. I shouldn't have just slunk away with my tail between my legs. I should have fought for her. I fucking loved her.

And I probably always would.

Now the question was, did I have the guts to say that into a TV camera? It wasn't like she'd see it.

Except maybe, somehow, she might.

"And Finn." The female interviewer recrossed her legs demurely. "How about you? Anyone special?"

It was just the kind of question nosy interviewers would ask us when we were kids, hoping to get some kind of precociously adorable quote. And Finn knew it, too. I fully expected him to roll his eyes, but he checked himself and just gave a mildly disappointed laugh. "Nah, nobody wants to deal with me."

"Oh I know that's not true," the female host interjected, giving him a decidedly appraising look.

He raised one eyebrow at her. Then, keeping his voice carefully neutral, he said, "I'm just grateful for the chance to play music with my family, and when this is all over, I'm going to go hide in the woods away from people for the rest of my life." He leaned forward, giving the host the full benefit of his quizzical eyebrow. "Seriously, how do you New Yorkers deal with all the people around you all the time?"

The host looked like she wanted to leap onto Finn and lick his face. Claire cleared her throat. "I'm single too," she piped up, her little sister syndrome kicking into high gear. "And loving it. All I need are my girls." She leaned forward, trying to break into the one-sided staring contest the female host was having with Finn, who was now studying his feet. "Isn't that right? We don't need men!"

The male host stepped in. I braced myself. "And of course, Beau. The Quiet One." I smiled and nodded in acknowledgment of my old moniker. "Don't think that by keeping silent we're going to forget you're here!" Chuckles all around. "Is there anyone special in your life?"

I leaned forward. "Yes, there is," I said immediately.

I felt my siblings turn to stare at me, but I ignored their shock. "And I love her very much." I took a deep breath. "And she's trying to figure some things out right now, but I hope that someday our paths will cross again."

Chapter Forty-Six

RACHEL

For the second time in a week, I was leaving in the middle of the night.

My legs throbbed with each thumping heartbeat, and with each one, I got angrier and angrier. I'd pushed through the pain, letting it propel me the dark four miles to the Greyhound station on the outskirts of Crown Creek. And with the last bit of money I'd somehow had the foresight to secret away from my parents and the greedy, grubbing hands of the Elders, I'd bought a one-way ticket to New York City.

Now I was on a slightly stinky, and dizzy-making bus, bumping and jostling my way through the night. My entire life, I had never left Crown Creek. Now, each passing mile was the farthest I had ever been from home. But I was too exhausted to think about this for very long. The bus's sway was lulling me as the last bits of adrenaline ebbed away, leaving me desperately sleepy.

Click.

My eyes snapped back open. There was that noise again. The man in the seat diagonally ahead of me had spent the past twenty minutes playing with a deadly looking folding knife. He'd flick it open and then twirl it lazily in his fingers before, *click*, he snapped it back shut again.

I stiffened and sat up straighter, glancing over at him warily. His wildly unkempt gray hair was corralled underneath a battered leather cap and he wore the leather vest I'd come to associate with the men who drank all day at the Crown Tavern, leered at me when Beau wasn't looking, and then headed out to their shiny motorcycles to shatter the peace and quiet with their loud engines. I quailed against the window, hoping he hadn't seen me looking at him.

I shifted in my seat, trying to find a comfortable way to hold my injured legs. As I moved around, I hissed as I inadvertently sat on my braid yet again, yanking my head back. The sting of it getting torn out at the roots along my forehead brought tears to my eyes and for a second I just wanted to give in to the tears. To curl up into a ball and feel sorry for myself. "Goddammit," I moaned, hugging my arms around my chest. But swearing held no power anymore. I reached back and lifted my heavy braid again in sudden irritation. I'd worn this braid every day of my life. It was a mark that set me apart from the world. It told everyone in Crown Creek that I was Chosen, that I belonged to that weird, secretive cult they'd all heard about. I stiffened just thinking of the word, having spent a lifetime being conditioned to reject it. But isn't that exactly what the Chosen was? A cult that brainwashed its believers into accepting corporal punishment for the sin of... *.singing?*

I yanked the tie off the end of the braid and then hastily combed my fingers through my hair, letting it fall loosely around me. I didn't want to ever be marked as Chosen again. Without the heavy braid tugging at my scalp, I felt freer. A headache I'd been living with my whole life suddenly eased.

But the bus was overly warm. And my hair clung to me as hot and itchy as a wool blanket. It hung down in front of my face when I leaned forward, a curtain to hide me from the world.

I didn't want to be hidden anymore.

Click. The biker's penknife flicked again. I jumped, and as I did my hair got twisted in the zipper of the secular jacket I had unearthed from my mother's sewing pile before she could cut it up for a quilt. "Shit," I hissed as another small clump along my hairline was torn out at the roots. Wearing it loose was even worse than wearing a braid.

Angrily, I reached back and braided it back up again. And then I mustered up all of my courage and leaned forward. "Hey? Excuse me?"

The biker turned and for the first time, I saw his eyes. They were kind. "You need somethin'?"

"Could I?" I swallowed. I was done letting other people make me feel bad without my permission. I wasn't scared of him, or anyone. "Borrow that knife for a second?"

He looked down at it, and then back up at me, and then shrugged.

Then he watched me take it and slice off my braid.

Instantly the weight was gone. I breathed a sigh of relief, and then whooped out loud. "Oh my God!" I breathed as I reached up to touch my hair, now swinging along my jawline. "I'm free."

The biker glanced up. "Better?" he asked.

I held it up, that thick ratty rope holding me down. Anchoring me to a life I was done with. "Yes," I breathed. So much better. I extended my hand and looked at it, wrinkling my nose. "I want to throw it out the window. "

"Nah, keep it." The biker sniffed and then snorted up something into a handkerchief before continuing. "You gotta always move forward, but sometimes it's nice to look back and see how far you've come."

I blinked. "You're right."

"Fuckin' A," he agreed. "Can I have my knife back now, miss?"

"Oh!" I handed it back to him. "Thank you."

He gave me another look that lasted so long I felt some of my fear of him creeping back in. Until he suddenly nodded again. "It suits you."

I looked out the darkened window and absently raked my fingers through it, marveling at how smooth and untangled it was. "I'm glad you think so." I thought of Beau and how he'd wrapped my braid in his hands before kissing me and a sudden pang of regret made me tuck my braid back into my purse. I closed my eyes and tried to picture his reaction when I saw him.

Several hours later, I suddenly jerked back awake from a jumbled and restless sleep. I blinked, and then blinked again, then rubbed my eyes to make sure I wasn't still dreaming. All around, glass towers jutted into the sky. Buildings loomed skyward like the walls of a canyon, and the bus was part of a river of cars that flowed along the canyon floor. And all around us were people. So, so many people.

Panic clawed at my throat, but I had to be sure. "Excuse me?" I leaned over to the biker again. "Where are we?"

He blinked up from the doze I'd startled him from and looked out the window. "Henry Hudson Parkway, looks to be. Gonna be at the Port Authority soon." He shuffled around, gathering up a surprising amount of bags. "Hey, thanks for waking me up, kid."

But I was still confused. "Henry Hudson Parkway in..." I hesitated.

A flash of sympathy crossed his face. "New York, kid."

"New York City?" I stared out the window, feeling faint. "*This* is New York City? It's huge!"

"That's a true statement, right there."

He went back to gathering up his things, leaving me to gape out the window. Somewhere, in this massive, bustling city, Beau was playing music with his siblings. But I had no idea where to look for him. I had no idea who even to ask or when he was leaving again.

I closed my eyes and silently cursed myself and my stupid, sheltered naïveté in thinking I could simply hop on a bus to New York City and immediately walk out and find Beau again. I was a fool. And now, thanks to the bus ticket here, I was a broke, penniless fool.

It killed me to know that somewhere in this city was the man I loved. But he'd be leaving soon, and I was trapped here with no money and no way of letting him know I had come for him.

I was never going to see him again.

Chapter Forty-Seven

BEAU

"I don't care if I look like a tourist, I *am* a tourist!" Claire stopped, *again,* and took a selfie, *again.*

I looked at my brothers and shrugged. Finn looked like he wanted to vomit, but then again, Times Square would do that to a person, especially a person who felt most comfortable in the silent woods. "How you holding up?" I asked, worried about him and his declarations that this was the cesspool of humanity, but he couldn't hear me over the city noise that assaulted us from every angle. Jonah was busy texting pictures back to Ruby, but Gabe looked over it all.

I agreed. It was our last day in New York. After a whirlwind of recording and special appearances, the reunion performance was all planned. In two months, we'd be playing three stadiums in the Tri-State area. Tickets went on sale today. It was happening.

I should have been thrilled.

But all I wanted was to get back to Crown Creek. I'd been rehearsing what I'd say when I saw Rachel again. Because that was happening. I would march right onto the Chosen compound and demand that she be allowed to speak to me. In my head, it was clear as day how it would look, with her walking up to me in those long skirts.

She'd watch me, warily. And then I'd take her into my arms and kiss her and dare her to push me away.

But I couldn't do that, stuck as I was in the middle of Times Square. I shoved my hands in my pockets to keep from balling my fists in frustration.

"Oh my God, it's the Naked Cowboy!" Claire shrieked, darting out into the street. Finn lunged and caught her by her purse strap, saving her at the last second from being mowed down by a taxi. "I have to get my picture with him, he is a *staple,"* she announced, ignoring her brush with death to merge in with the saner pedestrians who were wisely crossing at a crosswalk.

"Jesus polka dancing Christ," Finn snarled. But he followed her. We all did.

As we moved unrecognized through the throngs of people, little snippets of memory of my old life returned. Moving through strange cities on tour with my brothers filled me with a kind of melancholy nostalgia. I loved this. I missed this, and it took navigating the neon madness of Times Square to make me finally realize it.

A waft of warm air from the subway grate rushed past my face, making me wince. Gabe saw and chuckled. "Still getting used to being beardless, huh?"

I ran my hand over my chin. "It feels like I'm naked."

"Nah, he's the one who's naked." He lifted his chin in the direction of the Naked Cowboy. I looked to see him standing proudly on the street corner in his tighty-whities, guitar strategically placed over his crotch. Then immediately looked away because my sister was kneeling down next to him, miming an act I wanted to believe she knew absolutely nothing about.

As I turned, the hair on my neck rose, my heart quickened, then a second later, my brain caught up with why I was suddenly breathing faster.

Wafting across the breeze, over the noise of the traffic and tourists, was a voice.

A voice of an angel.

A voice I knew.

"What's wrong with you?" Finn leaned into my eyeline, but I shushed him and listened harder.

There it was again. "Rachel?"

"What?" Finn looked around too, but the voice had fallen silent. "Hey man, I know it's been a rough few days, have you gone mental on me?" He looked rather pleased about this prospect. "Maybe it's my turn to hover over you all the time?"

"Wait, ssh!" I hcld up my finger because the voice had started to sing again. "That's Rachel." I was sure of it. But how? "You hear that, right? I'm not hallucinating?"

"I hear"—Finn paused—"something," he admitted. Then he shouted, "Whoa! Wait! Where are you?"

But I was already sprinting as fast as I could toward that angelic sound. It couldn't be her, but I had to know for sure.

And if it was her?

Then maybe I believed in miracles after all.

Chapter Forty-Eight

RACHEL

I'd sat in the filthy bathroom stall at the Port Authority bus station for a solid hour as I wrapped my mind around the enormous mistake I had made.

Then I stood up. An hour was long enough. If I wanted to find Beau, I needed to get back to Crown Creek. I'd go to his parents' house, ask them to help me. Or, barring that, I'd walk to Beau and Finn's new house and just wait for them. They had to come home at some point, right? That's what home was. And once they got home, I would be there, ready to start over again.

But in order to do that, I needed money.

I wandered out into the thronging streets, letting the crowds carry me along like a leaf caught in a current. If I let myself, I knew I'd become overwhelmed in a second. There were so many people in this city, millions, it seemed, and though I searched every face that passed me, none of them was the person I wanted so desperately to see.

"Please," I murmured, not knowing who I was speaking to. Maybe I was praying. "Please, please, please." I took a deep, shuddering breath.

A sense of calm washed over me. Looking around was too much, so I'd kept my eyes focused only on what was in front of me. A man, with a broad back, carrying a backpack and a guitar case. He strode across the street and then crossed again, and I followed him. He was a musician, maybe he knew Beau? Maybe he would help me?

But he didn't turn, not even when I called out, "Excuse me?" I followed him and then stopped short when he suddenly dropped the guitar case. He opened it up and lifted his instrument, leaving the case wide open. Then he put the strap around his neck and began playing.

His raw, ragged voice was harsh, and he only seemed to know a few chords. I wondered what he was doing, suddenly playing there on the dirty sidewalk.

And then, to my astonishment, a woman dropped a dollar bill into his open case and then kept walking.

I gasped as another person, this time a man with matted hair hanging in ropes down his back stood and listened for a moment. He dropped a few coins into the case and then walked on.

My heart was pounding in my throat and suddenly I knew how I could get home.

I walked away from the guitar player, not wanting to have to compete with him. The street suddenly opened out into a canyon of neon. Blinking, scrolling signs in more colors than I knew were possible, strobed around me, and streams of people swarmed past.

This seemed like the best possible place I could find. I wrinkled my nose and pulled a discarded plastic cup from one of the trash barrels and set it down on the sidewalk in front of me. Then I took a step back and started to sing.

The ache inside of me was person-shaped, a hole the size and weight of the man I loved. I sang that ache, pouring my hope that someday I might fill it again with Beau's love. I sang the hymn that I'd sung for him when he called me an angel, and an old woman stopped and watched me with tears in her eyes. I sang the song we were supposed to sing at the open mic, and three teenagers ran up and dropped a five dollar bill in my dirty cup. I smiled my thanks and kept on singing every song I knew. I sang loudly, without worrying about vanity or sin. I sang with all my heart, but my voice was getting tired.

I glanced down at my cup. It was stuffed with dollar bills. Maybe there was enough to get something to eat, something to soothe my throat. That's all the time I would take, and then I'd come right back out here and sing until I had enough money to get back where I belonged.

With Beau.

I cleared my throat. One last song before I went. I closed my eyes and tried to remember how it had felt, standing there next to the piano as Claire played. When Beau had come in and watched that first voice lesson. Then I began to sing that feeling.

There was a shout and the screech of tires. A man was running, running right toward me and shouting my name even though I didn't know him.

Wait. Those eyes.

Yes, I did!

"Beau!" I shouted, rushing to the clean-shaven man who had vaulted to curb to stand frozen in front of me with his mouth open in shock.

"What are you doing here?" we both said at the exact same time.

"Where is your beard?" I asked at the same time he wondered, "What happened to your hair?"

Pure joy bubbled up in my chest. "We both lost some hair," I babbled, reaching up to touch his smooth face. "You look so different."

"You're still beautiful," he murmured, brushing his fingers along the hacked strands. "Maybe even more so."

I launched myself into his arms and he crushed me to his chest, then slammed his lips over mine. I kissed him back hungrily, ignoring the shouts and jeers from the people having to step around us on the sidewalk.

When he pulled back, he looked concerned and gently raised his fingers to brush away the tears that were now streaming down my face. "I fucked up," he confessed.

I wiped away my tears and laughed. "No, I'd say I was the one who fucked up."

He grinned to hear me swear. Behind him, Jonah, Gabe, Finn, and Claire finally caught up. "Holy shit," Finn gasped. "You really did hear her from all the way across the street."

But Beau wasn't even looking at them. His eyes were fixed on me, like if he blinked, he was afraid I'd disappear. "I don't care that you can't have kids," he whispered. "I just want to be with you because I—"

"I love you," we both said at the exact same time. He folded me into his arms again and I knew once and for all that I was exactly where I belonged.

Chapter Forty-Nine

BEAU

The church doors opened and the first worshippers streamed out into the bright sunlight. I scanned the crowd, watching for Rachel.

She emerged with a giant smile on her face and waved goodbye to a young mother who hefted her baby up onto her shoulder before leaving. I smiled to see that Rachel was almost dancing as she came down the steps before she stopped and looked around for me.

I held back. I wanted one more moment to look at her. Her sweet white dress should have looked demure, but there was no hiding my girl's curves. Nor was there any hiding her smile now that she'd cut the rest of her hair off. Her new pixie cut made her eyes look huge and they widened farther when she spotted me waiting for her.

"Hey!" I leaned down to kiss her on the cheek, keeping it polite for the sake of the churchgoers. "How was it?" Rachel had been searching for a church ever since we got back to Crown Creek three weeks ago. Her first two attempts had ended in frustration, but she was smiling now and that was a good sign. "Did you like it?"

"It was... different." She laughed and rolled her eyes. "I mean, of course it was." For a moment, my thoughts went to those marks on her legs and anger flooded my veins. She didn't want me to go find the man who had done that to her, and as much as I wanted to go storming the

Chosen compound with a stick of my own to beat people with, I did what she asked.

She took a deep breath and I forced myself to listen as she continued. "I think I could belong there, though."

I pulled her to me and kissed her again, this time on the lips. "I'm so glad."

"Oh!" Her eyes gleamed with excitement. "They ask me to join the choir!"

"Oh angel, that's wonderful! Do you think you're going to?"

"Yeah." She smiled shyly. "And I'm going to sing as loud as I want, too."

I nodded. "Damn straight you are. And I'm going to come watch you do it."

She looked surprised. "You'd do that? I didn't think you were religious."

I just kissed her. Maybe I was, maybe I wasn't. Or maybe my religion was Rachel. "I know it's hot as balls out here," I said with a stifled yawn. "But I'm dying for a cup of coffee."

Rachel wrinkled her nose as she fell into step with me. "Finn still not sleeping?"

I gritted my teeth. I didn't want to think about the bad turn my brother had taken. Ever since we came home from New York, he'd been broodier. He was awake into the wee hours of the morning, and then slept most of the day. After the high of the New York City trip, he had crashed back down hard. I was worried about him, and I hated feeling like I had to cut my time short with Rachel to check in on him. I knew he hated it too, telling me again and again that he didn't want to be a burden.

He wasn't a burden. He was my brother. "He got a few hours in I guess." I yawned again and smiled at Rachel's worried expression. "He was still asleep when I left, so I think we're okay."

She nodded and then the corner of her mouth curled up into a wicked little smile. "Good. Because I'm dying for a cup of Satan's brew too. After the caffeine withdrawal headache I got while at the compound, I never want to be without my coffee again."

"Spoken like a true addict," I teased her, then paused when I saw the way her mouth turned down. "What's up?" I asked, but I knew. She was thinking about it again. That nightmare week she'd spent. How she'd been hurt by the people she trusted and nearly forced into marrying someone she barely knew. She thought she'd been going back to the place she'd belonged because that's what they'd told her. "Hey, no one can tell us where we belong," I reminded her. "No one else can make that choice for us."

"I know." Her voice was faint at first, then she nodded with sudden resolve. She looked up at me. "And I know where I belong." She slipped her hand into mine and smiled. She didn't have to say it. I already knew.

Wherever she was, was where I belonged.

Chapter Fifty

RACHEL

Beau was being weird.

"Are you sure you don't need any help?" I stepped directly into his path as he dashed past me yet again. "Because you sure look like you could use some."

He gave me a quick kiss. "I told you to sit." He nodded to the kitchen chair where I had been parked for over an hour.

"I've been sitting," I complained, but dutifully went back over to his kitchen table and sat down again. "Hey, Beau?" He turned back at the back door and looked at me. "Why do you have a black smudge on your face?"

He reached up and wiped his cheek, smearing the black even more, and then sighed. "You're impossible to surprise."

I sat up. "Bonfire?" I sniffed the air, then jumped up in excitement. "Yes! You're making a bonfire!"

Car wheels crunched on the gravel drive. Beau ignored my shouted questions, most involving how many marshmallows he'd bought for the occasion to look out over the deck.

"There he is," he muttered.

But the car wasn't Finn's, it was Claire's white Jeep. "Claire is coming? Why is Claire here?"

Beau sighed and threw up his hands. "Fine! It's a Labor Day bonfire. I figured we could end the summer the way we started it."

I turned and looked at him. "Wow," I said, touched. "That's a great idea."

He smiled and wrapped his arm around my waist. "Well, it's been a pretty great summer." He kissed the top of my head. "One worth celebrating."

Behind Claire's car, his father's classic Corvette rumbled to a stop. His parents waved up at us and began the trek up the lawn. Behind them came Jonah's old car that their father had restored for him, with Ruby in the passenger seat. Gabe and Everly jumped out of the cramped back immediately. I squealed to see my friend again. "Everly!!"

"Look at what happens when I leave you alone!" she teased, gesturing to how I was leaning into Beau. I laughed and went thundering down the deck stairs to hurtle into her, knocking the bag of chips out of her hands.

The end of summer meant the nights were getting shorter and cooler. Beau herded everyone inside and orchestrated a potluck feast, but all the while he was checking out the window.

There was still no sign of Finn.

"How long has he been gone?" I murmured in Beau's ear when we met again at the refrigerator.

He looked pained. "Since last night, I guess. I don't know. He wasn't here when I woke up. We were up late talking about—" He caught himself and shook his head. "We were up late talking, so I slept in later than normal. I thought maybe he went for a walk, but his car's gone."

I felt a flash of guilt, remembering how Beau had gone looking for me and found that I had disappeared as well. I slid my arms under his, clinging to him for a moment. He sighed, then lifted one of my hands. Kissing my fingers, he flashed a smile. "He'll be okay."

"He will," I agreed.

Beau held my gaze in his hazel one for a long moment and then nodded again. "Okay!" he called over the din of his family. "I've got marshmallows and a bunch of toasting sticks, some of them better than others. Ready, set, go!"

Gabe shot out onto the lawn at a dead run, elbowing past Jonah, who tackled him around the knees. Which made it easy for Claire to shoot around both of them and claim the best marshmallow toasting stick for herself.

I nearly fell over the deck I was laughing so hard. "Come on!" Beau urged, waving for me to join them. "I snagged you the second-best stick."

It was a night just like the first one I'd spent with the Kings. A soft summer's night and the feeling of belonging. I went out onto the lawn and joined the family I'd created for myself.

Beau put his arm around me. I felt him stiffen when I went to slide my cold hand into his pocket. "What?" I teased. "Too much?"

He rolled his eyes. "Man, you really are terrible at keeping surprises from."

The chatter around the bonfire fell silent and everyone looked at us. My heart started thumping so loud I was sure they could all hear it.

"I wish Finn was here," Beau continued.

"So wait," I urged. "Whatever it is you have planned, wait to do it until he comes back."

"No." He took a deep breath. "I'm doing this now."

He dropped to one knee.

I heard Claire squeak, and a sigh from his mother. But the only thing I could see was Beau reaching into his pocket and pulling out the most beautiful ring I had ever seen. "Rachel Walker, we belong together. We both know it, fuck, we went through hell to figure it out." I clapped my hands over my mouth to hide my disbelieving giggle at the fact that he was cursing during his proposal. He grinned sheepishly when he realized. "Sorry. But yeah. We figured it out, and now I'm sure. I'm more sure of this than I've ever been of anything. I want to belong to you forever." He stood up and slipped the ring onto my finger. "Will you belong to me?"

I looked around at the happy faces watching us, holding their breath, waiting to find out if I would belong to them too. The only face that was missing was Finn's and I knew it had to be killing Beau that he was doing this without his twin here to see it. And that made me love him even more. "Yes!" I shouted, clasping his smooth face between my hands. "I'll belong to you. I'll marry you. Yes, yes, yes!"

Everyone clapped as I kissed him. Gabe whooped so loud that it covered up my whispered request so that only Beau heard it. "But only on one condition."

He pulled back and looked at me, worry furrowing his brow. "What's that?"

I cupped his face again. "You have to grow back the beard."

EPILOGUE

Chapter One

RACHEL

Five Days Later

Beau didn't want me to come with him to the police station. I pushed him, and when he still refused, we had our very first argument as a couple.

"I'm going to be your wife!" I shouted at him through confused tears. He'd looked startled and I understood his surprise because I'd felt shocked too. I'd never shouted at anyone before. I'd never dared. Beau's love made me feel safe and secure enough to let my true feelings come out. And they were coming out in a thick torrent of pleading. "I don't want you having to go through this by yourself," I pleaded. "I need to be there with you. For you." I hiccuped and knuckled away a fresh tear.

All at once, Beau looked defeated. "Rachel," he sighed, coming over to me and cupping my face with his hands. "My sweet angel." He pressed a soft kiss to my forehead, but I didn't close my eyes, and I held his gaze when he pulled back and looked at me.

Deep purple shadows ringed his grief-stricken hazel eyes, making them look bruised. He'd been trying to hide his sleeplessness from me, but it was written all over his face. His new beard was growing in wild and untrimmed, shadowing his newly hollowed out cheeks. They'd slimmed down from a steady diet of black coffee... and little else.

I knew full well what he was going through. He didn't need to explain. But since he was, well, him - since he was Beau King, the man I loved more than I could fathom - he attempted to put it into words anyway. No matter how badly he was hurting, he still put everyone else first. "Listen to me," he said now, with a heavy sigh. The storm had passed, our argument forgotten. "If something... happened." At that, his Adam's apple bobbed and he blinked before rushing to finish speaking. "I need you to be the strong one. If you're there with me when I get the news that -."

"You're going to try to take care of me," I finished for him. It was my turn to cup his face with my hands. His gaze had lowered as he disappeared into his worry, but I lifted his chin so that he had to look me in the eye again. I searched his face, then nodded. "Okay," I relented. "You go. I'll be right here when you come back."

He shivered when I said that and I wanted to kick myself. "I will," I repeated. "You're not going to lose both of us."

He nodded and then pressed a fierce, desperate kiss against my lips. I could taste his grief and fear and I wanted to fling my arms around his neck and cling to him. But there was something else too. "And someone needs to be here all the time, right?" I whispered against his neck as I rubbed reassuring circles on his strong back. "In case he shows up?"

"Right." Beau pressed his forehead to my shoulder before straightening back up. The strained, "gotta-stay-positive" smile he'd returned to his face. It was the same one his mother had been wearing, and Jonah too. Gabe had worn it for about a day before it had slipped into an anxious scowl. Claire hadn't bothered with it for more than an hour before succumbing to a fierce, ranting furor. And Mr. King had slipped almost immediately into a terrifying, distracted silence.

We were all eaten up with conflicting emotions, veering from anger to fear to sorrow. And without answers, there was nothing to do but speculate.

So when the chief of police had asked the King family to come into the station, we all jumped at the prospect of news. "That would be just like him, wouldn't it?" Beau went on. "Waltzing in through the door right now and getting mad at us for being mad at him?" He shook his head with a far-off look in his eyes. "Fucking Finn," he said finally. "What the fuck?"

"Go." I squeezed his hand.

He lifted it to his lips and brushed a kiss across my knuckles. His lips lingered on the ring that sparkled there. Then he turned and rushed out the door.

I knew he wouldn't look back, so I didn't head out onto the deck to watch him pull out. Instead, I headed back into the living room and sat on the couch, turning away from Finn's beat-up old easy chair. His absence had lingered in the air all week. Like a whiff of a far-off bonfire carried on the early autumn wind. But now it was a heavy, pressing thing that was impossible to escape by staying busy.

So I didn't even try. I sat and waited for the news. Fearing the worst and hoping for the best.

And a few times I found it in me to pray.

I was in the middle of my whispered entreaties when I heard the sound of wheels on the gravel. The fear that I'd tried to keep at bay hit me like a punch to the gut.

I was so breathless I couldn't stand. So I was still sitting there on the couch when Beau walked back in again.

The slump of his shoulders had me fearing the worst. But the expression on his face was not sorrow.

It was rage.

Before I could ask, he shook his head. "They closed it."

"What?" I couldn't make sense of the words. It was like he was speaking a foreign language. "Closed what? What did they close?"

Beau took another step into the room and then sagged against the wall.

This got me moving. I was up and rushing to his side, slinging his arm over my shoulder, then guiding him over to the couch. He dutifully sat down, but his body was too taut with anger to relax. He stayed perched at the edge of the cushion, his elbows on his knees as he rubbed his palms together over and over again. "The missing persons' case. They closed it."

"But he's still missing!"

He rolled his eyes. "He's a grown man who shows every sign of leaving of his own accord," he parroted, clearly quoting what he'd been told. He nodded at my openmouthed shock. "That was my face too, believe me."

"His car is still here. His clothes? You guys just bought this house together, how do they figure he left?"

"Because the bus is gone."

He dropped his head, his gaze fixed on his shoes. His shoulders rose and fell so fast I feared he was crying.

Until I saw the white-knuckled way he was clenching his fists.

He was furious. I had never seen him so furious.

The old me would have quailed and shrunk away, terrified. But I wasn't that girl anymore. I'd cut myself free of that fear when I'd sliced through my thick braid with a biker's Bowie knife. In one stroke, I'd cut the ties with my past as a meek and mild daughter of the God's Chosen compound. My braid had been a tether, keeping me anchored to the terror of what I now knew was a cult. When I hacked it off, I'd made a promise that I'd never live in that kind of fear again.

I had nothing to fear from Beau. I trusted him with every fiber of my being.

So I didn't hesitate to reach out and take his clenched fist into my hands. "Take a breath." He blew out a long exhale as I nodded. "What bus?" I prompted.

"Our old tour bus." He shook his head but squeezed my hand as he relaxed. "From back when we were playing. The thing is tricked out. We used to live in it for months at a time."

"I never saw it."

"Well, there's a good reason for that. We stored it at the Knights' garage."

I blinked. I'd heard of the Knights, though only in whispers. A rough, close-knit family prone to using their fists to solve their problems. "Why would you store it there?" Mr. King helped out at his friend's garage all the time. "Why wouldn't you leave it at Chuck's?"

Beau gave a helpless shrug. "They gave us a good deal?" It came out as a question and I knew he was kicking himself. The Knights were so secretive. I couldn't help thinking of them as their own little enclave. Sort of like a biker branch of The Chosen. "Gabe made the case that since Chuck was so close to the family, it wouldn't be a big leap for any super fans who wanted to track us down to head right to Andolino's garage."

"And the Knights wouldn't do that." I nodded slowly.

"They have space out of town. And it's heavily guarded - you need a key code just to get in. And getting one of them to talk - about anything - is like pulling teeth. Gabe used to ride dirt bikes with Rocky...." He gave a helpless shrug.

"They say Finn took the bus?"

"Signed it out. It was his signature too."

"But why would he do that?" My voice was rising. "Without telling anyone? Without telling you?"

Beau opened his mouth. And then his beautiful face just... collapsed.

"Shit. I'm sorry. Come here." He let me pull him to me until he lay cradled against my chest. I stroked my fingers through his hair and over his face, tracing the swirls in his beard. He sighed and closed his eyes, his hurt and anger at his twin brother's betrayal too enormous for him to even move

Beau did for those he cared for. It was how he showed his love. He loved through doing. Through action.

And I loved him. Breathlessly. Body and soul.

So I said nothing. There was no word, in any language, that I could speak clearly enough to express my love for him. My sorrow for him. My loyalty and my devotion to him.

I had to show him instead.

I traced the spiral of whiskers just under his cheekbone, then let my finger brush down to his lips. As I traced their shape, I felt them relax under my fingertip. The grim set line of anger softened further as I bent to trail my lips behind my finger.

His mouth was warm and supple under mine. I kissed him slowly, patiently, feeling him yield by degrees. Until finally, with a rough sigh, he reached up to me, clinging to the back of my neck the way a drowning man would.

Our lovemaking was a practiced dance by now. We moved together with the fluidity of two people perfectly in tune. I slid over the top of his body as he rolled over onto his back, but we never stopped kissing. Not even when my hands sought at his zipper.

I'd started out wanted to do this for him. But somewhere between that first slow kiss and this frantic tugging at his jeans, it had become for me too. I needed to feel his skin against mine. I needed to lose myself in the oblivion of him sliding inside of me - that first thrust and then the slow movement as we found our rhythm. I needed to feel his heart thudding under my hands as I pressed them against his chest, bracing myself to take him in deeper. I needed to feel that moment of union, where we were so connected I wasn't certain where I ended and he began.

Beau came alive underneath me. I'd always loved the way he watched me when I was on top. The worshipful parting of his lips, the blaze of pure lust in his eyes. It inflamed me, which inflamed him too, sending us both into a frenzy that had me crying out in seconds. He sat up and I wrapped my legs around his waist the way I knew he liked it. I groaned into his shoulder as he delved his hands into my hips, urging me deeper. His growls and groans were almost animal-like in my ear and he seemed impossibly hard inside of me. But I matched him, taking everything he had until he let out a ragged, gasping noise and his whole body went stiff.

"Watch me," I whispered as his eyes flew open. And then I lost myself in the sensation as we both clung to each other in a bid to keep the sorrow at bay.

Beau closed his eyes and tilted his forehead to rest against mine. His breathing slowed by degrees, ragged gasps deepening until he was drawing slow steady breaths.

Only then did I kiss his forehead and gently nudge him back. I saw his mouth tug a little at the corner as he realized what I was doing, but he let me guide him until he was lying back down on the couch. I tugged a cushion over to pillow his head and then brushed my fingertips over his eyelids.

"Rach -?"

"Sssh." I hushed him before sliding free and tugging one of the throw blankets up to his waist. Then went to the bathroom to clean up.

Just as I'd hoped, he was asleep when I came back out again.

I stood for a moment, watching the man I was going to marry. The slow, regular sip of his breathing stirred things inside of me, things that were fiercely protective and desperately in love. Betraying a man like Beau was not just unthinkable to me, it was impossible.

What the hell was Finn thinking?

I shook my head and tried to push the anger back down again. My rage wasn't what Beau needed. I didn't want him to think he had to console me or worry about me. Right now, the only thing I wanted him to think about was Finn.

I grabbed my keys off the hook and tucked them into my bag. I would make things easy. I'd start by taking over the cooking tonight. I would serve him his favorite comfort food - that thick potato soup he liked. And a side of the potato bread I could make in my sleep.

I'd loved him through sex.

Now I'd love him through carbs.

Nodding to myself, I wrote a quick note explaining where I was in case he woke up and panicked that I was gone. Then grabbed my keys and headed out.

Chapter Two

RACHEL

The drive back into Crown Creek was one I could do in my sleep by now. The twisting road wound through cornfields and pastures that gleamed gold in the slanting sun. Autumn was sniffing around the edges of late summer. Even though it was still warm, the oak trees were wearing scarlet red crowns at their very topmost branches. So I knew the warm weather wouldn't last.

It was the rhythm of the seasons I knew well. I'd grown up in the thick of them, out in the fields of the compound.

I knew that my childhood looked idyllic to outsiders. After all, my family was close-knit. I had scores of younger siblings, and a heap of cousins to play with. We were always running in and out of each others homes, playing tag and begging treats. With our longs skirts swishing and our long braids flying, we even looked like a page in a storybook. A fairy-tale.

No one knew it was actually a nightmare.

A little shiver crawled up my spine, raising goosebumps along my arm. I couldn't figure out why I was dwelling on this. The compound was behind me. The Chosen were behind me. I should have been thinking of Beau. Worrying about Finn. Worrying for the rest of my new family. The Kings were where my mind should have been.

Maybe it was the familiar whiff of cow manure in the air. Maybe it was the slant of the light through the just-changing trees . But something was dragging me back to the horrors of compound life.

I shook my head to clear it and then yelped. "Holy shit!" I screamed and slammed on the brakes as hard as I could.

I'd nearly slammed into the back of the car in front of me. A car that was stopped dead in the middle of the road where no car had ever been stopped before.

"What the - ?" I let go of the steering wheel and shook out the nerves from my trembling hands, " - hell?" I craned my neck, trying to see what the hold-up was.

But I couldn't see anything beyond a sea of brake lights. The smell of autumn leaves and car manure was now replaced with exhaust. The minutes ticked by and I tapped my fingers against the steering wheel as we crept into town at five miles an hour. Like the world's strangest parade. "This is... weird," I said aloud.

Ahead I could see the line snaking into town. I caught sight of a few of classic cars. Behind me pulled up an armada of motorcycles revving their engines as loud as they could. I needed to go straight through town, but everyone else was making a right at Five Corners.

Why? There was nothing I could think of that would warrant that kind of traffic up Johnson Street on a Friday afternoon. "Okay then," I said, shaking my head once I was clear of the snarl. What should have taken me ten minutes had now taken a half an hour. I hoped Beau was still asleep.

I pulled into the IGA and rushed in, hurrying through my mental list of Beau's favorites.

Standing over the dairy display, I debated between Muenster or Colby Jack - he liked both. I was so absorbed in the mental pros and cons that I nearly jumped out of my skin when someone called my name. I pasted a polite smile on my face and turned, expecting to see one of Claire's friends.

A young woman with a narrow face and terrified eyes was standing there, far too close to me. She'd pressed her hand together, as if in prayer.

"Rachel?"

I didn't recognize her at all.

"Hi?" I said, stepping back.

She blinked, looking hurt. Then her face registered understanding and she looked down. "I guess you wouldn't recognize me in these clothes." She was wearing an ill-fitting oversized T-shirt and corduroys so long the hems dragged on the ground. I looked back up at her face and then her hair.

Someone had roughly chopped her ashy blonde hair into a lank bob. Someone who was working fast and didn't have the right kind of tools. Someone who knew her long hair would mark her as an outsider in the secular world.

Someone a lot like me.

Someone who grew up calling herself one of God's Chosen.

Chapter Three

RACHEL

My first instinct was to run. Drop my potatoes and cheese and sprint as fast as I could. Get away from this apparition, this ghost from my terrible past.

For a second I could almost believe I'd never left the compound. The reassuring white noise of the grocery store fell away. All at once I was in the meetinghouse again, sweating in the suffocating heat, my steps hobbled by heavy skirts. I swallowed hard and tried to remember I was safe from all that. "Ruth?"

She nodded, still looking down at her clothes. "These are so hard to get used to," she muttered.

"Ruth, what are you doing here?" I darted a look behind me, waiting for - what? One of the Elders to leap out from behind the canned soup display? What was I so terrified of, really? I tried to steady my voice. "What's going on?"

"I'm so glad you're here." She dared to lift her gaze to mine and I knew what it cost her to do that. Who knew what vile, awful things she must have heard about me? The stories told at meeting of my disgusting sins? The lies they must have told about me to justify my defection? "You have to help me."

In spite of the chill of the dairy case, I was sweating. I felt a pain in my hands and realized I was clenching my fists so hard my nails were digging into my palms. I unclenched them, finger by finger. "Of course," I said, as steadily as I could. "But what is this? You're out?"

"I am."

"Since when?"

"Since?" She looked around. "This morning, I guess?" Her voice bubbled with suppressed hysteria. "Since you left, maybe? Since I realized it was possible to leave?"

"Oh, Ruth!" I shook my fear loose and wrapped my arms around her. She was stiff at first, then clutched at my clothes. "I'm so proud of you," I whispered in her ear, but my mind was reeling. "Is it just you? Are there others?"

I heard her swallow next to my ear. "There've been three, that I know of. Susanna went first."

"Susanna?" That was a shock. Susanna Baker had barely spoken to me, barely spoken to anyone. But shyness doesn't always mean cowardice. I knew that well.

Ruth looked over her shoulder again and she and I both stepped closer to each other. I kept my hand on her arm. "It's a whole network now," she mumbled, looking down and barely moving her lips. "Girls are leaving in the middle of the night."

"How?"

"A car comes and picks them up behind the dairy barn." There was a rutted pitted road, little more than a path, that led from the barn to the road. I'd thought only Chosen knew about it. "It's supposed to take them to a safehouse."

I felt dizzy. "A safehouse? Who's running it?"

Ruth shrugged. "I don't know. No one does, I don't think. In case someone talks. It's better, they say." She reached up to tug at her braid and jerked her hand back in surprise when it wasn't there. "That's where I was supposed to go today but... but it was *closed*."

"Closed?" I echoed.

She clutched at her arm, hugging herself. I wrapped my arm around her shoulder and pulled her close as her fear made her words tumble over each other. "The driver honked the horn, gave the signal. I guess the gate was supposed to open, but it didn't, so he got out and told me to get down." Her body shook with tremors. "We were late getting out, it wasn't dark enough, it was my fault, my husband - ," she spat the word and I jerked in sympathy. I hadn't realized she'd been married off. "He was up half the night coughing. I thought I was going to miss my chance. But the driver waited for me until it was near dawn. He was so angry with me though, Rachel." She was shaking harder now, and I swallowed hard to see her terror in the face of angry men. "And then when it was locked, he wanted to take me right back again."

"No...," I breathed. To have that chance and have it snatched away would be unbearable.

She shook her head. "No. I wasn't going back. I had no place else to go, but I wasn't going back to Zacharias." She shuddered again and her fingers played around her neck in a way that made my stomach turn. "I made him drive around until we found a place that was open. He wouldn't stay with me, said it wasn't safe for us to be seen together. So I've been here since this morning, trying to look like I blend in." She snorted softly and touched her ragged hair. "I thought, somehow, if they find me, it's better if I'm around people, right?" She looked at me, pleading. "Right? If they come to find me here, someone will see have to see me. I won't just disappear."

"They're not going to find you," I declared. "No. You're coming with me."

She let out a soft cry and fell against me. "Shh," I whispered. We were no longer alone. The old woman who carried her little dog everywhere was watching. She looked like she was about to greet us but thank God and all his angels her dog chose that moment to attempt a leap for freedom. It gave me cover to hiss, "No, none of that now," to the sobbing Ruth. "You get your head up, okay? Look, you're my cousin, got it? You're helping me do the shopping. Here." I grabbed a brick of cheese and put it in her hands. She looked down at it like it was a bomb, but nodded. "Right, now let's go get you a pint of ice cream, help you get over that asshole," I declared, loud enough for the dog-carrying woman to overhear. "No more crying over a cheater, you hear me cuz?"

It was an Oscar-worthy performance that I sort of wished Beau, or even Claire, was there to see. I led Ruth over to the frozen section and picked out two pints of the most decadently secular ice cream concoctions I could find. (Salted Caramel Pretzel with Fudge Ripple for me, and Birthday Cake Funfetti Spectacular with Marshmallow Swirl for her) Then I marched us both to the checkout and paid with a smile, daring the bagger to question Ruth's clothes or her red-rimmed eyes. "Nothing better than ice cream for a broken heart, am I right?" I chirped to the checkout girl, before grabbing Ruth by the wrist and leading her out the front door.

She was fine until we exited the safety of the store. But once we were out in the daylight, she quailed, dragging her feet as the terror took hold. "No one is going to come for you," I whispered, but I quickened my steps all the same. Relief flooded me when we reached the car.

"Merciful heavens," Ruth moaned, sagging into her seat. She curled up against the door, tucking her knees to her chest like a child.

I swallowed. The sight of Ruth's terror was making me re-think my plan. I'd meant to drive us right to the house. But Ruth was in the throes of a sudden, paralyzing fear. Fear takes over the second safety is at hand. In that moment, the evil you endured didn't matter. Because it was what you understood.

Ruth had left behind everything that made sense to her and now the unknown was closing in. I'd felt this terror.

I didn't want to cause it.

I bit the inside of my cheek. I'd wanted to run back to the house and put this all in Beau's hands. I knew he'd take over. I knew I could trust him.

But Ruth didn't.

She only trusted me because she knew where I was from. Beau - my wonderful, loving fiancé - would scare her into muteness. I could see this now. It didn't matter that he was good-hearted and sweet. She would take one look at his leather jacket and low-slung jeans and see Satan himself.

"Ruth, I need you to listen to me," I told her, intruding into her thoughts as gently as I could. "You've been so brave, all day." I reached out and took her hand in mine and tried to still the fluttering. "You're safe, do you hear me? But I need you to listen."

She took a deep breath and opened her eyes. When she finally looked at me, I nodded. "Now. I can take you to my house -."

"Yes," she answered immediately, but I held up my hand.

"Ruth, I'm engaged." I held up my left hand for her. Her eyes widened when they fell on the sparkling ring. "His name is Beau, and he is the kindest, most loving man I've ever met. But he is a man." She was already getting paler. "And his brother lives-," I caught myself, started that I'd forgotten about Finn's disappearance. "Well... his brother isn't... there right now. But he usually lives with us too." Ruth was white as a sheet now. "Ruth, I promise you. They will not touch you. They will want to help you as much as I do."

"They're secular?"

"They're secular," I agreed. That word had once been enough to inspire terror in me. I could see Ruth struggling not to succumb to that same terror now. "And I don't want you to be any more frightened than you already are." Her trust in the outside world would come slowly. Like mine had. I knew that rushing it might send her running terrified back to The Chosen. Like it once had for me. "Would you like me to try and take you to the safehouse instead?" I asked her. "We can try again? Do you think you can remember how to get there?"

She widened her eyes. And then closed them, exhaling a painful sigh. "I don't," she moaned.

"Try to remember. What did it look like?"

"There was a fence all around," she said, keeping her eyes closed as she tried to conjure the picture. "A low building, big rolling doors like on the barn, I think."

"A garage?"

"Maybe? I saw a few motorcycles, but then my driver came back and shouted to get my head down. He jumped back in and turned around so fast the tires screamed."

I wracked my brain. "Was it here? In town?"

She shook her head hopelessly. "I don't know. He started taking all these turns, saying we were probably being followed. I got all turned around."

Andolino's garage didn't have a fence around it. Not that I could remember. Of course, I'd only been there with Mr. King, and he went in around the back. Maybe a different entrance? I started the car. "I'm going to swing by the place I'm thinking, okay? You can tell me if it's what you remember."

Ruth nodded and I couldn't help but notice the way her shoulders lowered a fraction. I didn't want to disturb her silence, so I kept my questions to myself as I drove.

But with no place to go, they ended up swirling around in my head in a frenzied tornado of worry. "How is my family?" "How are my sisters?" "Is Rebecca with a good man?" "Is he righteous?" "Is Miriam okay?" "Levi, oh my heavens, has anyone found out that he's gay?" "Did I expose him by leaving?"

"Why aren't the Chosen coming to the Saturday markets anymore?" "Has there been a crackdown?" "Do you know where Susanna ended up?" "Is she safe?"

"Who on earth is running the safehouse?" "Are they secular?" "Why are they helping us?"

"Why do they care?"

With no answers forthcoming, the questions clogged my throat. I had to say something to dislodge the lump that was forming. "Does this look familiar at all?" I asked.

Ruth sat up. We were turning onto Mill Street now. She stared intently at the bridge that spanned the upper set of rapids and shook her head. "No, we didn't cross the creek, I don't think."

"How about this?" Andolino's garage was ahead on the right, a neatly whitewashed building with three bays all open. Inside, Chuck and his sons were bustling about in their navy coveralls, using all three lifts at once.

Ruth looked and immediately shook her head. "It was closed. Locked. Like it was out of business or something."

I pressed my lips together, thinking. The only other garage around here belonged to the Knights, but it wasn't in town and I wasn't sure how to get there. I handed my phone to Ruth. "Can you type in 'garages'?"

"Where?" She looked down that the phone like it was a snake poised to strike.

"Never mind," I laughed and took it back from her. I'd have to teach her about smart phones. "Sorry. I doubt that's the place anyway. Maybe it was a warehouse? Somewhere in the old part of town?"

Ruth shrugged. I turned and headed back into town, driving slowly in case anything sparked Ruth's memory. "Did you go past here at all?" I asked as we turned onto Johnson Street.

At the corner, the big Catholic church rose, its steeple the tallest structure in town. "I think?" Ruth breathed as she gazed up at it. "There weren't so many cars though."

She was right. Gleaming motorcycles lined the street. Cars, both regular and classic, filled both the church lot and the lot of Lowry funeral home right next door. "So that's what it was," I muttered to myself.

"What?"

"I got caught in traffic on the way to the store," I explained. "Whoever's funeral this is, he must have been an important guy. I didn't think there were even this many people living here."

"Maybe it's people from out of town?" Ruth wondered, then gestured. "She doesn't look like she's from here."

I turned to look where she was pointing. A blonde woman was standing at the door of her hatchback, staring at the front of the funeral home. The wind lifted her hair away from her face, and even from this far away I could see the confusion and sorrow on it. Her shoulders were rounded in defeat. But as we slid past, I saw her straighten them before she pushed her door closed and started walking across the lot.

"She's secular," Ruth said, a touch of wonder in her voice. "But she's scared too."

The sight seemed to have a strange effect on Ruth. She sat up straighter, seeming to draw herself together again. Empathy warmed her voice. "Who is she?"

I dragged my eyes away from the rear view, but the image of that stranger trying to pull herself together was seared into my brain. "I've never seen her before," I mused aloud. "I wonder why she's here?"

"We passed that!" Ruth cried, pointing to the Crown Tavern and derailing my train of thought. "I know because I remembered seeing it when we'd come in for Saturday Markets." She shook her head and closed her arms over her chest. "I used to think the people inside had to be the worst kind of sinners. Now I'm one of them."

I grabbed her hand. "Stop. You are a good person, Ruth. There are more ways to be a good person than the Elders taught us."

She gave me a small, tight-lipped smile. I nodded and smiled back in a way I hoped was encouraging. But inside I was losing hope. We'd driven up and down nearly every street in town, and Ruth still had no idea where her driver had taken her.

Just then I heard a rumble. Ruth let go of my hand and hugged her stomach. "Sorry," she muttered. "I haven't eaten in a while."

"Okay." I turned the wheel sharply to the left before I missed the turn. "You're hungry. I'm hungry. My fiancé is probably starving." I nodded with each sentence, trying to convince myself as much as I was trying to convince Ruth. "Let's eat something, okay? Just a dinner so you can have your head clear." And I can clear mine too, I didn't add. My whirlwind thoughts were spinning faster and faster with each moment. Each worry was trying to drown out everything else. Finn's disappearance. The secret underground railroad of Chosen. The locked up safehouse. The funeral. The strange girl in the parking lot. The fear on her face. Nothing was connected. Yet everything seemed linked.

I shook myself so hard that Ruth gave a yelp of surprise. "We're gonna eat now, okay?" I repeated. I glanced at her. "Sound good?"

"Okay."

"Okay." I pressed the gas pedal a little harder. It wasn't much of a plan, but it was the best I could come up with. "That's what's going to happen. We're going to all eat together. And then we're going to figure out what happens next."

THE END

BOOKS BY THERESA LEIGH

The Crown Creek Series

The Kings

Sweet Crazy Song

Jonah and Ruby's story

Cocky Jonah never wanted to come home to Crown Creek. But a chance meeting with kindergarten teacher Ruby has him wanting to stay forever.

Lost Perfect Kiss

Gabe and Everly's story

A risk taking bad boy. A girl-next-door nurse. And the kiss that never should have happened. Gabe has to convince Everly to take the biggest risk of her life. Him.

Soft Wild Ache

Beau and Rachel's story

Growing up in a repressive religious cult meant that Rachel always believed the outside world was evil. But when sensitive rocker Beau opens her eyes to life outside the compound walls, she learns that he's the sweetest sin she's ever seen.

His Secret Heart

Finn and Sky's story

Sky was certain she knew everything she needed to know about volatile, unpredictable bad boy Finn King. But when her world turns upside down, she realizes everything she thought she knew is wrong.

Crown Creek Standalones:

Last Good Man

Cooper and Willa's story

Willa hates Cooper. But when she wakes up in a hospital room, he's the one who's there waiting - rumpled, frantic... And swearing she's his fiancee.

Coming soon:

Ryan and Naomi's story

Sadie's story

Visit theresaleighromance.com for more.

ABOUT THE AUTHOR

Theresa Leigh is a romance author whose love of reading is so intense, she sometimes injures herself by walking around with her nose in a book. She loves writing stories that have you feeling every emotion... sometimes all on the same page.

Theresa lives and writes in the beautiful Finger Lakes region of New York State (not the city) (that distinction is important to her), where she lives with her husband, twin sons and twin orange cats, Pumpkin and Jackie O'Lantern. When she's not writing or reading, she enjoys eating too much Thai food, walking around barefoot, and cooing baby talk at her cats.

Get in touch!
www.theresaleighromance.com
authortheresaleigh@gmail.com
facebook.com/booksbytheresaleigh

Made in the USA
Lexington, KY
29 November 2019

57861997R00142